Ugly Daddy

A novel by
Queen Phoenix

ISBN 978-0-578-26361-8
Second edition

Printed in the United States of America

This is a work of fiction. All characters and incidents are of the author's imagination.

liveinlove1111.com

Table of Contents

I dedicate this book to my deceased mother Colleen Stridiron, who was the strongest person I ever knew. She's the reason for my many accomplishments. I'm proud to be her daughter, and I know if she were here she would be proud of me. If she weren't such a good mother, there would have been no way I would have kept my sanity and become successful after she left me and life did what it did to me. I go on to keep you alive, and so you can keep your recognition. I love you Mom and our love is forever.

Special Acknowledgements

These acknowledgements are for the people who have made a difference in my life.

First, thanks to God who is the center of my life and the one who makes all things happen. I know without you none of this is possible.

I want to acknowledge the deceased in my life:

My mom Colleen Stridiron, I love every precious moment we had together. Sometimes I feel like I'm suffering down here without you. I always thought we were bonded together forever. As a child I could never imagine life without you, and as an adult I can see why. I don't think anyone understands the pain I carry inside for you, and that I haven't got past you being gone. I will never accept the fact that you're gone. For in my heart and mind you are still here. I love you more than life itself.

Thanks to Leroy Rodgers my stepfather because of you I can say I had a father who taught me something. To my step brother Kareem Boulden who rarely had a chance in life, but remembering the times we shared as kids is a lifetime and even though we did not come from the same blood line, I will die with you are my brother. Thanks to my Aunt Goldie Dickey for giving me a chance in life. She tried to protect me from the system. God bless you. To my Nana Kathleen Stridiron, you and I never really had the chance to get close. But knowing you during the little time we spent is valuable to me. You have all the traits that a grandmother should have, and I'm thankful for you. And my Aunt Sharon who I most recently lost and the pain is still fresh. When I think about you, I try to hold back tears. I wish God had given you more time. When I think of you love and passion comes to mind. You are my favorite aunt on both sides of my family, and the most passionate relative I have.

You have never hesitated to help me, comfort me, or love me. You were always there for me when I needed you. I wish we could have spent more time together. I am very grateful to have had you in my life, and you are greatly remembered. To my grandpa, you were the best thing that came out of grandparenthood. You kept everything real. You called it as you saw it, and I can appreciate that. I appreciate your courage and also your company. You are definitely unique and definitely missed. I want to thank Philip Burnet for being a real friend and father figure to me all these years. I want to thank Jeff Miller who has been my career advisor for a lot of years.. He has supported me and had faith in me, in everything I believed in. He played a big part in all my accomplishments, and a professional friend who went out his way for me. The world needs more people like you. Mike Atkins, you are a powerful black man mentally. Your credentials and prestige makes you a president. You spoke to my class one day and I was amazed how one man could have so much knowledge and wisdom. You changed my life forever. Because of you I know that sky is the limit. Keep on moving my brother. To Adelsola, I thank God for you. I look forward to our Monday afternoon sessions. For each time I leave you I learn and grow. You are a therapist doing God's work. I thank you Miss Wanda Harris, who will always be my mother-in-law no matter who I'm with. You took me in and loved me like one of your own. The realest lady I met since my mom passed, and the only women to come close to a mother figure to me. I share a special love with you. To Patrica Bagget, the best English professor at OCC. I could never thank you enough for putting your life to the side to help me when you didn't know me. Just when I thought there wasn't any way, there you were. Thank you.

    To my father, I forgive you.

To my brother Michael Cory Lane, AKA Caseen, it's just us now. I promise I will never leave you. And a special thanks to your wife Melinda Campbell Lane, thanks for holding my brother down. And last but not least, I thank my kids, Willy, Jaquey, and my Queen. Each one of you is different and unique. If it weren't for you all, there probably would not be any existence of me right now. You three are what I'm living for. I know I'm not the perfect mother, and I never will be, because there are no perfect people on the earth. But don't ever think anything opposed to I love you. To my Divine Masculine I trust this journey.

Psalms 22:1, 2: *My God, my God why have you abandoned me? Why are you so far away from helping me, so far away from the words of my groaning? My God I cry out by day, but you do not answer- also at night, but I do not rest.*

Twenty-six years of pain. I finally lie down and let the devil attack me. I lie still—it feels like depression. I am a dysfunctional Christian. I live life today through my past dysfunctional life. I have skeleton bones in my closet that come alive sometimes. I know that life wasn't always like this. But for the most part, my past was fucked up. My experiences to me now feel tragic. When I look back at it, it's just too hard to bear. I use to meet with a therapist once a week, and tell that Caucasian all my business, only to find out that the bitch didn't give a shit about me. And technically what could she do for me, or understand me for that matter? I doubt she could get two feet in my shoes. She listened to me, but she also judged me. And the dumb mental health doctor with the junkie office, don't know me or never read my file. Got piles of folders to the ceiling.

He says, "What is your name? Oh Mrs. Thomas mentioned you." He's looking for my file, can't find it. "What seems to be the problem?"

I tell him I'm depressed from time to time and begin to fill him in on some of the symptoms I have.

"What medication were you taking? Well why you stop taking the doxepin?"

"I like the doxepin, but I can't get up in the morning when I take it and I have things to do.

"That's because you have to take it early in the evening." He reaches for his prescription pad. "Now, do you want some more doxepin or do you want to try something else?" I didn't want anything but some answers. How bout what's wrong with me, and will I ever get better. I didn't want to take medication for the rest of my life. When I realized that all he had was prescriptions for me, I took the doxepin in case I felt like I really needed it. I wasn't going to try different medications, I aint no fucking guinea pig. I am ready to talk about it. I can't stop thinking about it. Nobody will sit long enough with me and let me get it all out. My closest relatives don't believe some parts of it, and don't know the rest of it. I'm just going to have to keep writing so that I can tell my story. Maybe people who thought they knew me will better understand me. My associates don't know why I get depressed and why I act the way I do. The men that I dealt with didn't know why I put up with their bullshit, why I did not trust them and after a while simply dismissed them. My life began when I was twelve

Chapter 1
Mama

I didn't have any nicknames, Pooh, Keke, Miesh, or anything like that. My name is Shiree, Shiree Brown, and that's what I got called. I was the different one in the family. I often dreamed. Outside of our two-bedroom house that fit the description of a green shack on 625 Cary Avenue in Staten Island New York, I imagined it all. I could see the future. In my future I saw money, fancy cars, fancy houses and my mother. I was closer to my mother than she was to me. I tried to stay under her even at twelve. I loved her smell and her glamour. She was tall, yellow, with long thick sexy legs. Her lips were full and her eyes were dark pearly brown. Her hair was black, short and curly from the curl she had put in. If one word best described her to everyone she knew, it would be real. She always spoke what was on her mind, and it was never to hurt anyone unless you struck one of her last nerves. She was the sweetest person who never had an enemy. The closest she came to an enemy was envious bitches. Mama was someone everyone wanted to be like, but couldn't. She was a naturalist. Only real people respected her beauty, her intelligence, and her sweetness. Mama did not have one phony bone in her. Even though she was pretty, she was not afraid to kick her heels off, ball her fist up and whip your ass.

I didn't miss a thing. Being observant was one of my many qualities. I was so smart I understood everything. I was a child, but smarter than some adults. I was a straight A student in elementary and junior high school. I won spelling bees and made the honor roll every marking period. My mother must have had a folder bigger than the phone book with my honor roll certificates in it. Mother bragged about me. Her daughter was going to be a lawyer. I loved school, and at home I loved to play school and read books. In the bathroom I use to stand on the tub and look at myself in the mirror with a towel on my head. I use to talk to myself in the mirror swinging my head side to side, pretending I had long hair. I was yellow just like mama, with long skinny legs. Everywhere I went someone told me how cute I was. I had long hair that mama always kept up in ponytails, when I liked it down. I was twelve, but to mother I had to have been like seven. She made sure we stayed kids until it was time.

While I was happy as long as Mama was around, entertaining myself trying to escape poverty, my oldest brother Caseen was fourteen and the total opposite. By his facial expressions you could tell our living conditions were unsatisfying to him. He didn't like the rules, discipline or the structure. The facts were, we could not watch television or go outside on a school day. He appeared bored at all times. He was sneaky and set in his ways. We were close, because it had always been us. We shared a room since I was born. He did not like school.. I think he was one of those cats who preferred to work than go to school. He loved money and nice clothes. Dad didn't make enough to provide us with anything more than fila, or any cheap brand sneakers

from Payless at Path Mark. So Caseen began to get his hustle on anyway he could at school. His main gig was bullying. He would take the sensitive
boys' money and whatever else he could get.

But Mom and Dad were strict. We could not go in the house with anything they didn't buy or we would get clocked. The difference between Caseen and me was that nothing scared him; a beating did not faze him. One beating for me would set me straight. He often got in trouble in school; he was always fighting. Caseen was a difficult child, Mom and Dad especially thought. But to Caseen and me our two baby brothers were difficult kids.

Little Leroy and Troy were only ten months apart. Little Leroy was eight and Troy was seven. We could not hit the little brats because they were our baby brothers. The brats never stopped coming in and out of our room, throwing blocks at us and then running out. We were never to hit them under any circumstances. We had to tell Mom and Dad if they hit us even if we knew they weren't going to do anything.

Late one Friday night Mother was in the bathroom taking a bubble bath and Dad was out driving his taxicab. Caseen and I were in our room. I was sitting directly in front of the television. Troy came in and stood in front of the screen. Shetara was just about to show Lionel her new stunt on the Thunder Cats.

"Move Troy," I said, gently pushing him out the way.

"No," he said, calm and deceitful and back in front of the screen again.

I looked at Caseen who was sitting on his bed writing rap songs and chanting the rhymes out loud.

"Oh my goodness," I yelled, aggravated now. "Move." I pushed him to the floor.

"No," he yelled as he got off the floor, crying and yelling at me. "Puh," he went and spit splattered all over my face.

Caseen laughed, but I was so mad I pinched Troy and pushed him down again.

I could hear my mother from the bathroom. "What the hell is going on out there?"

I went back to watching the television. I looked up and saw Troy for a quick second. Then I saw the dustpan, before I felt it lodged in my forehead. I jumped up and started screaming. I pulled the dustpan out of my head and covered my head with my hand as I jumped on the couch and cried. I just lay there in fetal position.

Mama came out of the bathroom, "What happened?"

I was too busy crying and my feelings were hurt, so I couldn't really talk. Troy stood there looking like a midget. He stared at me with no remorse.

"What happened to her?" she repeated, asking anybody.

Caseen began to explain, "Troy stood in front of the television; she told him to move and pushed him away. He kept coming back, and she kept on pushing him away. Then he hit her with the dustpan." Caseen smirked, trying to hold back his laughs.

My mama looked at Troy. "Go get your ass in my room and get in my bed. Your daddy gonna whip ya ass when he get home."

All I could think of was, Why can't you?

She looked at my head then she nurtured it, and I went to bed.

Little Leroy was the biggest pest. He took playing to extremes. His favorite game was spitting on me. He would come in my room spit on me and run away. But Caseen didn't play that. One time Leroy came in the room and spit on Caseen, and threw a few blocks at him. Caseen picked one of the same blocks Leroy threw, and when Leroy turned around to run, Caseen caught him in the back of his head. Little Leroy grabbed his head and hollered all the way to Mom and Dad's room. Dad came out cursing at Caseen. Dad told Caseen to keep his fucking hands to himself, and if he did it again he would fuck him up. Caseen was a liar, so he came up with a story about how Leroy and him were playing with the blocks, throwing them back and forth and that the whole thing was an accident. Of course Dad didn't believe him, but he didn't do anything.

Dad was more hip to our lies and sneaky ways than Mom because he was sneaky himself. He always caught us in a sneaky act. He knew when someone was drinking from the juice carton, or when we snuck in the refrigerator for something. Dad's name was Leroy, and our baby brother was named after him. That's why we called him little Leroy. Big Leroy was not Caseen's or my natural father. We called him Dad because he played the role that our fathers were suppose to play but didn't.

Daddy Leroy was a light-skinned, medium-built pretty-boy. He had long silky hair he kept back in a ponytail that always reminded me of Steven Seagal. He drove taxicabs and cooked in restaurants to support us while Mama got her beauty sleep. She got up every morning to wake us up for school, iron our clothes, and fix us breakfast. On cold days she always warmed our milk up. Before Daddy Leroy came along, Mama lived on both sides of the world. We lived in a raggedy building on Vanduzer in Park Hill, Staten Island, New York. Caseen and I shared the only bedroom in the apartment. Mama had her bed in the living room. We had a huge kitchen with nothing in it. She was a welfare recipient receiving food stamps and WIC. I always remembered Mom as struggling. She was a single black, beautiful woman who just wanted to get ahead.

But the odds were pretty much against her. She left the apartment at night when she thought Caseen and I were asleep. I always got up and found Mama's bed empty. She was in the streets selling crack and snorting a little coke here and there. She tried somewhat by attending Drake's business school during the day.

What Mama didn't know was that Edward, who lived across the street, was never watching us like Mama paid him for. His seventeen-year-old son would fuck my four-and-a-half-year-old pussy almost everyday.

Caseen got tired of the boy poking him with needles to run him out of the room and told. Mama was hysterical and needed to calm down and think. Edward advised her not to go to the police or else he would tell that she was doing drugs. Mama's only mistake was telling her oldest brother, Juney.

Edward's son was nowhere to be found, so Uncle Juney beat Edward with a baseball bat until Edward stopped moving. Uncle Juney was sentenced to seventeen years in the joint for manslaughter.

That summer Mama took Caseen and me to her mother's house in Syracuse, New York, and she went back to New York to sign herself into a rehab. She came back with Daddy Leroy. After that she sat home all day watching the stories, and she never missed Oprah Winfrey.. One day I think she got tired of sitting around, and Dad did not bring home enough money for her. She was always independent and ambitious, so she went and enrolled in Staten Island College.

My mother went to school October 13, 1991 on a Saturday morning. By seven that night she hadn't showed up at home. We expected her home long before that. Dad took it as normal, only usually something like that would have never been considered normal to him. At least I didn't think he looked worried. But how could I tell? He stayed in his room the whole day. Dad seemed quite sick that day. The day was boring. I felt like any day spent without Mom was boring. The energy Mom sent out always kept me going.

When I woke Sunday morning, there was no sign of Mom. I was a bit worried, but not too worried since Dad was cool about it. Nothing dramatic had ever happened to our family except Caseen getting jumped his first day of Mukee High School by the regulators gang. They beat him with brass knuckles. He came home with both of his eyes closed. But that was normal; Caseen was always fighting in school or getting jumped.

Dad prepared breakfast that morning. I sat at the breakfast table with Caseen, Little Leroy and Troy. I kept watching the door hoping Mama would walk through and say, "I'm home."

I began to think about last weekend when I stayed the night at my real dad, Sam's, house. Sam lived in Staten Island on Wolkoff Street, in a condo down the street from the Big Apple Bazaar. Last weekend I stayed the night at his house. I fell asleep in his bed watching Eddie Murphy on tape. I must have been in a peaceful sleep, when all I remember was not moving but opening my eyes to pitch darkness. It was so dark I couldn't see, but I could feel my father's hand in my panties. I was shocked, and I was nervous. I slowly turned on my side toward the patio window. As I turned, he slowly removed his hand. I lay on my side quietly. I was terrified. A thought passed to get up and run down the stairs, out the door and down the street, but I was too scared to do anything, so instead I did nothing.

A few minutes went by. Sam sat up, turned on the lamp and the television. Then he tapped me and said, "Booby, you awake"? Then he looked at the television, complaining that it was hot in there. He knew that I knew, but I said nothing. I thought about that night until it bothered me. I knew I should tell my mom.

Leroy left the house for a few minutes and then came back. He looked confused, except he didn't tell us anything. That's how Mom and Dad were; they didn't talk to Caseen and me much. We stayed in our room and they stayed in theirs. Dad believed kids should stay in a child's place. He firmly believed that and never let up on his discipline.

Dad had two sons from a relationship prior to his relationship with Mom. Kareem was a year younger than I, and Lionel was three days older than I. They lived with their grandmother in Port Richmond in Staten Island also. We looked forward to seeing them on weekends, and summers. Dad even bought pull-out beds for our room. Dad thought we were the kids from hell when we were together, and he gave out more ass whippings than a regular day.

That Sunday went by rather quickly. When the night came my patience had run low, so I began snooping around and eaves dropping. The phone rang and I heard Uncle Andre's voice from the loud speaker. "Hey Leroy what's going on? Where's my sister?"

Dad hesitated. "Well I figured she was with you. She hasn't been here since she left for school Saturday morning."

"Leroy, it's Sunday night now. Are you telling me you don't know where my sister is since Saturday morning?"

"That's what I'm telling you," Dad answered. "And she hasn't called or anything?"

"No Andre, she did not."

"Well something's not right because this is just not like her. Why would she do this? She was supposed to be here for Stella's baby shower but she didn't show, and that's the real reason I'm calling. Did you try any of her friends?"

"You know your sister doesn't have any friends,"

Dad replied.

"Listen Leroy, I'm going to call you right back, okay?"

"All right, man."

I almost tripped over Troy's shoe trying to run back to my room when I heard Dad coming. I ran back to the kitchen when I heard the phone ring again. I heard Uncle Andre's voice again. "Leroy?"

"Yeah it's me."

"Yeah, man. I just called my mom, she's worried, man. She's going crazy. I'm coming over there and we can put in a missing-person report and try to call everyone we know because she never did this before."

After they hung up I went to lie down. I knew it would take Uncle Andre a while because he was coming from the Bronx. Uncle Andre and my mom were close because they were just about the only family members left in New York City. Mom's mother moved to Syracuse with the majority of mom's brothers and sisters. Mother had nine brothers and three sisters.

Dad and Andre called the police and told them Mother was missing. The police questioned me because the last time I spoke to Sam he told me that he was taking my mother Saturday to buy me a coat. The police went on their way to Sam's house to find out anything they could.

After the police left, Uncle Andre kept watching Dad. "Are you all right, man? You don't look too good?"

"I'm fine," Dad said.

"I think you need to see a doctor," Uncle Andre insisted.

"I'll be all right."

"But Leroy, look at you. You can barely walk. You're throwing up all over the place. I mean it's obvious that you're weak."

"Okay I'll go to the hospital. I can drive myself. I need you to take my kids to my sister Janna's house. You remember my sister Janna right?"

"Yeah, the one that lives not too far from the ferry in Stapleton?"

"Yes, and I'll call my sister right now and let her know you're coming."

Dad's sister Janna lived in Stapleton by the ferryboat. She was cool. She was our step aunt but you wouldn't have known that. She gave us whatever we asked for and allowed us to do whatever we wanted. She had brown smooth skin, and long hair. She was on the thick side and wasn't scared of anyone, not even a man. When we got there, she and my uncle talked while I went in my cousin Tanisha's room. We played on her bunk beds for a while. As I played I still had my mom in the back of my mind.

The hospital called about Dad; he was being admitted for pneumonia, which meant we would be staying at Janna's house for a few days.

At Aunt Janna's house I took showers; I ate; I got myself ready for bed. I played with my brothers and cousins, and I smiled like I was okay. I don't think anyone knew that I really wasn't. Inside I was dying. I had no patience. Each day I couldn't go another without Mama. All the grown folks were trying to get to the bottom of it all. They were searching and asking questions. I just looked in everybody's eyes searching for answers, trying to read facial expressions.

At night, when the whole house was asleep except me, I lay wondering, trying hard not to worry or talk to God. Because I knew something was wrong and every time I prayed to God and asked for something good, I got something bad, so I stopped praying. I lay there thinking Mama must have left us or found another man. She'll be back later to get us. Maybe she just needed some time for herself.

I was realistic. I dealt with logic and facts. So, of

course, I thought if she stayed out too long somebody might have hurt her. Growing up in the city you automatically knew, the streets were dangerous and the people couldn't be trusted.

I will never forget a detective called Janna's house asking her questions she couldn't answer, so she passed the phone to Caseen. He couldn't answer them either, so as he held the phone he asked me the questions. Caseen came to Tanisha'a room where I was sitting on her top bunk. I was already watching him and waiting anxiously. "Shiree" he said as he approached me. I sat up anxiously. "Do Mom have a scar on her stomach and do she have green ruby earrings. "Yes, yes," I said while nodding.

Caseen hung the phone up, and went back to what he was doing. But I was left puzzled. Mom did have a scar on her stomach from a cesarean she had with my little brother, and she did have green ruby earrings. If someone on the phone just described her, then they must have seen her.

I went to sleep confused and woke up confused. Mom was missing for approximately three days. Aunt Janna left the house for a while; Cousin Joyce and her boyfriend Manny were left to watch us. Everybody was dancing to Reggae music, including myself. I enjoyed myself for exactly one minute. And that was it, because this was no happy moment. I wondered, Where's Mama? Come on now I'm ready to go home. And so I sat down.

That's when the phone rang and Joyce answered it. From my seat on the couch, I could see Joyce. She dropped the phone and hollered all the way out the door.. All the kids ran behind her. We all watched her run up the stairs to someone's apartment. She didn't come downstairs until Janna came back. Janna walked in the door shaking her head in disappointment. I was one of the first people watching the scenes. I didn't miss a beat. Mama always said, "You can't tell Shiree something indirectly because she's gonna want to know everything. And she will question you until she is clear."

So now somebody had to tell me something. Whatever it was, I knew it wasn't good. I said to myself, "Oh my God, Leroy died in the hospital."

Manny took Caseen in the back room. I walked around trying to find some answers, asking people, "What?" while everybody was dealing with their own grief and shock. Nobody would tell me anything. I went to the back room and Caseen lifted his head, his eyes were full of water, and he had his hand balled up in a fist like he was going to smash something. I panicked and ran in the bathroom. I wanted to scream, "Mama come home now, I'm scared."

Aunt Janna walked in the bathroom and I read her eyes. She felt sorry for me. She did not want to tell me anything, and if there was any way she could have gotten around telling me, she would have. Because you just don't tell a little girl like me that her mother is never coming back.

"Shiree, your mother is dead."

The woman found in Far Rockaway on the side of the store, stabbed to death with multiple stab wounds, was my mother. At six o'clock in the morning a storeowner was opening his store when he saw my mother lying there dead and abandoned. As I cried, I began to tremble. Janna took me to her room. As I walked, I saw my little brothers, and I tried to imagine their pain. They were too young to understand. When I saw them, I cried harder. All kinds of things went through my mind. I knew this changed my life forever. I was really scared and I felt alone. I realized I had felt that way since Mom left for school. I didn't know how I could go on without her. I never was very good at being away from her. I was so close to Mom; I loved her as if I birthed her. That moment I felt sorry for my brothers, and my dad who was still in the hospital.

Janna tried her very best to comfort me, and I felt safe. She put a blanket around me as I trembled and cried. I asked her to close the shades on the windows I was so terrified. I lay down and continued to cry. Janna lay next to me with her arm around me. That night Janna was the first person I told about what Sam did to me.

She could not believe that my own father would put his hands in my panties. She just completely flipped. She went on and on to say, "Shiree, please tell me you're lying." But after looking in my sad frightened eyes full of water, she knew it was true. Aunt Janna jumped off the bed and placed her hand on her hip. "Get the fuck out of here."

I could tell she did not like what she heard at all. And for some reason I started to become scared of Sam. I was still trembling and I jumped at every sound I heard. I had this feeling he was coming to get me. I was sure of it.

I awoke the next morning from a deep sleep, with swollen puffy red eyes. As I staggered into the bathroom, Aunt Janna was nowhere in sight. Joyce was watching all the kids. As I was leaving the bathroom and entering the living room, Sam was in the hallway trying to get by Joyce. I started to tremble.

Aunt Janna was walking down the hallway when she saw Sam.

He played it cool. "How you doing, Janna? I came to get Shiree."

She barged right past him. "She ain't going nowhere with your nasty ass."

He gave her a look to say he didn't know what was going on. He was flashing papers around. "Look Janna the judge granted me custody."

"I don't give a damn what papers you got, get the fuck away from my door."

I started crying again. I couldn't believe all this was happening. It all felt like a long bad dream and I just wanted to wake up. Standing there and knowing my mom was not coming back, I hated Sam even more. I never knew much about Sam, except that Mom said he was my biological father. But if you came to me and asked me, who my father was, I would have told you Leroy. The man who took care of me, clothed me, fed me, educated, disciplined and loved me, the man I call Daddy.

I met Sam when I was eleven. He and Mother were still legally married, but separated since I was three. When I first went to his condo, it was like visiting a stranger. He also was a stranger I never wanted to meet, because I never really trusted him. I always sensed something about him wasn't right. He appeared fake to me. His whole personality seemed like an act, and I never cared for him much.

Sam left and to my surprise he came back fifteen minutes later with the police.

From the door Janna was cursing Sam out. "I don't care about the police you're not getting this girl."

The police walked right in. "Miss, miss, calm down. Let me talk to you over here. Okay, what is your name?"

"Janna," she told him with attitude and her hand on her hip.

"Listen he's got papers from the court a judge signed giving him custody of his daughter." His eyes roamed the house and he said, "Is she here?"

Aunt Janna responded quickly. "She's here, but like I said, she ain't going nowhere."

The police officer said, "Ma'am you let me handle this. Where is the child's mother?

"Her mother is dead." Janna was getting loud. "And that sick mother fucker right there put his hands between that little girl's legs."

The police told Janna to watch her mouth. "This is my mother-fucking house, you forgot? And without a warrant all of ya'll can get out."

"All right listen, let me speak to the girl."

"That girl's name is Shiree," she quickly reminded him.

I cried and cried and cried, and I was so scared. All that talking, I already knew the outcome would not be in my favor.

Officer said, "I am very sorry for your loss and everything that's going on, but I can't do anything to stop this guy from getting his child. Those are the judge's orders."

"That's a damn shame," Aunt Janna said following the officers as they escorted me out. She would not give up. "You mean to tell me you give a child to a rapist? Your suppose to be the police." "What do you want me to do ma'am?" "Arrest his ass." The police officer ignored her statement. "Goodnight," he said. "You kiss my ass, and the judge could kiss it too." She defended my honor to the fullest and talked a whole lot of shit to Sam. Manny had to get her before she went to jail.

After eight hours I realized I had no control over the matter. I cried and hugged everybody goodbye. The hardest part was leaving my brothers, the only family I ever knew. I loved them and at that time I needed them.

I looked at Sam in disgust, and then got in his car. He patted me on my leg. "You'll be okay. You are my child. You belong with me."

I just looked out the window as the tears rolled down my face.

From what I heard, a rumor going around that Sam

killed my mother. Mom's sister Gina was just at our house from Syracuse a week before Mom's death, and she said Mama told her that Sam threatened to kill her. I also heard that when Dad found out about Mom, he snatched all the tubes and needles out of him. Basically, Daddy went crazy.

Sam talked to me while he drove to the Bronx. He was taking me to his mother's house on Valentine Road. "Stop that crying. You don't have anything to be afraid of. I'm your father. I'm going to take care of you now, you'll be all right."

All the grandkids called his mother Nana because that's what she preferred. Nana was sweet, short and petite, very light skinned with long hair. She spoke with a Jamaican accent that I always adored. Nana was born and raised in St. Thomas in the Virgin Islands.

Sam and Nana got together at the kitchen table, drinking liquor and flapping their mouths. I sat down in the living room, staring at the television but not watching it. I grew up with five brothers, Mom and Dad, and so I never had the chance to feel alone.

Nana kept coming in asking me, "Shiree are you okay baby?" She smiled. "Your father told me that you told the police he touched you. Is that true?" She looked confused and ashamed of me.

"Yes," I responded in a very low tone, but a head nod to go with it so that she understood me.

"Why did you tell the police your father touched you?"

"Because it's true," I told her.

"Now darling, do you expect us believe that?" She pissed me off right there.

I turned my head away from her and back to the television, trying not to roll my eyes. Why can't it be true? I thought. Because your dear Sam said it wasn't. While he sat there looking like he was sad, or should I say pretending to be sad and hurt. I knew he wasn't. He had that please-feel-sorry-for-me look on his face. And it worked for Nana, but all I felt for him was disgust.

I slept with Nana that night, and I thanked God that we stayed at Nana's house that night instead of Sam's.

I woke up to two unfamiliar voices outside the door. I could hear them talking and I knew I was the subject of their conversation. I just lay there in Nana's bed.

Sam peeked in, "Are you up Shiree?"

I said, "Yeah I'm up."

"Your Aunt Sandra and Sharon are here to see you, okay?"

"Okay," I responded okay even though my tone was low.

In a sharp loud voice Sam replied, "Did you hear me, Hun?"

"Yes, I said yeah."

"Well speak up, Hun, I can't hear you. I'll be out here when you get up."

After he shut the door, I rolled my eyes and got out the bed. I stood there looking at the bed thinking I should make it up.

My Aunt Sandra came barging in. "Hey niece, look at you, you have grown so big into a little lady, and you look like your daddy with your pretty self." She hugged me and walked away talking about, "I know I got some fine nieces."

I looked at her and thought, lady I don't even know you. I seen you about two or what three times. And I wasn't trying to hear that stupid mess.

That's how Aunt Sandra was, loud and crazy. She was light-skinned, tall, with hair that touched her butt.

Aunt Sharon came in after Sandra and hugged me and asked me was I all right. She said, "Oh I'm sorry sweetie." And it was her sympathy I appreciated. She grabbed my hand and walked me into the kitchen where

Sam was sitting at the table calling me.

He said, "Your Aunt Sandra is going to take you to the beauty parlor today to get your hair done okay?"

I nodded.

"Open your mouth, I'm speaking to you."

"Yes," I said, growing impatient with Sam. He had me on the spot. I stood there gathered around the table with my Nana, two of my aunts and Sam. They were all watching me, smiling, so I had to throw on one of my fake smiles because I was not happy nor was I feeling the moment. Only one I was really feeling was my Aunt Sharon. I wanted to take her in the room and cry in her lap.

Aunt Sandra asked Sam, "What do you want done to her hair?"

Sam ran his fingers through my hair shaking his head as if he was disappointed. "Tell them to hook it up. It's a little damaged." He sucked his teeth and took a breath and said, "Actually it's damaged a lot. She had some good hair, but her mother didn't take care of it. Colleen let it fall out."

I looked at my Aunt Sharon, she felt my pain and I walked out the kitchen.

At the salon I waited my turn, sat in the chair without a word. I was a little girl, so Sandra gave the beautician orders. I sat still for way too long and when they got done my hair was way too short. Aunt Sandra told the beautician to cut my hair off. I thought, Is this a joke? I'm twelve-years-old, stepping out with a short cut. I was so pissed off I walked ahead of Aunt Sandra the whole way to Nana's. I could have cried because I wanted to give her a good piece of my mind but that wasn't my style. My mother would have never allowed me to talk to an adult like that.

I went with Sam to prepare for my moms funeral, and he let me pick out the casket. He got on my nerves the whole day. Sam acted like your average white boy. He tried to be so proper. He's sophisticated and intelligent, but nasty. He was always trying to change me. He wanted to tell me how to eat, how to dress, how to fucking sit. What got me was how could he tell me how to feel? He tried to manipulate me.

He sat at the table with Nana, drinking as usual. "Nana, can I get some homemade iced tea?"

"Sure honey, help yourself. It's in the fridge." Sam smiled at me as I entered the kitchen and turned back toward his mother shaking his head. "You know Ma, it's a damn shame Colleen put Leroy before Shiree and her brothers. She did not take care of them properly."

When I heard what Sam said, I accidentally swallowed a huge ice cube and nearly choked. I could not believe my ears. He talked about my mother in front of me. I wanted to spit in his face. He didn't consider my feelings as a young girl who just lost her mother. Was I supposed to agree with him? Was I supposed to choose sides? All I knew was I hated him. I didn't know him or his family. I didn't belong there.

His sister Sharon made me feel good and safe. She was more than sweet. I felt that she connected with me and understood me in a sincere way.

My family was on their way down from Syracuse, and I wanted to be with them. That was all I thought about. I often imagined my aunt's pretty faces and the pain they must be experiencing. Sam knew I wanted to be with them, but he didn't care. He felt like I was his child and so I belonged with him.

On the day of the wake, Sam took me to Mickey's Funeral Parlor on Lenox Avenue in Harlem. We got there before anyone else did. I could barely believe my eyes, to see my mom resting in that casket. I was shocked, but I knew it was some fucked up shit. I took a quick look at my little brothers. I spotted Caseen walking in with Grandma and all my family from Syracuse. I got excited and began to walk towards them.

"Shiree," Sam called me.

"Yes."

"Where are you going?"

"I'm going to say hi to my grandmother." I continued to walk off.

"Shiree," he called me again.

I turned back toward him.

"Come over here," he said. "Look, you can tell me you're going over there so I know where you are. You don't just walk off." He grabbed my hand. "Come on," he said.

"How are you doing Clara?" Sam wrapped his arm around her with a Kool-Aid smile.

"Hi Grandma." I hugged her.

"Hi baby." Grandma hugged me back. She was always so serious. This time I knew she was hurt.

Sam smiled at everybody, knowing he didn't like them. He was jealous because I showed Mama's family more love than I showed him and his family. "Well Clara I will see you at the funeral we was just leaving. Let's go Shiree," he said, pointing at me as if that was a signal to move now. Sam quickly took me out of there.

I did not understand him, but somehow I knew Sam was an evil man. He did not want me to be with my family and I was sad. I couldn't hug them or talk to them.

The day of the funeral was October 23, 1991. Everybody was dressed in black. Sam rented a limousine. I sat beside Nana, and Aunt Sandra sat across from me with a jacked-up men's suit on. Sam sat next to her with his Bacardi Rum in his hand. They were all drinking Hennessy.

I sat there wondering if Sam thought we were attending a funeral or a wedding. I didn't remember my mother and his wedding, but I would rather have attended his funeral than my mother's. My father was tall, about six two, very slim, and brown-skinned with good hair he kept short. It was slightly curly, but very soft.

The funeral home was filled with mourning people. Mom was loved by many people. There were family and friends from all over, upstate, downstate and different prisons. There were even some of mother's classmates from the college she was attending.

Uncle Ernest stepped in the door and saw Mother from afar and flipped. He hollered, "Take my sister out of there."

Somebody grabbed him because he was crazy. He probably would have tried to take his sister out.

He was bent over as if he couldn't really hold himself up and kept hollering, "Get her out."

Aunt Gina was six months pregnant; when she walked in the room, her first glance at my mother she passed out. Thank God someone was behind her to catch her.

As we all sat down and the preacher preached, Mother's baby sister Gale kept crying out loud. She sat in her seat holding her stomach like it just ached so badly while she kept rocking. And she kept screaming, "Why, why, why her?" Then she said, "Take me with her."

My two baby brothers were not at the funeral. I overheard that Troy was trying to get in the casket with Mom at the wake. And the both of them had bad dreams that night. I did not see Dad, and from what I knew he was still in the hospital.

I sat with Sam and watched every move that was made. Caseen walked up to our resting mom and stood there crying. Sam walked up behind him. Caseen turned around and Sam extended his hand, offering Caseen a handshake. And that's when I saw Caseen's hand go up and I saw Sam hit the floor. Sam crawled away from Caseen and then I watched him run from my brother.

My grandmother grabbed me and we ran out of the funeral home. My Uncle Juney's wife, Natural Earth, took me to her house, until later that night when Grandma came to get me. They called and kept me posted as to what was going on.

Sam continued to run from my brother and refused to move the casket to the burial grounds until I got back. But the police were going to arrest him if he didn't let them take Mom's body out of there.

I missed them putting my mother to rest in the ground. They buried her at Rest Land Memorial Park in East Hanover, New Jersey.

I was at Uncle Andre's house in the Bronx on Fordham Road. Caseen and all my family were there too. I knew Grandma was going to take me to Syracuse with her. Leroy and Troy were still at Aunt Janna's and were going to stay with their father Leroy when he got out of the hospital.

I was scared, but I was happy because I felt safe. I was around Mama's family who loved her and knew me.

Chapter 2
The Big Change

Syracuse was not quite like New York. Cabs did not stop when you waved; there were no trains to ride; and the weather was not that nice. There were no bright lights after hours, no loud noises, and nobody knew what a hero was. Syracuse was a small country town, and if you got out often, you would eventually notice the same faces. Cars didn't drive that fast or take up much room on the streets. I didn't see any projects.

Grandma gave Caseen and me each a bedroom and she signed us up for school.. Caseen went to Henniger High School, and I went to Lincoln Junior High. Our schools were not far apart, so we walked together every morning. I was popular in my school because I was from New York and had a deep accent. I was different, and I knew it. I knew that I had been through something. There was a dark empty spot inside of me. Some nights I lay in bed crying, realizing that I was not dreaming, my best friend was really gone.

Grandma was the person I wanted to be with for a variety of reasons. But adapting was beyond challenging. After school and on weekends I was always bored, and Caseen was always gone. Nobody filled the house but Grandma and Grandpa. I didn't exist to anybody and nobody talked to me. It was way too soon after Mom's death for me to be alone.

I tried going to my Aunt Savannah's house after school while I attended the library she lived next to. All my aunts resembled Mom and had a lot of her ways, being as how she practically raised them. I enjoyed being around my cousins, and I always went home before dark. But Grandma didn't like that. When I came in the door Grandma always had an attitude.

One evening she looked at me, rolled her eyes, and walked away, as if to say I disgusted her. She walked back toward me as if she had to get something off her chest. "You waited till you got up here with me to run the streets. You didn't do it with your mother cause you couldn't, she wasn't going for it."

I began defending myself. "Grandma, I went to the library."

She started screaming at me, "You were not at no library I called over to Savannah's house and you were over there. So stop that damn lying"

"I only stopped by because she lives near the library, and I wanted to see my little cousins."

"No, you just wanted to get your ass over there, so you used the library for an excuse. " She sucked her teeth and kept yelling at me while she walked around looking for something. "What the hell would you wanna go over there for in the first place? They sleep all day, don't do nothing with themselves, then they go out to the stores and be stealing." Grandma rolled her eyes again, sucked her teeth and threw her hands in the air. She said she was an old lady she couldn't take it and walked away.

She always walked around with the screw face, and talked about me behind my back. I could hear her on the phone, "All she wants to do is run the streets."

Grandma always had the look as if I got on her nerves.

My bed always felt good after a long day. I kept tossing and turning because of the sound of Grandma's voice in my head. I didn't know if she knew it or not, but her words really hurt me. She thought the worst of me. I really did go to the library. I did my work first, and I took out books that I actually read. But I also wanted to see my family. Was that a crime? I knew Caseen was not in his room so I went to use the bathroom and be nosy. When I found his bed empty, I got depressed. He was never home and Grandma never yelled at him.

Caseen's features began to sharpen he was getting older. He was a tall nice-looking light-skinned brother. He had a head like LL Cool Jay, along with LL's eyes and full lips. He had deep beautiful brown eyes. The type of eyes you would label him fine just for them. He had a lot of girls after him, my friends would always ask me questions about him, and they wanted the hook up. But he was crazy about this one girl named Melinda Campbell. She went to the same school as he did and was from Queens, New York. She was what we called back then a fly girl, because she stuck out from the rest of the crowd. She was slim, pretty, brown-skinned with long hair. She had a pair of door knockers in her ears and she was down for him.

Grandma was like a good mother. She worked hard, cooking and cleaning. The house was never dirty and we never missed a meal. She went to work and still kept the house up. You could look at Grandma and tell she was one of those hardworking women from the south. She never sat down and there was nothing lazy about her.

Grandpa got up every morning and sat in the living room watching cowboys, waiting for Grandma to serve him his breakfast. After he finished, he would get his coat and hat and he was off to the liquor store. He had to have a bottle or else he would get the shakes. Often he went around collecting aluminum he found the streets and traded it in for some cash. He wasn't a cool laid-back grandpa. He was the loud obnoxious type. He didn't like noise at all. He didn't like people moving around, whether sitting with him in the living room or walking around his house.. He would suck his teeth and say, "God damn it, what the hell is wrong with you gal, can't you sit still?" Or if you walked around the house he would say, "Damn, what are you looking for? Ain't nothing in there, Godly, ain't you got nothing to do?" If you brought a child around that wasn't too cute, he would tell you in a heartbeat. He would tell the child too. If the child was jumping around he'd say, "Oh, hell no boy, sit your ugly ass down; you got the nerve to be jumping around ugly as you is." Then he would call my grandmother, "Clara, whose ugly ass child is this? They just drop their damn bad-ass kids here, like this some daycare or something. Make him sit down before I kill him.

Every morning before school Grandma gave us a glass of orange juice and made us a breakfast that stuck to us. We sure needed it, because we walked a few miles every morning in blizzards. Each day I walked, I thought about the North Pole, while the snow covered my ankles and touched my knee caps, and the frozen wind smacked me in the face.

I decided to stay in the house to make Grandma happy, but it was just so boring. When Grandma had herself a drink, she was the world's best grandma. Grandma would laugh and smile. It was the only time she would talk to you and call you honey. I loved her like that, and one day I told her.

She said, "Oh yeah."

It got to be like, if she wasn't drinking, you were not getting a smile or anything pleasant out of her, just a screw face. That screw face made me believe that she didn't like me.

I used to hear her on the phone telling people, "She don't help me do anything, the girl is lazy and she sleeps all day."

What did she want me to do? I thought cleaning up after myself was good enough. Of course, I never saw anything to do. Everything looked clean to me. She would get up early Saturday and Sunday mornings, six, sometimes seven, o'clock to iron curtains and fold sheets. I never did those things before. And shit, Saturday and Sundays were days off from school, I was not getting up at those hours. I was usually tired, and I deserved to sleep. I got up every morning walked through blizzards for hours and got straight A's. What the hell was the problem?

When I lived with Mom, she never taught us how to clean. I used to say, "Ma, I'll wash the dishes, or I'll mop the floor."

She would say, "No," or "You don't know how." We had our chores and those only consisted of our room and the bathroom. Our daily chores took place every night after dinner. One person washed the table and the chairs down, while the other person swept the floors.

One night I tried to help Grandma out. I figured I would do something since she complained all the time. I saw a few dishes in the sink, so I put soap on a rag and started washing.

Grandma walked past me and took a double look when she realized what I was doing. She turned around and snatched the rag right out of my hand and turned the water off with her screw face. She said, "You wasting my soap."

I turned around and walked away. I was humiliated. Why couldn't she just show me how to make a pot of dishwater?

Then she started to pace the floor talking shit. "You like when I drink so you can take advantage of me, right? So you can get my money?"

I stood in my room doorway watching her pace around. I knew she was angry. "Grandma, I never asked you for any money. It's just that, when you drink you are so happy. How do you think I feel, watching you walk around with your face all grumpled up?"

She grabbed the broom and started running toward me. My eyes got wide and I ran toward Caseen's room. She ran behind me and whacked me across my back before I even made it. I could hear Grandpa in the backroom, "What you doing to that girl?"

I made it to Caseen's room and fell on his bed, after she whacked me again. That's when she whacked me across my back. Each time she hit me I hollered and jumped around. I just sat there crying, rubbing my back because it was stinging. She left me sitting there and got on the phone and told everybody I called her ugly.

Caseen started selling drugs, and he thought he was a real OG. He was rocking the hottest kicks. He had a closet full of clothes and his pockets were swollen. His jeans got bigger, and his seizers turned into fades. Word on the street was he had the whole Kennedy square locked down. He was doing all the things that Mom and Dad would have never gone for.

Dad never got the chance to formally say goodbye after Mom died, so he came up to Syracuse to see us. I was so happy to see him and my baby brothers. I felt sorry for them. I saw a lot of pain. I never, out of all the years, saw my father look so stressed, and like he had no control and like he had nothing. I was going to miss him.

Caseen was never crazy about Daddy because, for one thing, he was our stepfather. He never let Caseen get a fade. He always cut his hair all the way down, and he used to beat us.. We did not get away with anything. But Caseen stopped getting beatings the year he turned fourteen. Daddy took off his belt to whoop Caseen one night, and Caseen said, "Let's go outside, nigga."

Dad started fronting like he was going, while Mom was jumping around, going crazy. They never went outside, but Caseen never got another beating. I guess Caseen felt like he was getting to old for that shit.

It was the end of the school year and I was in class.. I was happy, just like every year, because I was getting promoted and still getting honors. That's when I heard my name over the loud speaker. The voice said for me to report to the principal's office. Class was almost over, so I packed my Jan sport and did the dip to the office. As soon as I got in front of the door, I saw Sam, Nana and the bitch that cut my hair.

I turned around and took flight toward the staircase. I dropped my Jan sport on the second flight. I kept going to the third flight, when a security guard grabbed me. He called my name out, "Hey Shiree, are you Shiree?"

"No I'm not," I told the man and began to walk away.

"Just a minute," he said, his hand on my arm. "I need you to come with me to the office.

I started shouting at him while I tried to pull away from the tight grip he had on me. "Get off of me." I sucked my teeth and huffed and puffed. "What you want, man? I'm not Shiree and I didn't do anything, so get off of me. I can walk on my own."

"I think you are, or else you wouldn't have run."

When I saw Sam standing in the office, I said, "Hell no, I'm not going with you."

The principal was standing by his desk. "Please sit down Shiree," he said.

"No, you sit down, I'm going home."

"Shiree," he said, looking very surprised, "I never

heard you speak like that."

"That man came all the way from New York to get me. I can't go I live here with my grandmother, and I got to go home right now or else she'll think I'm running the streets."

He grabbed me and I said, "You better get off me, man. You don't understand."

He said, "Okay, calm down. Stop crying and come inside my office. He's not taking you off these grounds."

After I told him, in tears because I was frightened and couldn't understand why he wouldn't leave me alone.

Grandma came marching into the office with her bag on her hip and we all got escorted to Family Court.

We were there for hours before a tall dark-skinned skinny lady walked up to me. "Hi Shiree, my name is Mrs. Shindle. I work for social services. What I'm gonna do is find somewhere for you to stay for a little while until the judge determines what he wants to do.

"Okay, so I can go to my aunt's house."

"No Shiree, I'm sorry. I have to find a place for you outside of family."

My tears dried up. "Oh you mean I have to go to a foster home?"

"Yes, Shiree."

"But why, why can't I stay with my grandmother?" Fresh tears began to fall.

"Because the judge wants to make sure you are safe. The judge could not decide what's best for you in one day. He needs to hear everybody out. Then he will make his decision where you will live."

I went with the lady and cried as I walked to a designated area. More hours went by until she found me a place to stay. As I waited I asked God, "Why?"

Miss Williams was a sweet but stern religious lady. She was short and dark-skinned, and she rarely smiled.

I did not know one person who loved the Lord more then she did. She truly believed in Him and feared Him. She had the qualities of a strong black serious woman, and you could tell she didn't take any shit.

Two girls were already there. Their names were Missy and Tiffany. Tiffany was adopted, but Missy was a foster child and twelve just like me. You could tell that Miss Williams had Tiffany broke in to her religious ways. The girl was almost a saint, but that's what I liked about her. She was sweet and cool, and I could talk to her as if she was an older sister because she was five years older than I. On the other hand Missy was a simple bitch. She had a big mouth and loved to front. It was obvious to a duck that she truly believed she was all that.

I told her quick, "You are not all that. Don't front for me."

She tried to get loud with me, and that's when I stepped in the middle of the floor and said, "We could do this."

She pretended like she was about something, but she wasn't. As soon as she saw Tiffany coming, she threw her hands up and asked me, "What's up."

I swung at her and missed because Tiffany was in the way. If Tiffany the saint didn't save her, I was going to mop her bald-headed ass all over that room.

I always felt lonely in that house. It was very big with six dark and gloomy rooms. The whole house was dark with no sunlight. The living room had furniture that looked like it came out when Granny was born.

Miss Williams was a very nice lady. She bought me stockings, shoes and a dress, and took me to church. I heard beautiful music, people danced for the Lord and even cried. People danced so hard, shoes came off, and glasses and wigs. When the preacher man preached about devils in disguise and jealous people, I looked at Missy and hollered, "Yes Lord."

For two weeks all I did was go to church and meet with my lawyers. Miss Williams said that Sam wouldn't have any good luck for touching me. But I wasn't so sure he needed luck with all the money he had. His lawyer made me look like a pathological liar in that courtroom. I got on the stand and told the truth, but Sam denied ever doing such a nasty act as that. The judge made his decision for me to return to Sam's house in two weeks.

I did get to go home with Grandma until then. My heart dropped, plus I cried, but there was nothing I could do about it. Even though I believed Grandma didn't care too much for me, I still wanted to stay with her. I loved her.

Chapter 3
Strange Things

I rode in the back seat of Sam's gray Lincoln, while Sam drove and his wife sat in the passenger seat. I cried out all the water in my body before they came. Then I realized that my tears did not change anything. My tears did not bring Mama back, nor did they keep Caseen and I together. Now I had to face my new life.

Sam must have recently married Stephanie because before Mama died he did not have a wife. I could see this lady had a lot of compassion, and I was wondering what she was doing with a man like Sam. Sam was an aggressive man who always forced his opinion on everyone. He and only he could be right. Perhaps you were right and he was wrong, but he wouldn't admit it. He was the type to criticize and put you down if you made any mistakes. And the worst side of Sam was his jealous attitudes. A man like Sam you had to praise and don't praise nobody else while he was around. Stephanie had the sweetest little voice and a Costa Rican accent.

I realized that Sam had moved to Brooklyn, in Midwood. Webster Avenue was a decent block. It appeared to me he was living in the best building on the block. The co-op building had glass doors, and the lobby had clean mirrors on the walls and a sofa and a love seat in the lobby. When we got to the door on the second floor, Sam put the key in and went in. I walked in after and noticed some furniture from his old place coordinated with some new furniture. I have to say, he had a very nice apartment and I was impressed.

When you first come in, you walk into the dining room, which wasn't that big. It was big enough for his glass table with six chairs. It looked so expensive. The glass table did not have legs like most tables. It had fancy cement pillars underneath it. There was no door to separate the living room and the dining room. Off the living room was the kitchen on one side and my room on the other side. Their room was off the dining room to the left. The living room had a fancy look to it. It had a brown soft three piece set in it. It had a sofa, love seat and a Lazy-Boy, end tables that were a mixture of glass and brown oak, and an entertainment center. He had real coconuts hanging from the ceiling. There was also a real stuffed turtle lying on the floor as a decoration. I had a nice cozy room with a thick mattress and box spring and soft blue carpet on the floor.

When I went to my room to unpack, Sam came in and said, "Hey Babe, are you all right?" Those were his favorite words. He was always asking someone if they were all right, and he was the type who always wanted to be asked if he was all right. He loved attention.

I was all right when I was in Syracuse, and he knew that. Plus, he knew I didn't want to be there, but I was so glad he had a wife there. I couldn't stand the thought of being alone with him. I was afraid of him. I thought he was capable of murder. He was like the terminator to me—he kept coming back.

I went to the bathroom and smiled at Stephanie on

my way. She didn't know how much I appreciated her being there and for not being like him. Something was weird about their relationship; they didn't seem like they were in love.

The next morning Sam came to my room an ordered me to get dressed. "I'm going to drop Stephanie to work and I'll be back to get you."

Stephanie had a job at the cleaners in Coney Island somewhere. I had the house alone for about thirty minutes. I ran some shower water while I unpacked my bags. It was definitely time to go shopping. All I had decent was the three outfits Caseen bought me. My Gap jeans, my Guess shirts and my Calvin Klein outfit were the only things wearable. I jumped in the shower and jumped out quick. I was paranoid in the bathroom because, for one thing, I wasn't used to that house and I was scared to death of Sam.

He got back just in time. I was dressed with one of my cute Guess shirts with a pair of faded Guess jeans and my baby blue Air Max. I was standing in the bathroom curling my hair. I had one more part to curl and my mushroom style was done.

"You ready Babes?"

"Yeah," I hollered from the bathroom. I rode around with Sam while he took care of some business, until it was time to pick Stephanie up. We ate Chinese food that night. They stayed in their room and I stayed in the living room watching movies all night.

There were no kids my age in the building, just a bunch of middle-aged Russian couples. I already knew there were a lot of kids who lived in the building across the street. I saw the kids playing in the Johnny pump yesterday.. I walked across the street to see everything, when one girl walked up to me. She was short, dark brown with a baby face. She wore her hair in ponytails like Mama used to do my hair. "Hi, my name is

Shakena." She approached. "What's your name?"

"Shiree."

"Did you just move across the street?" she asked, pointing to my building.

"I just got here, but my father's been living here." I told her.

Shakena pointed to Sam's Lincoln and asked, "Is that your father's car?"

"Yeah that's his car."

"I know your father. He's mean," she said.

"Why do you say that?" I asked. Even though she was a hundred percent right and I couldn't agree more, I had to ask.

"Just by the way he looks at us we can tell he doesn't like us. One day he called us all kinds of names for leaning on his car. How old are you?"

"Twelve. I'll be thirteen next month. How old are you?" I asked curiously because she looked young.

"Me?" she asked pointing to herself, "I'm eleven. I live in this building on the fourth floor. Come on let me introduce you to everybody."

I didn't go upstairs until later on that evening. Before I left, Shakena and I exchanged numbers. The next day she called me and I was back outside.

Making friends made a big difference in my life at that time. It helped me adapt.. I even tried giving Sam another shot at being a father, but he failed. He was just too controlling and weird. He just couldn't help himself. He craved attention. I gave him respect and began to open up to him a little. But that was not good enough for him.

So life was cool, just as long as Sam stayed out of my way and I stayed out of his. Since I started going outside and coming in late, I wasn't around him much.

He started complaining, "All you think about is your friends. You need to be in this house before it gets dark." And he meant that.

The next day when it started to get dark, I was only sitting outside the building across the street with the other kids. I saw Sam coming from across the street.

"Let's go," he said.

I rolled my eyes and got up and left.

Sam scolded me in the elevator.

"Why can't I stay outside?"

"Because it's dark. Can't you see?"

"But I was only sitting across the street. It's not even late yet. All the other kids are still sitting out there."

He got real nasty and said, "Let me explain something to you. Don't tell me about those other fucking kids. If their parents don't care about them, that's them. You are mine, my fucking child, and I want you in at a decent hour. You hear me?"

To me it was like, whatever. I understood what he was saying, but it was the way he said it that made me sick. Even though I did not like Sam, I respected him because that's how I was taught. I only paid him no mind.

I was serving myself a plate of one of Stephanie's meals from her country when the phone rang.

"It's for you, Hun," Sam hollered from his room.

I picked the phone up in the living room, and Sam hung his end up. "What's up Shakena," I said, while holding my plate, about to have a seat.

Sam was walking toward the kitchen when he said, "Tell her to call you back. You're eating. Damn, didn't you just see her? Have some class about yourself."

"Shakena, I'll call you back when I'm done eating."

He came back in the living room, where I was still eating. He said, "Whatever you did at your mother's house, and at your grandmother's, leave that shit there.

That's ghetto shit. People who don't have anything, or ain't used to shit. We don't live like that here."

After I ate I took the phone in my room and called Shakena back. As we talked, Sam picked the phone up in his room and said, "I need to use the phone."

So I hung up, and I'm thinking he's trying to fuck with me. I called Shakena back. From the noises I heard in the background I was beginning to think Sam was listening in on my conversation. And when the phone beeped, I tried to click over but it wouldn't go through. That's how I knew he was listening.

Sam was not around. Stephanie seemed like a nice lady. I peeked into her room. "Hi Shiree."

"Hi. Where's Sam?" I asked her.

"I don't know. He just say he'll be back."

"I like your accent," I told her.

She smiled. "Oh, thank you. So how have you been doing, you like it here?"

"No," I told her bluntly. "You probably already know I don't want to be here."

"He told me about your mother, I'm sorry for you," she said.

"Did he tell you that he put his hands in my panties too?"

"Yeah he say you make that up. He say you're a liar because you want to stay in Syracuse."

"Stephanie, I'm not lying. He really did that. I swear to God."

"Oh my God," she said. "He really do that?"

"What do you like about him?" I asked her.

"Well, you know, when we first met he was so nice. I don't know what happened to him. He changed a little, you know. Sometime he yell at me when I make mistake and he get real mad sometime."

She hesitated to speak and I knew she was leery about telling me that stuff. "I won't tell him anything you tell me."

"No, don't tell him. You know your father." She put her head down for two seconds and lifted it back up. "I stab him," she said. She put her hand over her heart. "In his chest." I was shocked. "Are you serious?" I asked. She nodded. "He was hitting me. The police came. I went to jail, and he came bail me out. Your father, sometimes evil man." This is the perfect time to ask I thought. "Do he listen in on my calls?" Stephanie smiled. "Yes. How do you know?" "Because I could tell," I told her.

As I walked away I remembered asking Sam about that scar on his chest, he told me he had to have an operation. He said he was so stressed he almost died. He was trying to say I stressed him out by taking him through the court matters.

Sam did not wear boxers, unlike most big boys; he was still wearing tighty whities. How do I know? Because it was summer and he did not wear shirts, just his bare chest and tighty whities. Stephanie wore t-shirts, and panties.

I bumped into Sam outside the bathroom.

"Shiree, why do you have on so many clothes?" He tugged at my Polo sweat pants. "This is hot."

"I'm not hot." I looked at him like he was crazy.

"You don't have to wear so many clothes around the house. You can dress like Stephanie, that's decent." He turned behind him and looked at the bathroom. "Did you just shit?"

"No, I didn't."

"Well you don't have to close the bathroom door unless you're shitting. We're all family in here, okay hun? Let's be a family now."

I looked him directly in the eye and didn't bother to respond to him. I knew better than that. What a weirdo.

"Shiree? Shiree? Oh, there you are. I thought you

were outside. My sister Joane is coming over today. I want you to be home."

Apparently his sister did not like Stephanie for stabbing the shit out of her brother, so Stephanie stayed in her room.

I left him and his sister in the living room, drinking and talking, and went to bed early. Stephanie's tap on the shoulder awoke me. I looked up to see Stephanie standing over me. "Your father wants you to sleep in our room tonight."

As I thought nothing of it, I got up and followed her to the room. I jumped in the space near the door.

Stephanie jumped on Sam's dick and started to ride it like a horse, making sounds of pleasure.

My eyes opened wide, and my mouth flew open. I sat up in a state of shock and yelled out, "What the fuck, what are you doing?" I hopped out of his bed and ran to my room. I sat up on my bed saying, "Oh my God." I was still shocked when I saw Sam walking in my room butt-ass naked, dick hanging, with Stephanie on his arm, and she was butt-ass naked as well.

Sam said, "Come back in the room or we'll do it right here."

"Why are you doing this to me?"

"Come on Shiree, just come on. I'm giving you one minute or we're going to do it right here." Sam would not leave me alone, so I went back to their room. They repeated that same episode, only this time Sam puts his hand under the covers and starts to feel my leg.

"Get your hands off me. Don't you touch me." I pushed his hand away.

"Shh," he said, with his index finger pressed against his lips. He kept trying and I kept pushing. Then he got up and went to the living room to smoke a cigarette.

I followed Sam into the living room and sat down. "What was that all about?"

He was sitting there acting too cool, smoking his cigarette. "Stephanie and I are trying to make a baby and we need your help."

I looked at him like he was crazy and got up and went to bed. I knew that Sam put Stephanie up to that; I knew something was wrong with him. I looked at it as weird. I didn't know how to tell anyone something like that. It didn't make any sense, but that is what happened. I didn't understand it, and I felt forced to deal with the situation.. It was a part of my life. I often wondered, who's going to help me. But I also knew Sam had the control. I knew how we lived was not normal. That was no way for a father to raise a daughter. I never really thought about the future. I lived by the day, and I knew that wasn't me. When I was with Mom and Dad, I had a future, things to look forward to, dreams.

I never told my friends what was going on in my household. I did tell Shakena that Sam was listening in on my phone calls. So later that night, Shakena called. "Why didn't you come outside yesterday?"

"Oh, because my aunt came over last night so I had to stay in the house."

"Where's your father?" she asked.

I knew that Sam was listening on the other end, so I said, "He can hear you." So quite frankly, if he was listening, he now knew that I knew, so that would anger him, and it did.

He came home on his lunch break with a mean look on his face. Stephanie ran to the door. "Sam, what's wrong? You look upset."

He didn't pay her any mind. His eyes were focused on me as he walked toward me. He waved a piece of paper in the air. "This is what your friends left on my car."

I jumped off the couch and removed the paper from his hand. The paper read: Dear Sam, you are a freak and we know all about you. It did not surprise me one bit. He must have thought that of himself, because I knew he wrote that letter himself. I stood there calm, staring at him.

He knew from my look I didn't believe him. He said, "Oh, you don't care. You're putting your friends before your father. I don't want them in my house no more and your birthday party is cancelled."

I truly didn't care. He was full of surprises and no good things came out of him.

Sam went back to work. Stephanie came out of the room smiling. "You know Sam made that up right?"

"Yeah, I know he's a liar."

"He was so mad last night when you were talking to your friend on the phone. He's mad because you know he listens to your calls."

I was in my room writing a letter to my grandmother. I was informing her about that night Sam was having sex with Stephanie in front of me. Sam stood by my door in his Transit Authority uniform. He had to have been suspicious as to what I was writing. That's why he asked me to go to the store for him. He handed me the money and stood there waiting for me to leave, but I was waiting for him to leave my room so I could hide the letter.

He never left; he just kept saying, "Are you going or what?" He turned his back trying to pretend like he wasn't watching me when he really was.

I took my first chance and threw the pad under my mattress and left. On my way to the store, I knew he was reading my letter. I hurried up walking to the store and back. When I walked inside the house, Stephanie and Sam were sitting on the couch and my writing pad was sitting on the coffee table. Sam pointed to the couch. "Have a seat," he said.

As I got to the couch, I grew frustrated and asked

angrily, "Why were you going through my stuff? That's my own personal business. Oh, my God."

"Sit down," he said. "Why are you spreading lies to your grandmother?"

"Lies?" I responded. "Those are not lies."

"You think your grandmother gives a fuck about you? She didn't even want to keep you. And you want to write her telling her our business in this house. Now you're not going to get what Stephanie had for you for your birthday."

"I don't care," I said.

He kept going on and on. "You have more than the average child. What is your problem?"

"My problem?" I looked at him like I saw a ghost. I sat back with my mouth all twisted up, and my neck was all crooked. Yeah, the average child doesn't have a freak for a father, I thought.

"You're living real good and you don't appreciate shit."

"I don't care about none of this. I never had this before and I was happy. What I don't understand is why you do nasty things. The average child doesn't go through this. Just like you put your hands in my pants and lied about it, remember that?"

"Don't you dare bring that up. I don't know where you get your stories from." Sam preached for a while and I listened. He went to the kitchen, grabbed his Bacardi Rum and his glass.

He started feeling nice. I could always tell. His eyes would look sunken in, and he was being real nice to me after I had pissed him off. He put in videotapes to show Stephanie all the luxuries of a cruise line. Sam traveled all over the world.

He was enjoying himself, until I mentioned I was hot. That's when he told me to take my clothes off.

"What?" I looked at him like he was crazy.

"I'm not saying to get completely naked. There's nothing wrong with walking around in your t-shirt and panties. We're all family in here. Stephanie does it."

"That's different. She's your wife."

"When you go to the beach or pool, you wear a bikini, right?"

I nodded. "That's totally different." By that time I'm wondering, what is this man's malfunction?

The next thing I knew he was threatening to teach me a lesson. He gave me an alternative. "Throw your bikini down the incinerator, or take off all your clothes."

I looked at Stephanie, and said to myself, "Imagine this shit." I went to my room, took my two-piece out of my drawer and threw it down the incinerator. I went back in the house and sat down in the living room.

"Take your clothes off, Shiree," Sam ordered me.

"No," I said, and that was that. There was no way he was going to get me to take my clothes off. He must have been stupid, or that Puerto Rican rum was souping his ass up.

He still insisted on teaching me a lesson. His pupils were fully dilated and he was acting cool. "Take your chains off, Shiree."

"For what?"

"Because we are going to be tussling."

"You know what, you're right." I took my shit off.

Now Sam and I just happened to be sitting right next to each other on the couch. He stood up in front of me and grabbed me by my shirt. I grabbed him by his shirt. He pulled on my clothes. I pushed him back by his shirt as I pulled myself up off the couch. And so I flung his slinky ass down, right where he was sitting.

He looked at Stephanie. "Go run some bath water." She jumped up and ran to the bathroom like she didn't know what to do. He grabbed me again and I did the same move on him. Only this time Sam was mad. He never knew a little girl could have so much strength. So this time he knocked the shit out of me with a closed fist and my nose leaked like a faucet. It hurt so bad I stopped fighting. He stood me up and ripped my clothes off me, and I stood there and let him. He kept telling me to turn around.

Stephanie came out the bathroom and said in her Costa Rican accent, "Oh my God, what are you doing? Sam, put her in the tub."

Sam responded, "Don't tell me how to raise my child. If you don't like how I raise my child, you can get the fuck out and I'll raise her myself."

She went straight to her room and never said another word.

I cried and the blood from my nose made a trail on the way to the bathroom. I got in the tub. I was shaking and I felt beat up. I wondered what Stephanie thought of her husband now.. I just knew what just happened didn't really happen. I never in all my childhood years imagined that.

I cried in the tub. "Shh, stop crying Shiree. Open your legs and let me take a look down there. Did you know I graduated from med school?" I shook my head no, and kept crying. "Your not gonna get out this tub until you stop crying." He tried to manipulate me. "You are very fortunate. You don't know what I have for you in my will."

Sam went in my room and found me a pair of panties and a t-shirt to put on. Now Sam wanted to lay down the rules to the house. "From now on you are to wear clothes like that. You are to keep the door open when using the bathroom unless you're shitting.

I got out of the tub. I had to sit in his room for another lecture.

"Are you okay?" Stephanie asked. "I have a headache." I told her.

"Oh you have a headache? Let me get you some Tylenol." Sam knew just as well as I did that I had never swallowed a pill before. I had a fear of choking, so I never successfully swallowed one. And that night Sam made me bend my head back as he threw the pill in my mouthed and poured water down my throat until I gagged.

I awoke the next morning thinking I had a bad dream that night. But when I felt my head throb, and my eyes felt swollen, I knew it was no dream. I sat up on the side of my bed staring at the walls in disbelief. I had to get out of there.

On my way to the bathroom I ran into Stephanie. Sam had already left for work. "Are you okay?"

"No," I said as I slowly walked towards her. "I'm leaving."

"Do you have some place to go?"

"I have a father who treated me right and some baby brothers who live in Staten Island where I grew up."

"I will give you some money and ride with you to the ferryboat. I will tell your grandmother everything once you get away. I'm leaving soon, too."

We got off at the Bowling Green and walked over to the ferry. She waited with me until the boat arrived. When I heard the boat pull on the dock, I gave her a hug goodbye.

I looked for a seat in a section where I didn't see any people, because I felt sad. And I did not need anybody looking in my face or trying to hold a conversation with me. I had a lot on my mind; my mind was working a hundred miles per hour. I thought about the relationship Sam and Stephanie shared. What did Stephanie think of Sam now? She sat right there and saw all he did to me. She knew how nasty he became, criticizing and telling her what to do. Why didn't she leave him? Maybe she was scared of him. I thought maybe she paid him to marry her for a green card, and she had to wait for her papers to come in the mail.

When I got off the boat, I took a bus that dropped me off in front of the house. I knocked on Dad's door. He opened the door and looked happy to see me. I stepped inside and stood by the door. He hugged me. "How are you?" My little brothers jumped all over me.

I told him what happened and his smile turned sad. His appearance had changed. Dad was a fine high-yellow man, now he was brown-skinned and had lost a substantial amount of weight. He looked sick, but I never thought anything of it. I just thought maybe he was stressing over Mom.

I went into the room that Caseen and I grew up in and talked to my little brothers until Dad called me. When I went to see what he wanted, he handed me the phone.

It was Grandma. I was so delighted and felt a little relieved, thinking now everybody would know how Sam really was and would come and get me. "Hi Grandma."

"Hi. Now, what's going on with you?"

I told Grandma the whole incident that started from the letter I was writing to her.

She said, "Now why didn't you just tell Sam to get out of the bathroom?"

I started to daydream as I started to explain to her again, because she couldn't have possibly heard what I said. After I hung up I told Dad I was going next door.

Next door lived Caseen and my Godmother and her children. Turene and Wendy were more than our God brother and sister; they were our best friends. The only reason we called their mother our Godmother was because she baptized us. Wendy and I sat next to each other in every class from kindergarten at P.S.19 elementary to seventh grade in I.S.27 junior high school. We studied together, walked the halls together, and fought together. People were jealous of the bond we had and often tried to break it, but failed each time. We spent all our leisure time together. And that's how Turene and Caseen got down, too.

When I told Wendy about Sam, she couldn't believe it. Before I left, I told Wendy I did not know where I would be staying, but I would keep in touch.

When I left, I saw Sam's gray Lincoln in front of my house. I stopped in front of his car, looked in, and saw Stephanie in the passenger seat and Sam looking stupid. He rolled down the window and said, "Get in. We're still going to have your party."

I thought, Party! Is he sick or what? I thought about how he went all the way to Syracuse and fought for me. I knew he would have never let me stay with Dad. So I went in the house to let my dad know I was leaving and to tell my baby brothers I would see them later. Dad hugged me and told me he loved me. I got in the back seat of Sam's car, and he gave me a dirty look through the rear view mirror. I knew he was mad at me for telling everybody about the shit he was doing. But Sam knew just how to get out of that. He had a way of manipulating people and most people believed that he was a genuine saint anyway.

I sat in the back seat feeling sad and lonely. How had he found out where I was? I thought about how good my stepfather was to me, even though he was a man of discipline and believed in setting rules and regulations. I looked at it as giving Caseen and me structure and responsibility. He wanted us to set goals and have dreams for our lives. It never mattered to him how I dressed. He wasn't interested in seeing me half naked. He didn't care what my twat looked like. And for that, I appreciated his fatherhood.

We reached the apartment building and Sam let us

in. On the elevator Sam stared me up and down, as if something was wrong with me. At that point I didn't care anymore.

When I entered, Sam's eyes were still on me when he said, "Go straight to my room, Shiree."

I followed Stephanie into her room.

He picked up the phone and dialed eleven numbers, which meant he was dialing a different city. I knew he was calling Grandma, and now I knew who told him where I was. He said, "Yeah she's here right now. She lied because I told her she couldn't have a birthday party." Then he passed me the phone like I was going to agree with him, to make him look good and me bad.

"Grandma he beat me up and ripped my clothes off. I'm not lying. Stephanie will tell you."

"Oh yeah," she said. "Let me speak to Stephanie."

All Stephanie said was, "No, no, no."

I felt so hurt, but it wasn't her fault; she was scared of him, but I wasn't.

After Sam hung up the phone he grabbed a belt and tried to beat me. When he swung the belt, I grabbed it and hung on to it. He had one end and I had the other. I let go and he swung it again, and I grabbed it again. I swung his skinny ass around, and at that time I cut my foot on a little mirror that was on the floor. I still would not let the belt go.

As he tried to pull it away from me he yelled, "Let it go."
JJ

But I didn't respond, nor did I let it go. When I got ready, I let it go and hopped in my room.

Before I could sit down he called, "Shiree.".

I hopped back in his room and asked, "What the fuck do you want?"

"Watch your mouth."

"What do you want with me now, Sam, huh? Are you

done trying to destroy my life?"

"You give me respect. You are still a child."

"Respect? You want to talk about respect? You don't have respect for a child. I don't even get any privacy in this house. What about that, huh?"

"I said watch your mouth or I'm going to beat your ass."

I paced his room floor like a maniac, ready to explode. I thought, if he touched me, I was gonna tear his house up and him, too. "You ain't going to do nothing to me. You did all you're going to do to me. You want to hit me? Come on. Come on, because I'm not going for it tonight. Yeah that's right you ain't shit for a father. Leroy raised me. And you know what, I want out of this fucking house. Send me to a foster home, group home, I really don't give a shit."

"Fine. I will arrange for you to go in the system."

I kept running my mouth until Sam said, "Shut the fuck up."

"You shut the fuck up." I hopped in my room and to my bed, thinking. He wouldn't let me stay with Grandma, but now I can go to a foster home. Why couldn't Sam be like normal fathers?

All day I sat in the living room watching movies. Sam had me on a punishment so I couldn't go anywhere. My birthday came. I didn't get anything, not even a happy birthday from Sam, not that it would have mattered to me anyway. Stephanie told me, "Happy Birthday," and then Caseen called. He was in Staten Island and he said he was on his way. I knew Sam was listening on the other end and I knew he was mad. He wanted my birthday to be as miserable as he was.

Caseen came with Turene and Turene's cousin Marlon. Caseen had big gold rings on every finger.

"Happy birthday," he yelled as he hugged and kissed me. He handed me a gold box. After Turene and Marlon hugged me and wished me happy birthday, we walked into the living room.

I opened my gold box and pulled out a gold chain with my name on it. I was so happy.

Sam kept putting tapes in the V.C.R. He was trying to be cool with Caseen because he was scared of him.

Grandma must have not told Caseen what Sam did because she knew he would have come all the way from Syracuse just to whip his ass. The whole while Caseen was there Sam did not leave us alone. He was scared that I would tell Caseen about what he did to me.

"You know your going to be an auntie right." "What are you talking about Caseen?" "Melinda, is pregnant and we have our own apartment now." After Caseen left I was so sad because I wanted to leave with him. But I was happy that God sent me an angel to brighten up my day on my birthday. That one day made up for all the prior days I hurt.

It had been a whole week, when Sam came to my room and told me to pack my shit up. I thought to myself that he was serious. I didn't know if I was happy or sad. I was happy to get out of that insane place, but sad because I did not know where I was going. As I rode in the back seat of his car, I thought of all the horrible places I could end up.

Chapter 4
Placement

I stood in front of the building. I looked up and read Urban Strategies. Sam stood next to me while we waited to get in. I didn't have any feelings at that time. I didn't hate Sam. I didn't panic. Stephanie waited in the car. I loved her, and I felt sorry for her, but couldn't imagine anyone alone with Sam and happy. Maybe that's why I stood there feeling empty, because Sam took a lot from me.

As I entered the building, I learned that Urban Strategies was a boys' and girls' facility. I saw boys and girls eating in the kitchen as we were escorted upstairs. I waited in the lounge while Sam went to the office to fill the staff's heads with lies.

When he was done a staff came to get me. "Hi Shiree, I'm Mrs. Patti. Will you come with me please?"

I walked to the office and noticed that Sam was already gone. He never said goodbye or anything. Not that I cared, it was just a point.

"Please sit down, Shiree."

As I sat down I noticed her long stare, like she was checking me out. I wondered what Sam told her. Maybe he told her I was delusional.

"I know this is hard for you, Shiree. I know how you must feel. I have young kids here who have all been through something. I myself was a young child just like you guys. This is a shelter for young teens. As you probably already noticed, there are young men here as well as ladies. The guys sleep on this level, and the girls sleep upstairs. The lounge is right across from here where you were sitting. This place is temporary, and thirty days is the limit. We will work on finding a permanent place for you. We look for family members first. Now we have your grandmother's number here. Do you have any questions for me?"

I shook my head. She answered everything I needed to know. I had to sit there for thirty days if not less. She basically told me she would call my grandmother, and that's all I needed to know.

"Come now, I'll show you your room."

She left me upstairs in a room with three beds in it. "This is your bed and dresser here. When you're done unpacking, you may go down to the lounge. Everyone is on the first floor finishing up dinner. There was a plate put up for you. We were expecting you. So, if you're hungry, you may eat."

I sat on my bed wondering who else shared this room. I looked at my brown wicker suitcase that had been with me every step of the way and still had a ways to go. I didn't want to eat or go downstairs. I just sat there staring at the raggedy suitcase.

The door opened and a short dark-skinned girl walked in smiling. "Are you the new girl?"

Before I could answer her, she said, "My name is Precious. This is my room. Well, it's our room now. That bed over there doesn't belong to anyone yet. And I hope it stays empty. You seem like a very nice person. You're very pretty."

"Thank you," I finally spoke. She was so sweet; I

wished I could say the same for her. She was so dark, big-boned and she had nappy extensions in her head. They must have been in for a year, and they probably couldn't come out. She was ugly, apparently didn't have a damn thing, but she was happy. And for that she was beautiful.

"What is your name?"

"Shiree."

"How old are you?"

"Thirteen," I told her.

"I'm twelve. I'll be thirteen next week. Who was the man who brought you here?"

"That was Sam," I said.

"Who is he to you?" she asked.

"He's my father."

"Did he get tired of you?" Precious asked.

"I guess so, or more like I got tired of him."

"Where's your mom?" she kept asking questions.

"She's dead."

"So is mine," Precious said. "My mom and my dad are dead."

"How did they die?" I asked, suddenly getting interested in the questions.

"I don't know if they're really dead or not. But to me they are. I don't really know them. I was left in the hospital when I was born."

"What? That's fucked up," I told her.

"Yeah, it is if I think about it, but I don't care. Can't care about two people I don't know."

"How did you know you were left in the hospital? Because I don't think you remember that, and who would be sick enough to tell you that?"

"My uncle told me."

"Where is your uncle now?"

"He left me, too, after awhile. I been all over the place, and I can't stay here either."

I balled up like a ball on my bed and listened while Precious told me some more of her fucked-up stories. I felt sorry for her. I had my own sorrows, but I felt her pain like it was mine. Sometimes you don't have to be in a person's shoes to understand. If you truly felt pain before, and knew what love felt like and had an imagination, you can feel the depths of anything.

At the breakfast table I listened to everyone laugh and joke. Mostly everyone was older than Precious and me. Precious said a lot to me but not to anyone else.

On my way upstairs a girl stopped me. "Shiree," she yelled as she came toward me.

I stopped for her.

"That's your name right?" she asked.

"Yeah," I said.

She was around nineteen. She had my attention. She was tall brown-skinned, small up top and big on the bottom. Her hair was straight and bouncy. "Welcome here, my name is Monique." Her voice was so sweet. And her smile was sincere. She seemed older than nineteen. She wasn't wild. She had an old spirit. "Come up to my room."

I followed her to her room.

"Sit down," she said. She was classy. I looked around her room. Her closet had skirts, blouses, slacks and some dresses. I spotted at least fifty shoeboxes. Her dresser was decorated with expensive perfumes. She was a lady. "You just had your hair cut, huh?"

I nodded.

"I know what style you had. I could do it for you if you want."

I smiled. "Oh yeah," I said. "Do it." By the looks of her style, I trusted her.

"I do hair," she said. "Sit in this chair right here. You are so pretty," she said.

I smiled. "You're pretty too."

"Girl, I was very pretty once upon a time." I just listened to her, she sounded like she was old. "I been through so much and I'm lucky to be here, by the grace of God. These people really helped me out. I'm not supposed to be in this place after eighteen. My parents neglected me as a child. I was raped. I used to prostitute, and use heavy drugs. My pimp put a gun to my head when I wanted out, or just because. But God is so merciful. He turned my life around. These people are helping me and I'm alright." She said it again. "God is an awesome God."

I couldn't imagine all that happened to her. But then I imagined how. She was so sweet she could have easily been taken advantage of in a weak moment.

"Look at yourself," she said as she turned my chair around so I could see myself in the mirror.

When I saw my hair, I couldn't believe it. I trusted her, but I didn't expect her to be so professional. It looked exactly like a beautician did it

"You are very pretty, I'm not kidding. And let me tell you something. It's a price you pay for being beautiful. Your beauty will bless you, bring you a lot of good things, but it will bring you bad too." Her conversation was so deep I respected her. She was not only smart she was experienced, which made her wise. On my way out the door she grabbed me by my hands and smiled. "Come to me if you need anything okay?" I nodded with a smile and walked away.

I crept down to the lounge and sat next to Precious. "Ooh Shiree, you look even prettier. Don't tell me Monique hooked you up."

"Yes," I said. Why don't she hook you up, I thought. Everyone in the lounge did what they did in the kitchen: laughed and joked.

"Where did Monique go?" Precious asked me.

"She left."

"Monique is always gone. She don't sit around here, and she has a job."

Precious told me about everyone in the house. I was listening to the guy who was always cracking jokes. He was the funniest guy in the whole place.

Precious noticed me listening to him. "His name is Ernest," she said.

His face was smooth and the color of caramel. He was tall, thin and his face had a tight structure. He was talking to another boy by the name of Derriko. "Look son, you're not fucking with me. I'm the man and you already know." They were playing cards. He looked my way and noticed me paying attention. "What's up, Shorty," he said as he walked over to me.

"Shiree."

"Oh, my bad, I'm not trying to be funny. I didn't know your name."

"Then you should have asked me," I said without sounding nasty.

"Do you know how to play spit?" he asked.

"No, what's that?"

"It's a card game. Come over here I'll show you. Now the object of the game is to get rid of all your cards." While dishing out the cards he sparked up a conversation. "I saw you when you first came in. You came in and then you disappeared."

"Yeah, I went to unpack and fell asleep."

"I was waiting for you in the lounge."

"What were you waiting for me for?"

"So I could introduce myself. I'm the king in this place. I watch everything moving. If you have any problems you come to me. I get respect."

I smiled, as if I was not listening, but I was. Everything about him was sexy, especially the way he catered to me.

"Precious?" I whispered. "Precious?

"Huh?" she whispered back.

"Do you hear someone knocking?" I asked.

"No, why do you?"

"Yeah listen." And we heard a tap on the door. I jumped up and opened it. "What are you doing here?"

"Shh," Ernest hushed me to be quiet.

"You're not supposed to be up here, Ernest."

"Yeah, no kidding, why do you think I'm whispering? Let me in."

"No, for what? I'll get in trouble."

"No you won't. Trust me. I just want to talk to you."

"All right, come on in," I opened the door wide, giving him entrance. "Ooh you skinny," I said to him." He had a muscle shirt and boxers, revealing his long skinny arms and legs.

"Oh you got jokes, huh?" He helped himself to a seat on my bed. "I was lying in bed and I couldn't get you out of my head."

"What?" I said in a disgusted way.

"Nah, not like that," Ernest said. "I was trying to figure out what are you doing here. Everything I thought of didn't make sense."

"It's not supposed to make sense," I said. "Think about it. It doesn't make any sense that any of us have to be here? We're just kids."

"But what I'm saying is," Ernest cut me off, "you should be at home tucked away in your bed. You should have brothers and sisters, and a beautiful mom. You don't look like a troubled kid."

"I'm not a troubled kid," I said. Leave it up to Sam, I am. Ernest brought up the life I used to have without the sisters. "I lived like that before," I said. "But I never had any sisters."

"So what happened?" Ernest was persistent to know my story.

"Well my beautiful mom died, and it all went downhill from there."

"I'm sorry to hear that. I really am sorry for you. I could look right at you and tell you lost someone."

"What are you, a psychic?"

"What I mean is, I could see your pain. I can tell you hurt. You seem tough though, as if you hold your head up. And you carry yourself differently, too. Who was the guy who dropped you off?"

"My father," I said.

"What's up with him?"

"He's sick in the head, but he tells everyone I am."

"That's why he brought you here?"

"I guess, to cover up his bullshit."

"He touched you, huh?"

"How did you know?"

"That's usually what the case is when a father is sick. I hear stories like that all the time. I don't like to hear it though, especially coming from you. I could tell something was wrong with him. Next time he comes here I'm gonna knock him out. Is that all right with you?"

"Yeah, do it. I don't care. I wish I could have knocked him out when he made my nose bleed."

"He hit you too?"

"Yeah. Why are you here?" I asked.

"I rather be here than at home. My mom told me to get out, anyway. She tells me to get out every now and then, and I come right back here. I'm popular here. I run this place. Psych! Nah, my mom is a beast. You ever heard someone screaming every single day, 'I hate you. I wish you were never born?'"

It seemed like saying all that took energy out of Ernest. He lay down and began to doze off. He jumped when I nudged him.

"You can't sleep here. We'll get in trouble."

"I know. I'm going downstairs now. I'll see you in the

morning."

"All right," I said. Before I closed my eyes I thought about how nice it was to talk to Ernest. He understood me out of all people. Whether he understood me or not, he believed in me.

At breakfast a guy name Elijah walked over to me. "You can load the dishwasher."

I looked at him dumbfounded.

Ernest overheard and made his way over. He laughed at Elijah then he put his hand on his chin. "Why are you trying to get her to do your chore? She don't have to load the dishwasher, you do. Nobody gave her a chore yet, she's new."

"Oh, she's new?" Elijah asked.

"You knew that," Ernest said, walking away.

"Come on," Ernest said when I reached the lounge. "Let's go outside. You don't want to sit here all day."

"All right, hold on." I went upstairs to throw on my Air Force One's.

We walked to Ralph street train station to the end of the platform. Just when I was wondering where the hell he was going, he jumped down in the tracks.

I put my hand over my mouth. He shocked me. I always thought you would get electrocuted, but he was definitely down there. "Are you crazy?" I asked him.

"Come on down." He offered his hand. "Just come on. Look at me, I'm down here."

I jumped down and stood there.

He began to walk. "Come on," he said.

I just stood there.

"Come on, scary." He took my hand into his, and we walked off.

"Oh my God, it's dark. I can't see."

"Just walk. I got you."

Just then I saw light. "Look a train is coming," I

yelled.

Still holding my hand, he jumped on the wall. The train made so much noise, and it was so close I thought for sure it would hit us. But the wall was a few feet from the tracks.

When the train came and left, Ernest hugged me. The hug was nice, tight and warm. I felt safe.

He pulled out his marker and tagged on the wall: Tunnel Rats. "We are the Tunnel Rats."

When we went back it was dark.

We had got a new boy in the place named Carl. He was originally from Compton. He had a way about himself like he was too good. Ernest tried to be nice and was not at all trying to be funny when he tried to talk with him. But he was getting smart with Ernest.

Ernest looked around and grinned. I guess he felt himself about to get ugly. We all looked around amazed too.

Carl talked about his colors, what people could and could not wear. He talked about rules and regulations that took place in Compton.

"This is Brooklyn, son and we don't do that shit here," Ernest told him.

Carl got loud. "You telling me what to represent?"

"Pipe down, son, and cut that tough shit out before I fuck you up," Ernest told him.

Carl's exact words were, "You aint gonna do shit to me, nigga."

"Let's go outside," Ernest said.

Carl jumped up and headed toward the steps. Derriko was holding Ernest.

Carl had already made it downstairs when Ernest broke loose and ran downstairs. I looked out the window and saw Ernest punch Carl. Carl tried to block and Ernest punched him again. Ernest was moving fast, like a maniac. He turned around and grabbed a two-by-four.

Carl turned around and ran. Ernest chased him.

Carl ran right into a car, so he stood in the middle of the street.

It all happened so fast. Ernest hit Carl with the two-by-four across his back in the middle of the street. Carl went halfway down. Ernest hit him again and he went all the way down. Carl got up and ran and Ernest chased him.

One of the staff yelled, "Ernest, you're out of here. Don't come back."

Tears rolled down my face.

Ernest walked back down to the place and spoke to me out the window. "Don't cry. I'm going to my mother house. I'll be back tomorrow."

It wasn't long after that they told me to pack it up; they found me a place. They told me my Aunt Goldie, who lived in Tarrytown, in Westchester New York, was going to be my new guardian.

Chapter 5
Aunt Goldie

I was taken straight to my aunt's apartment. One River Plaza in Tarrytown, New York. It was a nice clean brick building. We went up the elevator to the door. I had a stupid look on my face with a stupid feeling to match. I did not know anything about Aunt Goldie. I heard the reason she was taking me in was because my mom was her favorite niece.

She opened the door with a great smile and a red wig.

I put my fake smile on for respect and appreciation. But truth was I was a lonely girl, and homesick from a lot of places.

After Aunt Goldie hugged me in the living room, she took me to my room and went back to the living room to speak with the people who brought me. I sat on my bed looking at my room. A huge window had a view of the front of the building. There was a twin bed and a small dresser and also a silver radio with a tape player. I sat on the bed in depressed state. The house was dark and gloomy, and boring. I didn't think I couldn't get used to this. I thought about Ernest and how far apart we were. At least I had his number.

Later that afternoon Aunt Goldie took me to her friend's apartment in the building. I met a good old friend of hers named Shirley. Her friends were delighted to meet me, as if they heard so much about me.

I was just quiet and innocent looking, as always when I got in a new situation around new faces.

After we ate dinner Aunt Goldie brought me back downstairs, then she went back to her friends. I crept around the apartment, which was not big at all. The dining room was in the living room; kitchen was off the little dining room; there was a long narrow hallway and off the hallway were my room, Aunt Goldie's, and the bathroom. I peeked in Aunt Goldie's room. It looked like it was being used for storage, but you could tell it was a room. She had a very nice bedroom set. Her bed had a bunch of clothes and bags on it, and on the floor was a bunch of boxes.

After creeping I picked up the phone and called Ernest. I felt at home when I heard his voice. I sat comfortably on the couch and the house suddenly became interesting. I told Ernest what Tarrytown looked like and how I wished we were still at Urban Strategies together. After I heard the elevator door close, I told Ernest I would call him tomorrow and hurried up and hung up and ran to my room.

Aunt Goldie came in. "Are you okay?" she asked. I nodded. "Okay, I'm in the living room if you need me."

I got up and put my radio on the bed and got back in. I lay there watching the light out the window, listening to sweet slow jams down low. I was very depressed. I hated the feeling of being somewhere I did not want to be. I guess Sam was right, Grandma didn't want me. If she did, why am I here and not there?

I woke up to pancakes, eggs and bacon. I sat at the table eating that good meal, while Aunt Goldie sat on her sofa looking at the television, drinking coffee and smoking a cigarette. There was not much conversation in the air.

When Aunt Goldie realized that all I had was answers to her questions for conversation, she began telling me about the town. "You will be going to Sleepy Hollow high school. Did you know this is the town the headless horseman ran around?" I sat at the table puzzled. "This town is not big, but you'll like it. There's a center down the street. All the kids your age go there."

That day I met some more people that Aunt Goldie knew. I would not say these people were friends, from the looks of it, just some folks she knew very well. A white lady named Dedra lived next door with two mixed little boys, and the big black dude I had seen go in and out of the house must of been her boyfriend.

Aunt Goldie knew so many people and was much liked. She was my great aunt, in her sixties, with great big hips a big wide ass, and little legs. She had an attitude, which meant she did not play that. Her red skin was natural and she wouldn't be caught dead with black hair. She wore glasses that never seemed like she was looking through them. Her head always shook like she had a nervous condition, and when she stared it was with her head down shaking, looking out of the glasses. This lady never sat still. She was either at bingo, playing cards with her friends, drinking, partying. She was single since she and Uncle Melvin separated. But she didn't care about any man, and this was a woman who did not need a man.

I sat at Shirley's boring apartment with Aunt Goldie for a few days and in my boring room a few days, too. Then she finally signed me up for school.

The other kids from my school were very friendly and very interested in New York City people. So I became pretty popular. I walked home with Nea because we lived in the same building, and Kemi and her sister Ieisha, African Ada all lived in the courts past my building, so we all walked home together.

All the friendly people I met had nothing on Ernest. He was all I thought about and all I wanted. Every time Aunt Goldie stepped out, I snuck and called Ernest. If she knew I was calling long distance, she would never have let me. After awhile Ernest started calling me. She seemed confused at first, but it didn't bother her. Then she became moved when he called. Maybe because he called too much and we talked so long. She knew he was long distance and got the impression I was using her phone to call him, too.

I met Katie Cutler, a white lady who lived across the hall. She had two sons, one was mixed and one was pure white. Katie asked me to watch her boys for a price. I didn't mind sitting at Katie's house, it was ordinary. She had a screen TV, leather love seat and sofa, soft carpet, and she had a lot of channels on her television. Katie was nice to me. She treated me as a little sister, and that's how I felt around her. She had grown feelings for a little girl.

Katie and the lady next door, Dedra, had a lot in common. They shared that big black dude who stayed at Dedra's. His name was Philip Burnet. He lived with Dedra and they had two kids. But Katie had Phil more than Dedra.

I began sitting at Katie's even when I was not babysitting. Phil used to walk right in and sit in his seat and run Katie's house.

I sat in the living room all the time with the both of them. We always talked; I told them my story about how I got to Tarrytown. They already knew about my mother and found that heart breaking. But I went a little further and told them the Sam business. I mean they were asking questions and I felt no need to lie.

From that day on Phil adopted me, not legally, but

spiritually and souly. It was no misunderstanding how he cared for me. I knew he felt sorry for me, but he never treated me like a pet. Katie was like my big sister, but Phil treated me like a daughter.

Phil owned his own towing business called Midnight Towing. He had his own tow truck and a lot where he towed all the cars that didn't belong in the Grand Union. That was pretty smart, and he made a lot of money. People left their cars in Grand Union all the time and got on the train.

Katie helped Phil in his business; she kept on the look out for cars. She would even do some of the tows by herself. She worked hard for Phil to help his business grow, and it did.

I know because I was the receptionist at the lot. I answered phones and people asked me about their cars that Phil towed. All I had to do was look for the slip and tell them, "Yes we have it" and make arrangements for them to get their car.

Life started moving fast and becoming quite interesting in Tarrytown. I didn't forget about Ernest. He called me at Katie's house. I told Katie all about Ernest. She understood as long as she had her Phil she was always fine. Phil meant to Katie more than she meant to herself. Anything Phil wanted her to do she did, and anyway he felt he was right.

Phil was never wrong. She would not dare argue with him. Her own painful feelings from the bottom of her heart were wrong if he said they were wrong. He never abused her or was mean to her for her to be like that. It was just, he belonged to someone else. And I think she believed that if she treated him like the king that she treated him like, he would eventually leave Dedra for her.

Katie was with Phil all day because they worked together and he was at her house in the evening real late. But regardless what time it was, he went home and woke up in Dedra's bed.

When my life started coming together, Aunt Goldie's was falling apart. To her I was spending too much time at Katie's; I was never home. I did go to school and still maintained A's.

Kemi, who lived in the courts, befriended me. She made our plans and I kept them. Almost everyday we stood in the Grand Union on the pay phone. That was one of the reasons I hung around Kemi; I always got to talk to Ernest for a long period of time. She had this phone trick that worked for her all the time. She would pick up the phone, dial a lot of numbers, and her call would go through. She could do this at any pay phone. I sat at Kemi's house talking on the phone with Ernest until it got dark.

I was marching home because I was so tired I was going to slam dunk in the bed. I figured Aunt Goldie would be out somewhere. The door was open; I walked in to find my aunt sitting on the couch pissed off. I saw a demon in her eyes. Her expression puzzled me, so I first said, "Hi Aunt Goldie, what's wrong?"

She stood up like she was coming toward me to take my head off my shoulders. "Don't you hi me." Her whole body shook. Her red wig and her body were shaking, saliva was shooting out her mouth while she stood there cursing me out. "You and that damn Kemi ran my calling card up. You sneaked and wrote my number down. A thousand damn dollars, how am I supposed to pay that? You just can't be nice."

She was hysterical. But I didn't know what for. I hadn't taken anything from my aunt. I would never do that. She called me all types of witches; I was a liar, sneaky, my no-good-ass friends and I.

I tried to explain to Aunt Goldie, "I swear I did not do

it."

She hushed me and pushed me out of her face, and promised me that she would fix me.

When I got to my room it came to me, Kemi got a hold of Aunt Goldie's card. She never knew any phone tricks. All that time she wasn't pressing any numbers, she was pressing my aunt's numbers.

Aunt Goldie had steam for me. She brought the new day in with yesterday's news. She walked around pouting, talking shit, looking evil. I was scared to eat, and wouldn't dare use her phone. In fact, she was on the phone talking about me, trying to be low. I overheard the names she called me, and how she felt toward me. I felt bad so I got up and left. When I went across the hall, they had already got the news.. She told Katie, Dedra, and the whole building knew.

Philip always made me feel welcomed when I walked in the door, "Hey Shiree," he would say. He was really happy to see me. In fact, he treated me like he was really my dad. Wrong was wrong and right was right. He gave me that courage, that confidence and esteem. When I went back home, Aunt Goldie was gone. I noticed she took her phone with her. I guess she was downstairs at Shirley's talking about me.

I was supposed to have been on a punishment and Aunt Goldie and her friends were going to Atlantic City. They were not due back till the next night. She meant punishment, because when I woke up that morning, she was gone. So was the phone. I was on my way across the hall, till I noticed there was no knob on the door. She locked me in. I thought, this woman is crazy. I felt like an animal in a cage, as I stared at the door. I thought about Ernest and how, if I only had a phone, I could talk to him. I went through everything in that house looking for the phone. I definitely could not jump from the fourth-floor window. Then I thought, she will be gone for two days. If I could get out, I could get another phone, plug it in and talk to Ernest for two days.. Aunt Goldie knew that, that's why she locked me in.

I started searching through things. I didn't know what I was looking for until I found a screwdriver and stuck it in the place of the knob, turned it and the door popped open. I stood there for a minute laughing.

I went across the hall and got a phone. I called everybody I knew and invited them to my party. I thought this calls for a party. I washed the living room tables down with Pine Sol to give the house a fresh smell. I tidied up and went next door to Katie's to get some air fresheners. Katie's house always smelled good. I never knew why, but Aunt Goldie's house had a stale smell to it.

With all the boys and girls from the hood and my school there were enough. My party had music and it was a basic get-together.. People laughing and joking, only the joke was on me, because they were laughing at me. I was coming from the back room with my new reggae tape. Nobody saw me standing there listening. Ronnie from the courts kept asking what was that smell.

Dominik picked up one of the pillows off the couch and sniffed it. He turned up his nose, threw the pillow on the floor and everybody started laughing.

I stood with my hand over my mouth. Oh shit. Nobody ever recognized me standing there. I took a sniff of the air and noticed the fresheners had worn off. They laughed about how my apartment smelled and I knew it was true. Every time I walked in Aunt Goldie's apartment, I smelled cigarettes mixed with booty and old-folk socks. But her apartment was not the only thing smelling bad; I noticed the smell got into my clothes.

It got to the point where I started taking my clothes to Katie's apartment so they could stay fresh. I would shower at Aunt Goldie's and dress at Katie's. That finally worked. First I use to spray my clothes with perfume and stick them in a bag so the smell wouldn't get out. But that never worked, I believe it made it worse.

I talked to Ernest that whole night before I returned the phone. When Aunt Goldie came back the next day, she already knew what went on. Some nosy person in the building told. Aunt Goldie really couldn't stand me anymore; at least those were the looks she threw at me. She always talked about me to all her friends in the building.

Things changed around the place. I stayed home more often because family was coming to visit a lot. My cousins, Durrell and Tyniesha, used to visit for a weekend. Durrell was Aunt Goldie's grandson, in his early twenties, and Tyniesha was her granddaughter in her late teens.

First thing they wanted to know was why I was driving their grandmother crazy. After I told them a few stories about how she would flip on me, they laughed and said that's Grandma for you. They loved their grandmother and wouldn't let anybody play her. But they understood me as a child. They knew I was a child growing up, and Aunt Goldie would be old fashioned and there were limitations to what I could do.

Ty and Rell began laughing amongst each other as they were putting their jackets on.

"Where are you guys going?" I asked them. "And what's so funny?"

"We're laughing at you," Tyniesha blurted out and began laughing again.

"Why are ya laughing at me?"

"Because you're crazy," she said and she ran her index finger under my nose. "My grandmother thinks you're the baddest child she ever knew. Grandma said, 'What's wrong with her Ty? She doesn't care about anything.' Are you really that bad Shiree?"

"I'm not bad," I said in a convincing tone.

We busted out laughing.

"Hey where ya going? I'm going too." They walked out of the room. "Hold up," I yelled while I was trying to find my sweater. I was always cool at night.

When I got to the elevator, Rell was holding it for me. "Come on you bad-ass slow poke. We got something for your ass." We all laughed.

"I know what ya'll about to do."

"Look, look at you." Tyniesha said. "That's why you so grown."

"Leave Shiree alone," Rell said. "She's a gangster."

We got to the parking lot where all the cars were parked on the lower level. We stood against the wall.

Rell pulled out a ready rolled phat-ass Philly blunt with the tree of life in it, some funk. "Here you light it," Rell said to Ty and passed it to her.

Ty puffed on it five times then passed it to me.

I laughed, took it and puffed it. I inhaled and two seconds later I was bent over choking. I could barely talk. "Here Rell get your blunt." I shook my hand with the blunt in it, which meant get it.

Ty patted my back while she laughed. She ran her index finger under my nose again. "You all right Cuz? Now when we go upstairs, go straight to the back. Don't even look at Grandma. Look at Shiree's eyes, Rell, they blood shot red."

Suddenly everything appeared funny, and smelled funny. "ILL, what's that smell?" I blurted out.

Ty laughed out loud. "You bugging, girl."

Every muscle in my body was relaxed. My eyes felt heavy. I stood against the wall, reminiscing about some of the good things in my life.

"She's high, Rell," Ty said. She pulled out her Newport shorts. "Here have a stolg. You feel good, huh

Cuz?" She threw her hands in the air hollering, "Ahhhhh!"

On the elevator Rell said, "Straight to the room, all right Shiree?"

"All right, "I said smirking.

We got to the door and Rell pushed me. "You go in first."

I walked in and Aunt Goldie was the first person I saw. She was sitting on the couch watching the television. "Hi Aunt Goldie," I said real loud, as if I was excited to see her. I walked up to her and stood there watching her make her face up that read, "What the hell is wrong with your stupid ass?"

Rell and Ty walked in.

I turned to look at them entering and remembered what they said about going straight to the room. All of a sudden it was so funny to me.

They shook their heads at me and went to the back. I covered my mouth and busted out laughing uncontrollably.

"What's wrong with you, girl?" Aunt Goldie asked me.

I stood there giggling.

"What did ya'll give this girl?"

Ty came out. "We didn't give her anything, Grandma, and she's just bugging. Come on, Shiree." She grabbed me.

As I walked away I heard Aunt Goldie mumble, "I'm not stupid. Her eyes are red, she acting stupid. That's that damn reefer."

Tyniesha was light-skinned and thick. She wore baggy clothes, kept her natural hair done and was mad cool with a gangster style and didn't have a phony bone in her. She was different from most girls I knew her age. She rolled alone and always took care of her business. It seemed to as if she wanted things in life. Her whole attitude was smooth, and sweet. She always listened, and I could tell she really felt my pain.

Durell was the same way; he kept his shit real and gangster. The thing about him was he was the type that kept your stomach hurting. He was too funny, always had a joke. He was tall brown-skinned, rocked a seizer and stayed fresh. Fresh kicks, fresh gear, top of the line shit, and he was fine.

They used to come up and stay a weekend sometimes. I always enjoyed their company. Aunt Goldie enjoyed them as well. I could tell she was proud of them, but it was me she despised. I guess she couldn't get over the phone bill. After I started smoking weed, my behavior got worse. I was getting bad reports from school; I told the secretary in the office to kiss my ass. I was not trying to hear them. I starting wasting time in class, as well as being rude.

I never talked shit to Aunt Goldie or disrespected her, because my mom and father were big on that. They didn't play that disrespecting elders. What my aunt didn't like about me was I stopped caring about things.

I was in the office waiting for the principal to speak with me. "Do you like this school?"

I looked to my left where the voice was coming from. I didn't notice someone was sitting next to me. "It's all right with me, but I don't think they like me too much."

"Why do you say that?"

"Because I'm always in this office."

She laughed. "My name is Patrica. I'm new."

"My name is Shiree. Where are you from?"

"I just moved here from Osning. I need to go to Osning tonight. You want to go with me?"

"Are you coming back tonight?" I asked her.

"Yeah I'm coming back. I have to go to school."

"How are we getting there? I'm broke right now."

"I'll pay your way there and back. Do you smoke

weed?"

"Hell yeah, I smoke. Shit, who doesn't."

"We gonna get high then, all right?"

"Hell yeah."

The principal opened his office door and pointed at me. "Shiree Brown, come in here please. Sit down."

I laughed to myself. Did he think I was going to stand?

He pulled on his tie as if it was choking him. He was definitely frustrated. "You know, Shiree, I'm getting really tired of seeing your face in my office. Now I know something is going on with you. What is it, Shiree?"

I looked around the room and then back at him. He was silent, as if he really wanted an answer. What did he want me to say? I'm bad because I hate Tarrytown, I hate Sam, and I don't give a damn about much?

He opened his file cabinet and pulled out a folder with my name on it. "Well, I can tell you now, something is definitely going on. When you first came here, you were sweet and nice to everyone. I can tell you were brought up right. You are one of our gifted students. You got straight A's for two months straight. Then you went downhill. Not to mention you're lashing out at the students and the teachers, and you're barely even here anymore. I'm going to request some counseling for you. We need to get to the bottom of this, because I would hate to lose you. You are a bright intelligent young girl. You can be anything you want in life, don't throw that away. Rarely do I see a student who's advanced in every subject. I can guarantee you an academic scholarship to some of the best colleges. Promise me you'll shape up."

"Yes, Mr. Solomon." I smiled at him. I smiled from ear to ear on my way out the office.

Patrica was still sitting there waiting. "Hey Shiree, are you going home now?"

"Yeah, why?"

"Here take my number. Call me in an hour so we can go."

"All right." I took the number and left. I was still smiling out the door. Mr. Solomon said I was smart and intelligent. I knew that. Mama used to be proud of me. She believed in me. She always said, "Shiree, is going to be something."

"What's up Patrica?" A big chunky girl came to the door. Even though she was fat, she had a pretty face. She was Puerto Rican with long jet-black hair.

I sat down on the couch and watched them kick it with each other. Apparently that was Patrica's home girl.

"Shiree, this is my friend Jenny, and Jenny, this is Shiree. Shiree goes to my school. She's mad cool."

"So what's up with you, girl? What's been going on?" Jenny asked Patrica. "Are you really going to stay in Tarrytown?"

"Hell yeah, girl, I got to. Larry is a trip."

A whole hour went by. I sat there listening to them reminisce and wash clothes. Even though I was miserably bored, out of respect I presented myself as patient. I felt like maybe she needed to get her stuff together.

The horn blew outside and Patrica said, "Come on Shiree, we're about to get high."

I hopped in the back seat of a raggedy filthy no-name four-door station wagon. I couldn't wait to get to the place we were going to. I was so tense I didn't think it was fair to me to sit in that car.

"Shiree, this is Larry, Larry, Shiree." She looked at him smiling while he continued driving.

I watched her from the back seat stare at him with puppy eyes. I began to peep her style. She was corny and a fraud. She wasn't real. What was strange to me was, I was on her time. I was following her. I didn't remember ever following anyone. Either we moved on the same level, or I was calling the shots, making the moves. That was not my style at all.

When we got to Larry's house we all sat in his living room. When he began rolling the blunt I exhaled finally some chronic and it was just what I needed.

The blunt rotated. Larry spent the longest time smoking the weed. I guess he figured it was his shit, so he got to baby sit it. Patrica was his girl which he had the upper hand and I wasn't shit.

I judged him as selfish, rude, corny, and he damn sure had game. There wasn't much conversation in the air at all.

They went in the room because that's what they wanted to do all along. They were in the room for almost an hour, while I sat in the living room.

I was not with that. So I stood up and yelled toward the room, "Let's go, I'm ready." Shit, if she wanted to lay around with him, why did she want me to come for?

"I'm coming," she yelled from the room.

As I sat there waiting, I thought about the boring day I had already with her, and this shit was rude. I started getting paranoid. It was dark outside. The boy's house was dark and lonely. I stood up again I felt like smacking the shit out of her. "Come on now. Shit, I'm leaving then."

The boy came out. "What's wrong with you?"

I rolled my eyes at him. What the hell did he mean what's wrong with me. "Tell Patricia to come here."

I took Patricia in the corner. "Listen I'm scared. I keep thinking about my mother."

"Girl you bugging. You all right, you just high. Sit down and let it wear off a little bit. We gonna leave in like an hour."

That's what she told me an hour ago. I sucked my teeth. "Just give me the directions to the train."

Without a hesitation she explained. "When you step outside you want to go left. Then you keep going straight about four blocks down. You will see the train on the right." She smiled at me and went back in the house after I said bye.

I walked out in the dark, and I couldn't believe she let me go by myself. I didn't know what they gave me because I never felt that way with Ty and Rell. I was paranoid. I thought the people who killed my mother were going to kill me. As I walked fast, I thought people were following me. The wind blew hard and shifted my body from left to right. It was the November wind, so it was quite breezy out there.

I got to the train station and stood there for twenty minutes, scared, thinking I was going to die that night. Somebody was going to come and take me out. I had no money. I didn't even know if I was going to make it back home. I thought about Patricia and felt hurt. She gave me something other than weed, probably dust, and then you might as well say she left me. I had a boring time; she stayed in the room with the boy the whole time. She knew I didn't have any money. She totally disrespected me; she must have thought I was a sucker.

My train arrived and I got on as if I had money, sat down and waited for the conductor to come around to collect the money. My stop was only three stops away. I was hoping he got to me on the second stop. That way, if he kicked me off, it would be my stop anyway. I got lucky; he got to me the second stop. As high as I was, I explained that I lost my wallet, which left me broke, and the next stop was mine anyway. As soon as I got off, I began to feel much better.

I went straight to Katie's apartment. I knocked on the

door and Katie opened it. "What's up, Shiree? Come in."
I walked into the living room where Phil was sitting.
"Hi, Phil."

"Hey Shiree," he said, excited to see me. "How's my little daughter?"

I flopped on the couch. I began moaning as I held my head back. My head was spinning. "Uh oh, your eyes are red. Shiree, you high, ain't you? You look fired up, girl."

I could hear him giggling.

When I didn't respond, he got serious. "If you can't handle it, why do you smoke it?"

I opened my eyes while I continued to lay back. "Nah Phil, I just got back from Osning with this new girl from my school. I don't know what the hell she gave me. I never felt like this with Ty and Rell."

"You can't be smoking everybody's shit, Shiree. You shouldn't be smoking at all. But you ain't gonna listen to me. You still my little daughter. If I was you, I would whoop that chick's ass."

"All right you guys, I 'm going in now."

"All right my little daughter you take it easy okay? And don't be getting high with that girl anymore."

"Okay Phil." As I walked across the hall I thought Phil didn't even know the half. The little bitch left me dolo.

On the way to school, all I saw was Patricia's face. I wanted to run right into her. I just couldn't get her off my mind. I felt played.

I went to a few classes and skipped the rest. I sat in the hall with the other kids who weren't trying to learn a damn thing except who had half on a bag of weed. For a minute I thought Patricia didn't make it to school until I saw her coming down the back hall stairs. She avoided the back hall stairs the whole day. And the only reason she came down then was because she must have thought I wasn't in school because she didn't see me in the front hall. She had to go through the back stairs to go home unless she was going to walk all the way around.

My eyes caught hers, but she pretended she didn't see me. Then I knew she was wrong about that night— she felt guilty. I called her and she met me half way.

"What's up, Shiree, are you all right?"

"Do I look all right?" I asked her.

She just laughed.

"You must of thought I wasn't all right last night if you're asking me now am I all right. Why did you let me go by myself with no money, knowing I was fucked up, and you brought me there?"

"Girl you was bugging out. I didn't know what was wrong with you."

"Oh, I was bugging, huh?"

"No, you kept talking about your mother and you said you was scared."

That's when I caught her right in her eye, and soon as she fell I stomped her. I could hear in the background "fight, fight, fight." She lay there hurt with no intentions to fight back. My first blow dazed her. I just kicked her in her head real quick, grabbed my bag and left before the principal came.

I was getting out of control with what should have been the importance of my life, and that was school and Aunt Goldie. She and I did not have any communication. I went and came as I pleased. She never said anything to me. Instead I got funny looks. I eventually got kicked out of school, for disrespecting the teachers, principal and the class. I didn't like school anymore. I found wasting time fun. Only, the teachers hated it and sent me to the office for it.

The blonde lady secretary scolded me when I stepped in the office. "Shiree you are going to be suspended." I turned around to head back out the office. "Aint no skin off my ass." That got me a hearing to get kicked out of school.

Aunt Goldie had to attend the hearing. She walked up in there like it was the last thing she wanted to do; she had better things to be doing. She sat at the end of a very long table, and I sat at the other end. A staff member with a tight-ass suit on gave me a long look. "How do you feel about not being able to attend school anymore?"

I shrug and told the man I didn't care, and I really didn't.

I used to hang out with a Dominican girl my age sometimes named Niome. I often went to her house where I met her sweet mother. She was pretty and had a lot going for herself. She wasn't a girl who got into trouble, or even knew what trouble was for that matter. Only sometimes she felt like she didn't want to be bothered for no reason.

This day she was hanging out with these girls that didn't look familiar to me in front of my building. I walked up toward them and Niome did not speak. So I stood there staring at her for a while. "Oh, you can't speak, Niome? I didn't do shit to you."

She didn't pay me any mind. So I said, "You ugly bald-headed bitch."

She knew and I knew she wasn't ugly or bald-headed. So she ignored me.

Now I wanted to fight. I'm too good of a friend to get treated like that. I jumped in her face, but she walked away from me, so I pushed her.

She started huffing and puffing, coming at me like she was going to take my head off. She began swinging all crazy at me, like she wanted to catfight.

I hate when bitches start swinging like they don't have any sense. So I backed away from her and came in at her with a blow to her right eye. That shit swelled up instantly.

She paused and I paused. Then she came running toward me. That's when I kicked the wind out of her. She fell down quick.

Immediately I grabbed her by her hair with both hands and I kept banging her head sideways on the brick building.

I heard my aunt calling my name out the window. "Shiree, are you down here? Your brother is on the phone." I dropped Niome and ran upstairs.

A few seconds went by after hanging up with Caseen, when Aunt Goldie told me to get the door. I knew who it was, so I pretended not to hear my aunt.

"Got damn it, Shiree, I know you heard me." She stormed past me and went for the door.

I was sitting at the table with my back toward the door when Niome and her mother came. I turned around to see Niome's angry mother standing there and Niome's eye was blood-shot and swollen, and the rest of her face was scratched up. I immediately turned back around, so I didn't have to look at them.

Her mother said, "Shiree, why did you do that? You guys were friends.

"Miss, your daughter was acting funny toward me, and plus she swung at me first, so she did it to herself."

Niome screamed, "Stop lying."

That whole time I was sitting at my kitchen table, calm, with my back still facing them. I turned around and started screaming at her. "Liar? You in my fucking house, don't talk to me like that because you can get the hell out."

Aunt Goldie sat on the couch looking at me with her

head twisted looking out her glasses. She was surprised, but then again she wasn't.

I looked at her, put my left palm in the air and said, "Excuse me Aunt Goldie, but she's tripping."

Niome's mother said, "Shiree, look at her face."

Her face looked terrible but I didn't have any remorse for her.

I got dressed quickly and began looking out the window anxiously. Ernest called and said he was on the train and Tarrytown was the next stop. I sat in the living room with Aunt Goldie. She stared at me from across the room suspiciously. She was watching Knot's Landing, but she couldn't keep her eyes off me. She went back and forth from the television back to me. Finally she asked, "Where are you going this time of night, child?" She sounded frustrated and plain sick of me. "You know that tutor is coming here tomorrow to meet you, so you need to stay in."

"I know Aunt Goldie. I'll be back, I'm just going outside for a little while."

"I'm not stupid, Shiree. You're going to meet that damn boy. And don't lie either, because he just called here. And you jumped up to get dressed. And I don't want him calling here anymore either."

Defensively I said, "But why, Aunt Goldie? He didn't do anything to you."

"I have a phone bill that cost more than my rent. Now what sense does that make?"

"But Aunt Goldie, he didn't do it."

"You just shut your mouth, okay?" She jumped up fiercely and walked over to the black wall unit in the dining area. She began searching through some papers. "You ran my bill up talking to his sorry ass. You don't want to do right in school or anything. And I don't like him. I know he ain't shit."

We both heard a low tap at the door. We both turned to look at the door. I got up because I knew who it was.

Aunt Goldie ran to the door before me and opened it. She didn't see anyone. When she stepped out and looked down the hall, she saw Ernest standing by the elevators.

I stood in the doorway behind Aunt Goldie.

Ernest started walking toward us.

Aunt Goldie flipped on him. "You get your stinky ass away from my door boy before I have you locked up."

I slid past Aunt Goldie and headed toward Ernest.

My aunt yelled, "Oh, you're leaving anyway, Shiree? You won't get your ass back in here, I'll fix you."

It was far too late to stop me from doing anything I wanted to do. We sat at the train station for hours, and it was so cold. We just wanted to be together. We cuddled and kissed and talked until I thought about Katie's house. Katie let us in and we went to her bedroom. We continued to talk, hug and kiss, but we did not have sex.

He came to see me a lot and we did different things, but sex was not one of them.

When the morning came, I called Kemi and told her to meet me at the train station. I wanted Ernest to meet my home girl. They got along fine because Kemi got along with everybody. That's one of the reasons I liked her. She was open-minded and wasn't afraid to take risks. And Ernest was straight thorough. So he was use to dealing with all types of people.

Ernest and I hugged constantly like two lovebirds until Phil pulled up. "What's up Shiree? Hi Kemi, how's your parents?"

"Oh they're fine" she responded.

"That's good, tell them I said hello."

"Phil, this is Ernest."

"Oh, what's up, man? I heard so much about you."

I gave Ernest a hug. "I have to go to work right now. I'm going to call you tomorrow if I can't call you tonight."

"Aight Kemi."

"All right Shiree."

I left with Phil. Ernest looked sad to me, but shit, money is money I thought. And I needed it.

I had Ernest on my mind the whole night. I couldn't sleep. I could still feel his hands wrapped around me. I wanted to hear his voice so bad. That morning I jumped up, got washed and ready and was out the door. I went to the closest pay phone and called Ernest.

"Shiree? That's you?"

"Yeah it's me."

"What's up?"

"Nothing," he said.

Nothing, I repeated to myself. What the hell is wrong with him? He didn't sound himself.

"Why did you leave me yesterday?"

"Ernest I had to go to work yesterday. You know that. You were getting ready to leave anyway."

Ernest got silent. "So, how long did you know Kemi?"

"I don't know, since I moved here why?"

"That's your home girl?" he asked.

"Yeah, why you asking me all these questions about Kemi?"

"I'm just asking."

"No you're not. I'm not stupid, so stop talking to me like I am."

"You know I love you, right?" he added. "

"I know you love me and you acting real stupid, too."

"For real though, let me stop playing. I love you and Kemi is not your friend."

"Why do you say that?" I asked.

"Because I fucked her."

I stood there with my mouth open. I was shocked for

three seconds. Speechless, after I realized it wasn't a game, I hung up.

I went to Kemi's house. She came running to the door. "What's up Shiree." I did not return her smile. "You slept with Ernest?" "What? Did he tell you that?" I didn't respond. "Don't believe that Shiree. For real. I wouldn't do something like that." I walked off. "Where you going?"

I went home. I knew she was lying. I felt betrayed by the both of them. She knew I loved him, and I thought he loved me.

Later on Aunt Goldie called my name. "Someone's at the door for you. It was Kemi. I went into the hallway for privacy. "I did it Shiree, I did. I'm so sorry. I didn't mean it. If I could take it back I would."

I forgave her and we continued our friendship. Kemi was experienced with sex. I was still a virgin. I didn't yet understand the life of sex. I respected Ernest in a way and was not that mad at him. He always was sweet and patient with me. He defended me and would go to the moon for me, and he didn't have to tell me, but he chose to. I still continued to talk to him at Kemi's house.

I left Kemi's house Sunday at seven o'clock. I had spent the whole weekend over there. I just wanted to take a hot shower and hit the sack. A nice phat spliff would be nice, I thought as I got off the elevator.

"Hi, Aunt Goldie."

She was sitting at the dining table. She looked at me and rolled her eyes. "Hi, Eugene." I spoke to her grandson as I noticed him sitting on the couch looking at me like I walked in with shit on my shoes.

Without greeting me back he said, "Where have you been all weekend?"

Before answering him I was trying to figure out, did he really want to know or was he trying to be funny. "I was at my friend's house."

You were at your friend's house for the whole weekend?" he asked.

I walked away and headed to my room. I wanted to scream at him. I wanted to say, "You don't live here, so what the fuck are you questioning me for?"

I already knew Aunt Goldie was complaining about me to him. Eugene was Aunt Goldie's grandson in his late twenties. He lived in Brooklyn with his boyfriend. He was a faggot and it seemed like it didn't bother anybody. He was not too fond of me, and neither was I of him.

I was clearing off my bed when Eugene walked in. "Don't you hear me talking to you?"

"I don't even know you," I snapped. "You just walk in my room and don't knock."

"That's not the point. This is my grandmother's house. Why are you stressing my grandmother out?"

"I'm not stressing her out. I didn't do anything." I said defensively.

He snapped out of nowhere, "She is my grandmother, not yours."

I rolled my eyes and went back to cleaning my room. My aunt loved every minute of him harassing me.

Eugene stood there watching me. "Why would you let your boyfriend disrespect your Aunt Goldie?"

"What?" I got loud with him because I was pissed off. I kept watching Aunt Goldie walk around, and she let her grandson get in my face and bully me. "He did not disrespect Goldie."

That's when he punched me in my face, and my nose started bleeding.

I fled down the hallway and almost made it out the door until he grabbed me with his faggot hands. I was going to get Phil. I'm sure if Phil had seen my nose, the faggot would have been holding his nose. I couldn't stand him or my aunt's son named Dick.

Dick was a true bum, he wore dirty clothes, never had money, or a place to stay. He stunk and my aunt would let him come and live with us sometimes. He acted sort of retarded, how he walked around, smiling for nothing and talking to himself. He would come in my room while I was in there. "Get out Dick." He smiled in my face. "No," he said.

I stormed in the living room where my aunt was. "Dick won't leave my room." "He don't have to leave. It was his room before yours." I took a double look at her and walked away.

I was very mad and thought, why couldn't he go in her room, she didn't use it. When I went back to my room, he laughed at me. So I left, and came back later. I was really getting tired of Dick because he was always testing me to see just how far I would go. He knew I didn't like him, so why didn't he stay out of my way.

"Come on, Shiree, hurry up." Tyniesha was rushing me.

"I'm coming, Ty."

"All right, hurry up before I leave your little ass."

"Where ya going?" I heard Dick ask Ty.

"To get some grub," she said.

"Oh ya'll going to Mc Donald's?"

"Why, Dick? You can't come, you don't have any money."

"I'm going, shoo."

"Okay, I'm ready," I said rushing out the bathroom. ILL, I said to myself.

Dick sounded nasty and he looked nasty too with all that cold in his eyes.

I ordered pancakes.

Dick followed me around while I collected napkins and silverware. Ty was already seated. Before I could sit down Dick stood in front of me. "Let me get some of your hotcakes."

"No Dick, get out of my face."

"Let me just get one."

"No, get out my face."

"Oh, you gonna give me some."

I nudged him out of my way and he struck me in my face. Then he smacked my pancakes in the air and left.

I knew the dude had a problem; I just couldn't convince his mother. She never did anything when he messed with me. Maybe it was her way of getting back at me since she didn't like my ways.

She kept saying, "You keep messing with Dick, he's going to put his hands on you," but he messed with me.

A week later Aunt Goldie cooked a big dinner, including collard greens, chicken, potatoes and all that good stuff. I sat in the living room with Ty and Aunt Goldie's daughter Marlene.

Marlene was real cool. She loved me like I was family, and she knew I was just a child. She never acted as if she was against me, or as if I was always wrong. She was just a cool person who always minded her business. She laughed with me and never judged me. She was a pretty light-skinned lady in her thirties and plenty of men were always interested in her.

We were all sitting in the living room just after eating. I was sitting on the long couch, watching everything as usual. Dick was walking around mumbling. Marlene was sleep on the small couch.

I was about to get up to get a paper cup. Dick brought one to me instead. When I looked in the cup I noticed dirt in it, so I got up to get another one.

Dick got up again to get another cup. On his way to his chair, while passing by me, he smashed the cup in my face and kept going.

I jumped up and, before he could make it to his seat,

I charged him.

He fell into the wooden chair face first, and the chair broke.

I stood back and gave him time to get up. I was ready for him.

He got up and swung at me.

I grabbed him by his sweater and swung him around until he landed on Marlene.

Marlene jumped up like she didn't know what hit her. When she realized what was going on, she and Ty broke us up.

I fixed him and my aunt. She was expecting him to beat me up like her grandson did. My aunt put faith in a lot of people to beat me up but the opposite always happened, like her granddaughter, Kenya.

Tyniesha and Kenya are sisters, but by their attitudes you could never tell. Kenya had sort of an evil soul; she didn't care about no one but herself. She was a fast girl, quick with the boys. She was sixteen and had a baby already. We hit it off when she first came. We went to a party one night, and we hung out. She taught me how to put on make-up, but I was not a make-up fan. We went outside together a lot, I introduced her to my friends, and we would have fun.

I grew tired of her early, and I felt she needed to take herself back to Peekskill. She was jealous of me and wanted to boss me around, but I think she found out soon enough, I was not the one. Although she was only two years older than I was, she talked to me like I was a child. She wasn't grown, and she definitely was not my mother.

I had a friend named Singing Dwayne who sang real well. He came around for me a lot because he liked me. She would flirt with him to get me mad. One night she stayed out all night at Dwayne house, and he fucked her. I didn't care like she thought I would and that's why she did it.

The part I cared about was how she ran around the town talking about me. Then she cut up my clothes without my permission to make her some shorts and short-sleeved shirts for her to wear.

She came in my room getting loud. "What you mad or something?" She was feeling guilty. "Because I do what I wanna do." She started going through my stuff, as she was talking like she was tough. "Yo, who do you think your talking to?" I asked her. "You can get up out my room with all of that shit." She twisted her head and said, "I'll whoop your ass."

"You ain't going to do shit to me," and I meant that. As she started to come towards me, I got up off my bed and threw her up against the window. She could have gone out of it.

We grabbed each other and fell on my bed. I had her hair and bent her head down, as I kept punching her.

Aunt Goldie watched for a minute. I guess she was giving Kenya time to get me. When she noticed her poor Kenya couldn't beat me, she broke it up.

I left for a while then came back. Half my clothes were gone and the chain was gone to my locket my mom bought me on my twelfth birthday before she passed. All I had was the locket, but at least I had that. Still, I was raged because I could never replace that chain. Kenya left and my life went on the same.

My tutor taught me at home, since I was not allowed at school. Every day before we got to work, she always asked me questions about my life prior to moving to Tarrytown. She wasn't being nosy, just concerned. I knew she felt sorry me because a lot of folks did.

I tossed and turned from all the commotion I felt in the apartment. It wasn't enough to make me get up, but I felt it.

I woke up to my Aunt Goldie's loud obnoxious voice. "Get up, Shiree, and pack your bags. You're out of here now. You don't want to stay here. You don't listen, and you think you're grown. No grown kids live in here." Aunt Goldie stood in my doorway with her hand on her hip and her head down, glasses hanging off the nose.

I glanced at her for two seconds before I lay back down, pulling the covers over my head. I heard her walk away from my door into the living room.

I heard her walking hard around the living room, talking shit. "She thinks I'm playing with her. I'm not playing with you today, Shiree. I'm gonna show you." She stood in front of my door again. "You're not gonna get up, Shiree?"

"Get up and go where, Aunt Goldie? Where do you want me to go?"

"Just get up, because you're getting out of here. Someone will come for you."

I lay right back down.

"Hello, hello, Shiree, please get up." The voice was loud and deep, and whoever it was banged on my room door.

I sat up to a tall, big white dude. "Who are you in my room, banging on my door, ordering me to get up? Get out of my room."

"My name is Detective Mark and your aunt here wants you out of her house. Now you're going to get up, get all your belongings together, or I can arrest you."

I sat completely up. "Where am I supposed to go?" I whined.

"I'm going to wait out there for you. You get up, get ready, and come out and we'll take care of the rest."

I was getting more depressed by the minute. As I packed my last bag I heard a familiar voice coming from the living room. I grabbed my bags and went to the living room. "Sam?" What the hell is he doing here, I wondered.

He didn't speak to me, and I didn't speak to him. He signed a bunch of papers and spoke with the detective and Aunt Goldie. I could tell by his expression and his language that he was glad things were not working for me and that my aunt was getting rid of me.

Detective Mark took me to the little Tarrytown precinct. I sat there for a very long time, until some people came to get me. They were strangers who came to take me some place new.

Chapter 6
The Foster Home

The tall dark-skinned heavyset guy introduced himself to me as Kenny. He greeted me with a handshake. The light-skinned thick lady with long curly hair asked me was I all right?

I followed them into a tall building. The room was filled with young girls and boys. A lot of the kids did not look happy. I sat next to the window where I could see the sun and hope to feel it because they had the air conditioner on full blast. The building was huge and broke off in different sections. There were a lot of offices and business people there.

Kenny came into the waiting area where I was, sat my suitcases down next to me and said good luck. Then he turned around and walked away.

I sat and sat. I ate the bag lunch they brought me that had a bologna sandwich, cookies, milk and a banana in it. I waited. Nobody told me anything.

I got up and walked over to one of the ladies dressed in a sundress with flowers on it and a polyester sweater. She sat behind a desk talking on the phone, which rang constantly. I stood there, waiting for her to hang up so I could ask her a few questions.

She looked up at me, "Yes can I help you?" The phone rang again. "Oh excuse me," she said. When she got off the phone, she asked me what did I want and the phone rang again. She said, "Why don't you have a seat. I will be right with you."

I shot back at her, "Why do I have to wait? I was standing here before those people called. First come first served right?"

"Listen," the lady grew frustrated. "This is a business we run here and these calls are very important."

"What are you saying, what I have to say is not important or I'm less important than they are?"

"Ma'am," I did not say that. What I'm saying is that you are already here, you are safe, and we are trying to find you placement. There are kids out there that need to get here and I have to get all the calls coming through because it can be a placement for you or someone who is here waiting."

"That's the problem," I said. "I'm tired of waiting."

"I know dear. It's a long process. That's why I need to answer the phone to get you guys out of here."

I walked away and headed back to the room. There were four people ahead of me. I sat next to a young black girl who had been crying since I got there. "What's wrong with you," I asked.

She had on a pair of home-made shorts, the kind you make by cutting a pair of jeans, yellow construction boots that were twice her size, and a nappy ponytail. Somebody wasn't doing her right, I thought.

She was crying because she wanted to go home. Shit I wanted to go home too, when home was home. "Well why can't you go home?" I asked her.

She stopped crying, wiped her face and said, "Because I got tired of my mother's boyfriend putting his penis in me and I told somebody."

As I listened to her, I became really angry. "So why

did you have to leave the house?" I asked her. "Because my mother didn't make him leave. She didn't believe me. BCW made me leave. They said we couldn't be under the same roof together."

"Didn't he go to jail?" I kept asking questions.

"Yes, but my mother bailed him out."

"What?" I jumped to my feet. "Your mother bailed him out while you walking around here with raggedy shorts, your older brother's boots and in desperate need of a perm."

She began to cry again.

"I know how you feel. Life is fucked up. I got the shitty end of the stick myself, and that's the reason I'm sitting beside you." But in time she you will feel a lot better. I'm sorry your mother aint shit. I know your crying because you want to be with her mother."

Naturally she shouldn't want to be with her, but that's how it is when you don't know anyone else. I wondered where I was going to be placed. I liked the fact that I was going be closer to Ernest. With the thought I got up and called Ernest's house.

His mother answered the phone, "No, Ernest is not here. Who's calling?"

"This is Shiree," I responded.

"Oh Shiree, I heard so much about you. Ernest is in jail. Are you in Westchester?"

"No, I'm in Brooklyn now waiting to be placed somewhere."

"Okay, Ernest will love to see you. Call me tomorrow and you can come over. We'll take you to see Ernest."

"Okay," I said. "I will call you tomorrow then." I hung up.

That was music to my ears. I didn't care where I was going, as long as Ernest was in my life. Ernest was all that mattered to me. He became my inspiration and happiness. He was all I looked forward to.

In the morning they woke me up to leave. I was taken to a small apartment building in Bestuy, on Stuyvesant between Monroe and Gates. An older lady in her fifties, short with big eyes and big bifocal glasses welcomed me in. The people who brought me left.

She tried to be so polite, and I appreciated that, but I did not like her house. Atmosphere was very important to me and I was getting more depressed by the minute. It was a very small apartment. As soon as you came through the door there was a little dining area on the left; the small kitchen was in front of that. On the right was the small living room with that plastic furniture a lot of people had in the city, that uncomfortable hot shit. When you walked in the door, straight ahead was a short hall. Off the hall were my room, her room and the bathroom.

She was a single lady, no man and no other kids. Boring. I knew she didn't think I could get used to that. My room was small, like every other part of the house, but it fitted two twin beds and a desk. She spoke to me for a while, maybe she told me about the area, and maybe she gave me a few rules. I never really heard a word that came out her mouth. All I heard was her name was Miss Galloway. She was a nice lady.

I sat on my bed thinking about everything. I had been to many places already. What this would turn out like?

The next morning she told me I could fix myself something. I could have had waffles, or cereal or something, but I wasn't hungry.

She spent her whole morning at the bar across the street. At the bar you could eat, drink and gamble. Galloway seemed to spend most of her time there.

I called Ernest's house and spoke to his sister, Lawanda. She told me how to get to the projects they lived in. I got to the Wycoff projects. The lobby doors were always locked but someone was always leaving the building, so I went in after someone. On the eighteenth floor, I knocked on 18B, and a little girl said, "Who is it?"

A brown-skinned big-boned tall lady opened the door. "Hi, are you Shiree?"

I nodded.

She smiled and said with excitement, "Come on in. Come on in here, sit down." Three girls were already sitting in the living room. "This is Ernest's sister, Lawanda, Ameanie, and this is Tarsha. Isn't she so pretty?" his mother continued. "Oh, and I'm his mother, Wanda. Ernest is crazy about you, girl." She looked at her daughter for agreement and said, "Right Lawanda? All he talks about is her. That boy be around here, Shiree this and Shiree that."

I sat there blushing from ear to ear, but I was content. I felt like I knew these people for a long time.

His mother was still talking. "He had that other girl here and he couldn't stand her. He said, 'Ma, make her leave.' I let her stay here because she had nowhere to go. She told us she was pregnant, but she wasn't. When I found out I threw her right on out of here."

Miss Harris started asking me questions about my life. I could tell she liked me, and from her very first greeting I took a strong likening to her. I sensed her realness. I called her Miss Harris because Ernest's last name was Harris. His sisters were cool too. While Miss Harris talked, they smiled at me.

"Do you want to go see Ernest today?" she asked me. "He's on Riker's Island. They gave him a year."

After I heard that, my heart sort of saddened. But the thought of seeing him had activated my joy. Yes I wanted to see Ernest. I was just thirteen still; no prison would let me in at my age.

She walked out of the living room telling her daughters, "Ya'll know ya'll have to go to Linderies' house to get that money. I will be back," she said and left the apartment.

I followed the girls to one of the back rooms. They had to get ready to go to Bushwick first. I stood by the bathroom door while Lawanda put her gray contact lenses in. This was the first time I learned about contacts.

Lawanda was sixteen. She had brown skin, and slim long modeling legs. She took her time and made sure she looked right, and had all the right criteria she knew would make her look good. She took her time to fix her hair; she had special talents to do hair. We talked like we knew each other for years.

Ameanie was brown-skinned short, thick, long hair. She was very observant, and very sweet. I was kind to her and so she gave me kindness back. She had a hiss in her talk, she stuttered a little and had an accent. Her father was Haitian from Hawaii and she lived with him for some time. Ameanie was very pretty.

Ernest's little sister, Tarsha, was the cutest, sweetest little thing. She had a squeaky voice, talked a lot, and danced her tail off. Her steps were fascinating. Her whole style was fascinating. She was a four-year-old little girl you could fall in love with in minutes.

"Are you coming with us to Bushquik?" Lawanda asked me. "We have to go to my aunt's house to pick up some money. Do you smoke weed?"

"Hell yeah, I smoke," I told her.

"I got to pick some up for Ernest, so we'll get us a bag too."

"Sounds good to me."

We got high on the way back. When we finally got back, it seemed like the whole day was gone. It was dark outside, and we were so high we were moving slow. We laughed all the way back.

Miss Harris was in the lobby waiting for us. Her voice

was so loud. "What took ya'll so long? Turn around, go right back out the door. There's no need to go upstairs. You better hope we make this bus to Riker's Island." She looked at Lawanda and rolled her eyes. "You high, ain't you?"

Lawanda laughed out loud. I kept giggling because I was high and Miss Harris was cracking me up. We were a block away from the building.

"Lawanda, do you have everything you need?" Miss Harris asked.

"Yes Ma," Lawanda responded.

"Are you sure? Do you have your I.D.?"

Lawanda's eyes grew big as she searched her back pockets. "Oh, I forgot it on my dresser."

"Lawanda hurry up and go get it."

Lawanda headed back toward the building.

"Hurry up girl, run." Miss Harris paced the sidewalk while she talked out loud. "That damn girl is high. I knew she was gonna do this. We're not gonna make that bus. Come on, Shiree, let's go back. We'll go tomorrow. Can you go tomorrow?"

I grinned at her and said, "Yeah." Shit I can go anytime you want to take me, I thought.

"You think your foster lady will let you stay the night?"

"I don't know," I said.

"Call her and ask her, okay? And we'll leave early tomorrow."

I called Miss Galloway and asked her could I stay. I told her I was at friend's house and that it was late and I was tired. She agreed to let me stay.

"Come on let's go down the hall to the Fortunato's," Lawanda said.

I followed her down the hall. "What's the Fortunato's?"

"It's a Dominican family. That's their last name."

Rita answered the door. "What's up Lawanda?" she said, and waved hi to me. She let us in and led us to the living room.

Lawanda introduced me. "This is Rita, Jodie and Jamie. And this is Shiree, Ernest's girlfriend."

Everyone said hi, except the fat girl named Jamie.

"Come on, Shiree, let's go get high." I followed Lawanda back to her apartment.

"I don't think that fat girl like me," I said.

"Who, Jamie? She probably don't because she like Ernest."

Ameanie was in the living room with her boyfriend, Mike. Mike was short, dark-skinned, stubby, and shabby looking. But that was her boo.

Lawanda's boyfriend, Lee, was waiting for her in her room. He was brown-skinned, medium built with dreads and chinky eyes. When Lawanda introduced us, he looked at me like I was invading his privacy.

The next morning I heard a loud voice and stepped out of the room. "So this is Ernest's girlfriend. Hi, I'm Dee Dee, his older sister. She's cute, Mom." She pulled her younger brother by his shirt. "This is Dashawn, our baby brother."

Dashawn just stood there staring, like he had a head full of thoughts but barely spoke a word.

I couldn't take my eyes off Dee Dee because she was unique. Her voice was loud, but it was a humorous loud. She was definitely a fashion chick. She looked good in everything she coordinated. She wore gold earrings, rings and chains. Her hair was dope and so was her style.

She told me she didn't live there. "I got my own apartment in East New York on Linden and Sheffield. I got two kids, Samantha and Devon."

Every day and night it was the same thing; Lawanda did my hair, and not just did it, she hooked it up. We got higher than high. We hung out; we jumped the train turnpikes. We started trouble on the trains. She had my back and I had hers. Mrs. Galloway never saw me, and Miss Harris saw too much of me. Lawanda and I were two peas in a pod.

Miss Harris woke up one morning, and spotted me in Lawanda's room on her way to the bathroom. "Hi Shiree, I didn't know you were here." She gave me a phony smile. I knew she felt I was wearing out my welcome, but she was giving me the benefit of the doubt that it would end soon. As she walked away, she began screaming that echoed and made things shake. "Ameanie? Lawanda? I want my fucking house cleaned. Why do it look like this in here?" Her words dragged as she screamed.

Lawanda got dressed quickly and we left.

Lawanda came with me to my foster home from time to time. I checked in with Galloway and left. Galloway was not happy, either, but what could I say.

Miss Harris stood in front of Lawanda's door. She didn't move or say anything for one whole minute. She stood with both hands on her hip and stared at us, as if she was trying to intimidate us with her looks. Then she took her hands off her hip and said in a nice tone, "Shiree, you're still here? That foster lady let you stay out like this?"

I shrugged as if to say I don't know and I really didn't care.

She shook her head and walked away. "Lawanda come here," she yelled obnoxiously. She yelled again impatiently. "Lawanda?"

"I'm coming."

"Lawanda, she cannot stay here like this. She's got to go home. She's nice, I like her, but she's got to go."

"But Ma," Lawanda tried to speak before getting cut off.

"I don't care. I don't want to hear it, get out of my face now."

On our way out the door Miss Harris stopped me. "Shiree? Come here, Shiree."

I stopped in front of her door.

"You're leaving?" I nodded.

"I didn't know you were going right now. Ernest should be calling."

"No Ma, we're leaving," Lawanda yelled.

Miss Harris noticed my gold watch. "Ooh, let me see your arm. That's beautiful."

"You want it?" I said, taking it off.

"Oh, you're giving it to me? Thank you, thank you, Shiree." She hugged me. "Okay, see you later. You coming back later 'cause Ernest is dying to talk to you."

"All right Miss Harris." I smiled and walked away.

Sometimes she would talk to me very nice, and then she would switch and start screaming like a maniac. I just sat and listened to her without paying her any mind. That's just how she was, but I knew she loved me. The way she treated me was how she treated her kids, no different. She was a very good person deep down, but she had a problem expressing it sometimes. I out of all people understood her and took a strong liking to her. She was real, said whatever was on her mind. I came around as much as I wanted, because Lawanda was my road dog.

The store man caught me stealing perfume in Rite Aid's downtown Brooklyn. He grabbed my arm and told me to go with him, and led me into a room that had cameras in it. He refused to let Lawanda come in when she followed behind us. I saw myself on the TV putting the perfume in my pocket. Lawanda kept knocking on the door asking the man could she pay for it and we leave.

The man kept opening the door being an asshole. He refused to let me go and was very persistent to send me to jail. The way he was talking to me, I knew he did not like thieves and he had plans to take me to jail, no ifs or buts about it. But I didn't feel like sitting in jail and I really never knew my stealing would amount to that.

He opened the door to face Lawanda. "Look Miss, if you don't stop knocking on this door, you can go to jail too."

"I ain't going nowhere." She rolled her eyes and jumped stupid. "All of this is uncalled for. I said I would pay for the stuff."

"It don't work that way ma'am. Now go away your friend is going to jail." He slammed the door.

Lawanda kept knocking, which made me more impatient and ready to go. The store clerk swung the door open with force. "Look, you ignorant ass, you should of thought about paying for it before she stole it. It's a little too fucking late. Now do you want to go?"

I stood behind him for about two seconds while the door was wide open, and he was talking shit to Lawanda. I saw every opportunity to leave, so I flew like the wind out of the room, through the store, to the front and out of the store.

I got outside to Fulton Street and I kept going straight to the train station. I did not stop, pass go, collect anything—I was out. It was amazing how icy it was outside, but as I ran I balanced myself.

Without looking back, I heard Lawanda's voice. She was keeping up with me and he was keeping up with her. The store mans voice got closer and so did his touch. He grabbed my arm and I grabbed the pole.

Lawanda jumped in his face. "Get off of her." She was breathing heavy when she threw her hands in his face. "Get the fuck off her I said." Every time she swung her hands in his face, the store man flinched.

It was apparent that he was scared as he hollered, "Call the police, thieves, thieves."

"What the fuck do you want? We're far away from the store, you got your shit back, so what the fuck do you want, some blood?"

"No you bitches going to jail. You too now, bitch."

"Bitch?" Lawanda repeated him. "Oh yeah, you want some blood." She pulled out her pocketknife. The store man's eyes grew wide.

She aimed at his hands that were holding me to the pole. "Let her go now asshole," she screamed as she swung the knife like a maniac.

He immediately let go and we ran.

"If I'm going to jail, it's going to be for a reason, you faggot," Lawanda yelled as we ran to the train station.

We had dusted him, but he was still running after us. He was too late because by that time we jumped the train pike The train was still there about to leave and we got right on it. By the time he had got through the turnpike and to the train, the train was pulling off. We laughed at him with our middle fingers up as the train rode away.

I went to Miss Harris' room for my everyday greeting. "Hi Miss Harris," I said excitedly. She just stared at me with no response. I did what I always did when she was in her mood. I walked away.

Lawanda was sitting on her bed when I walked in. "What's wrong with your mother?"

"You already know she get like that sometimes."

I walked back in Miss Harris' room because I wasn't scared of her. "What are you cooking for Thanksgiving?" I asked her.

She looked at me like she was about to bite me. "Get out of my face, Shiree."

"What's wrong Miss Harris?"

"Do it look like there's food in there to cook, Shiree, huh? Don't play with me."

I stared at her for two point five seconds then went to check the kitchen. I stuck my head in Lawanda's room. "Come on get dressed. Let's go to the supermarket."

"What for?" she asked.

"To get some food to cook for Thanksgiving."

"Oh yeah," she said. "But how are you supposed to steal food?"

"Girl, if anyone knows me better, it should be you."

We laughed on the way to Path Mark.

"Okay we're gonna get the turkey last. Now you got to tell me what to get because you know."

"All right," Lawanda said.

I shoved cheese, breadcrumbs, noodles and a few branches of collard greens in my pockets, sleeves and pants. We exited the store and I emptied everything out.

"Wait right here," I said. I went in the store and asked for a bag. I told them my bag ripped, and they gave me one.

We hid our food bag in the bushes and went back in. I put a turkey in my coat, and laughed all the way out of the store, hollering, "I'm in labor."

Lawanda laughed at me all the way to the projects. "Girl, you are crazy."

"Were gonna eat though, right?"

"Oh, my God, Shiree, how did you get this?" Miss Harris had her hands over her mouth. "Thank you, Shiree."

Lawanda and I left the weed spot high and rode the train to my house to chill. Miss Galloway was not home, as usual. We made egg salad and went to bed. She slept in the twin bed in my room that was not occupied. We laughed about the whole day.

When morning came, Galloway cursed me out. "You

know your not grown but you are just a little child. And you cannot stay out with your friends, and they cannot stay over."

I didn't utter a word back. But as soon as I picked up the phone and she yelled. "Put down my phone." I ignored her at first. "Get off my phone." "Alright Miss Galloway, when I'm done." I continued to dial out.

She came toward me to grab the phone. She reached for it and I pulled away from her. "Give me my damn phone, little girl. You are too much."

I put the phone up to her head and swung.

Lawanda grabbed it out of the air before I could knock the shit out of her. When we left, I knew she was going to get rid of me.

One night I called Leroy and told him I was coming over. He told me he moved and gave me the address. Lawanda, Lee and Ameanie came with me. We got so lost it wasn't funny, but it was cold. It was snowing; our hands and feet were frozen. We were going to turn around after two hours lost in the snow. I decided to call him back, because I didn't want to go all the way back home. After all, we came from Brooklyn to Staten Island and it was cold. If we could have just found the house, our bodies would be so warm. When I called he gave me better directions. We walked in the house smiling because I was so happy to be there.

As soon as I spotted Dad, my lips hung low and my smiled turned to a frown. I couldn't even keep silent. I screamed, "What happened to you?" I was in a state of shock. I lowered my voice, but still looking surprised I said, "You look different."

"Yes, I know. I have cirrhosis of the liver."

"Oh," I said in slow rhythm and went to greet my baby brothers. I didn't know what it was. I just thought it meant sick, but nothing major. But he looked like a pregnant anorexic with no hair. Dad was something to brag about but I didn't know any more. But something just was not right. He had dark spots on his face. He had a whole beautiful house. We never lived like this before, I thought. I walked upstairs admiring the house and I noticed Dad had a hospital bed in his room. In the bathroom the medicine cabinet was filled with perm repair for your hair and over fifty bottles of medications.

It was late so we went downstairs to my brother's room to sleep. I was amazed how grown and mature they were. Troy seemed real cool. His style was smooth and cool. He took his time in everything and had few worries.

Leroy seemed to be falling apart. He spoke about the little boy's nose he broke on the school bus, and he had plans to beat Troy's girlfriend's brother up. I knew he was going to be something else. I felt so sorry that we were apart and things were the way they were.

I felt sorry for Dad he looked so bad. I felt bad for looking at him. In the morning a cook came and cooked us all pancakes and eggs. A nurse came and helped Dad as we were leaving.

I went home that night and called Miss Harris. "My dad has cirrhosis of the liver."

"Oh my God Shiree he's about to die."

My heart dropped into my pants somewhere. How could I have been so naive? I should have known. Instead I made Dad feel bad. Maybe he knew I didn't know what it was, He'd forgive me.

Miss Harris explained it to me. "Cirrhosis comes from drinking so much."

"But he did not drink like that." When I hung up I lay across my bed on my backside like a stiff stick, looking up at the ceiling. I couldn't feel my body the tears rolled down my face. I saw Dad then I saw Mom. I remembered like yesterday.

Mom screaming, "Ya'll stop making all that noise in there. Keep it up I'm coming in there with my belt."

I'm walking home from school with butterflies in my stomach, scared to death Mrs. Bullock called my house because I misbehaved in school, showing my ass in front of the class all because of the fine-ass new boy. I walk in the door. "Hi Mom, Hi Dad."

Here go Dad, "What happened at school today?"

I come out with a story almost close to what happened, but never exactly. In my story I make myself look good.

He doesn't buy it, so he tells me to get in the room and wait on him to come tear me up. Why did he ask me what happened if he was going to beat me anyway?

I got those flashes of me and all my brothers going to the store, everybody except my baby brothers.

Me, Lionel, Kareem, Caseen, we running, racing to the yellow store. We hop on the back of the bus geasing down the street. We all sitting around the dinner table. Mom's fixing our plates and Dad's at work. That's when all the snitching and bribing goes on. Somebody's always unhappy at the dinner table. All you hear is, "So what? Shut up, nigga, I'll tell you went geasing."

"So what? I'll tell you stole from the yellow store."

Then someone always calls, "Ma!" and she screams "What?"

She always came and got some information out of somebody, and that's when all the snitching went on. The more I thought the more my tears couldn't help themselves. I cried myself dehydrated, and I fell asleep sad. I was a brokenhearted little girl. I wanted to go back home to Staten Island. I wanted to continue I.S.27; I was doing well there. I missed Caseen, Lionel, Leroy, Troy and Kareem. Slowly but surely we lost each other.

Galloway was acting mean toward me, which she never had before. She only paid me no mind like everybody else I went to live with. She was mad because I was supposed to be home and I wasn't. That was impossible. For one, I was introduced to the streets I liked to run. I had too much on my mind to sit still. And two, that little-ass two-bedroom apartment, her room, my room, the little-ass living room with plastic couches that nobody sat on. Nobody else was home. She expected me to sit in my room all day staring at the empty bed next to mine and the desk in the corner.

I did not think so. So my next step was out the door with my bags. She called the people to come and get me, and guess what, I did not care. "Bye, bye, ship me to my next placement."

Chapter 7
The Group Home

444 Cozine Ave, on the corner of New Lots in East New York stood a two-story building. I carried my bags inside the building by myself. My two chauffeurs were rude to me. They did not speak to me, look at me, or offer a hand with my bags. While standing in the hallway waiting, I could hear yelling and screaming from inside the house. It sounded like a zoo of bitches.

A Jamaican lady opened the door looked at us and sucked her teeth as to say she didn't have time. She threw her hands in the air and said, "Hold on one second all right?"

Two police officers barged by me and the two staff who were standing in front of me blocking the doorway.

The Jamaican lady came back to the door. "You guys come on in now. I'm so sorry. These girls in here are something else. We got police officers coming here every night." She took a deep breath. "Hello young lady you must be, um..." She put one finger on her chin and raised her eyeballs to the ceiling.

"Shiree," I cut her off.

"Yes," she shouted now realizing my name. "Well okay, Shiree, welcome aboard." She looked at the two chauffeurs and said, "You guys can leave now she'll be all right."

I thought they wouldn't give a damn if I were all right or not. And just like I thought, they left without a goodbye, see you later, good luck or anything.

I didn't make it farther than the door, which was where the two sides of the house were divided. The living room, where my bags were, was the first part of one side and the dining room, where the girls were fighting, was the beginning of the other side. I stood in the pathway between the living room and dining room and watched one girl flip another girl on her head. Every girl who was in the house was in the dining room. Every staff that tried to calm the situation got disrespected.. So much commotion was going on I didn't get attended to. The police left and had to come back again. After one fight another fight was going to get started between a few girls and the staff.

I just sat back and watched everything that moved. I caught on to the show offs, the suckers, and the slickers. This place was different from any place I been to. There was nothing but all females, and they were disrespectful and didn't have much to do.

After what seemed like a riot was over, I was told to go to the office. The Jamaican staff was walking fast toward me. "You, in the office," she said pointing at me as she continued to walk toward me.

I mocked her under my breath, "You, in the office." That was rude, I thought. I thought I told her my name. I plopped down in the seat on the other side of the desk. I listened to her go on and on about the girls in the place.

She went as far to say, "These girls in here think they can try me. They can go right ahead. I don't need this job." She laughed. "And I have family. My daughters will not go for these girls disrespecting me."

She was beginning to overwhelm me. I didn't want

or needed to hear the mess she was talking.

"Anyways," she said as she breathed in and out one good time. "Welcome here. I guess you got a preview of what it's like in this place. I mean, it's not like this all the time. We do have some good times. We go on trips a lot. The young ladies usually go out during the day. Now, you're not in school, correct?"

I shook my head. "No."

"You probably will be going to Thomas Jefferson on Pennsylvania Avenue." She flipped through a book that had my name on it.

I wondered what was in that book. I wondered if it had information on me, and all the places I'd been. If so, it should have been a lot thicker than that. When I finally got to leave the depressing office, I walked out to head toward my room.

"Pss, hey you, over here."

When I finally caught eye contact with the girl trying to get my attention I stopped.

"Come in here," one girl said with just her head sticking out the door and the rest of her body in the room.

Mrs. Riley, the Jamaican staff was two steps behind me. "Uh, I'm about to show her where she will be sleeping. You can meet her later," she interrupted.

The girl rolled her eyes and stuck her head back in the room.

We walked to the other side of the house, passing the living room and dining room. "This is your room. Your roommate's name is Darlene, and I don't know where she's at right now. Use this dresser and you guys have a bathroom in here. There's also a bathroom in the hall for this side of the house."

I was putting my things away when I turned around and the girl was standing by my door. "Come over to the other side of the house to meet the girls."

I was thinking to myself, I don't want to meet them, but I appreciated the offer."

"My name is Dee." She was one of the girls who were fighting. She kept smiling. She was tall, light-skinned, and big-boned. I remember thinking that if she didn't have all those brown spots and bumps on her face she would be a lot prettier.

She walked me to the room where everyone was. As soon as I walked in everyone said "Hi", at the same time. "Sit down," one girl said.

I looked at her and noticed she not only had hazel eyes, but she had gotten beat up that night. "My name is Cookie." She smiled sweetly.

Yeah she was a sweet little cookie, I thought. She got beat up by Dee and now they were talking like nothing happened.

One girl stood up and said, "You see that shit, girl?" She stopped all the body movement she was doing along with her loud mouth. "What's your name?"

"Shiree," I told her.

"Your name is Shiree?" Cookie asked nicely. "We had a girl here before named Shiree."

"My name is Melonie," the loud-mouth girl interrupted. She began using body movements again, talking with her hands, hips, fingers, neck and head. "That lady out there is a cunt. I told her to kiss my fucking ass. She always talking about her daughter. Like I would let her daughter whoop my ass."

The girl next to her stood up and said, "I don't think so."

I took a double look. They both were short with huge heads and identical faces. Twins.

"We're sisters," Melonie said. "Do you smoke weed?" one of the big-headed sisters asked.

"Yeah, I smoke."

"You want to smoke?"

"Yeah, I'll smoke." I didn't see anyone moving to go outside, so I said, "I know we can't smoke in here."

"Shit, why not? We do what we want to do in this camp," Melonie said. "We're going to open the window. This place is like prison. They have to open the door with a key to let us out. Melonie opened up three tea bags and emptied the herbs on a book. Then she ripped a page out of the bible and rolled a joint. As she was smoking it, it was burning fast but they all got a few hits.

When it came around to me, I turned it down. "I thought you smoked weed?" Melonie asked.

I looked at her and said, "That is not weed. That is tea."

I thought I was dreaming. "It's Princess Rain to you, Cookie. No, as a matter of fact, it's Miss Princess Rain."

"Oh please, Rain, sit down you're always talking," Cookie said.

Rain began making noises with her mouth. "You know I'm the shit and you wish you were me."

I opened my eyes. It was not a dream. The unfamiliar voice was coming from the dining room. The voice was soft, but yet squeaky and, whoever she was, it was obvious that she was beyond conceited. As I got out of bed, I felt irritated. I didn't want to meet the stuck up girl. I couldn't stand people of her kind. Because even if you were that pretty, the attitude almost always made you ugly and nobody wanted to be around you. I went to the bathroom to brush my teeth. I looked in the mirror and rolled my eyes. I grew more frustrated by the second, especially listening to the girls talk. That's when I realized I didn't like females too much.. Females are cool in general, but living with them was totally different, especially when they had nothing to do. After I got done I walked into the dining room and slipped into an empty seat.

"Hi Shiree," Cookie said, welcoming me to the table. Cookie was a sweet person when she wanted to be. She was tall, medium built, light-skinned with hazel eyes. And she knew she was pretty. She was conceited, but she had nothing on Rain. Cookie was just prissy and classy. She wore nice clothes and she was a show off. But it was cool with me. She got her mood swings every now and then, but that just meant she wanted some space, but ultimately she was sweet.

Dee shouted out loud to Rain, "Rain, that's Shiree, our new girl."

Rain did not respond. Instead she gave a look as if to say, "What's that suppose to mean?"

Dee said it again, which pissed me off, because I didn't need a bitch to recognize me.

"I heard you," Rain said and smiled. I gave Rain a look that I gave all my pre-enemies. It was a long stare that, if you could read, read "Don't fuck with me."

"You must be the new girl. Hi, my name is Mrs. Stewart. I'm a staff here." She stood there smiling. "When you're done eating your caseworker is expecting you in the office. He wants to see you, okay?"

I nodded and said, "All right." I couldn't wait to leave the table anyway, so that was a good enough reason for me to get up and go.

"Hello ma'am, you can have a seat." Light, bright skin with big head and glasses sitting behind a desk was all I saw. "I'm Mr. Jordan, your worker. I will be making sure you get what you need and that you do what you need to do. Is that all right with you?"

I shrugged. I didn't care. I wasn't the least bit interested.

"If there's anything you need, any problems, you come to me. Oh, and one more thing before you go.

Every Wednesday it's mandatory for you to go to the agency. It's in Manhattan. Someone will show you. It's mandatory for all of our placements to go. You will have group and meet with your worker afterwards, which will be me."

I learned the rules quick. I just wasn't sure I could follow them. I got used to doing what Shiree wanted to do. This was how I grew to be. I hadn't been shown love and attention since Mother left. Besides that, everybody talked about me like I wasn't shit, and my own father thought I was his ground he could easily walk or piss on. So I began to guide myself. I made my own rules and I chose what the fuck I was going to do when the fuck I wanted to do it. And there was nothing anybody could do to me that wasn't already done.

On my way back to my room I sniffed the air to smell the sweet aroma of Jam that was attacking my nose. That morning I had unpacked all my hygienes and cosmetics. I went straight to my room to check my Jam. I spotted it sitting on the dresser where I put it. Jam was a greasy gel that would slick your hair down like it was no tomorrow. And it smelled good. I opened up the Jam and noticed fingerprints in it. I closed it up, slammed it down on the dresser, and walked around the house to follow the smell. As soon as the smell caught my nose, I walked up on it. "What is your name again?" I asked the one of the loud-mouth twins.

"Melonie," she said while trying to keep it moving.

"Um, did you go in my room and use my Jam?"

"No," she said with a guilty look on her face.

"So why do I smell Jam in your hair?"

"Girl, they made more than one bottle of Jam." She waited for me to say something else.

"Well, let me see yours." I stood there with my lips turned up which meant, Yeah right, bitch, you're lying.

"Oh, I let Sonia hold mine. She just left." She looked

me up and down, like What?

I rolled my eyes, turned around and bit down on my lip.

I pouted all the way to my room, and then threw myself on my bed.

"What's wrong with you?" A voice came from the other side of the room.

I looked over and noticed my roommate was back.

As I was too mad to respond, she spoke again. "Don't let this place get to you. My name is Darlene, by the way."

I suddenly calmed down. Darlene was medium height, medium built, brown skin, short hair, and your average girl. From the looks of her she wasn't into looking good or dressing to impress. She really didn't care how she looked as long as she was clean. That was good to me. That way I didn't have to worry about her fucking with my shit. I got up and began unpacking my stuff.

"So what is your name?" Darlene asked, persistent to get a conversation out of me.

"My name is Shiree." I noticed that Darlene didn't smile much, nor did she have any expression to her words. I took her as serious.

I sat around the house for a few weeks. I was on probation period. It meant that I couldn't do anything for a while. Phone calls were from six until eight in the evening. Stipends were giving out every Friday. I heard it was about one hundred and sixty dollars. I never saw one. You only got one if you did your chores and followed the rules. I didn't like the rules. I didn't like the fact that Lawanda called me and I couldn't speak to her just because it wasn't six o'clock. I didn't like that we couldn't get out unless the staff opened the door with a key. And cleaning any shit other than my own was out of the question. So I did no chores and got no stipend.

On Friday morning Dee and I were sitting in the living room. Mrs. Wallace, known as the coolest staff the group home had, walked in. She was so short that if it hadn't been for an inch or two, she would have been a midget. She worked the graveyard shift. She came in at eleven at night and left at seven in the morning. She always sat around laughing and joking with the girls. "So what are you girls doing today?"

"Hi Mrs. Wallace," Dee said excitedly.

"Oh don't you give me that phony baloney innocent crap. You're no saint and you know it."

Dee giggled.

I looked at Dee and thought she had the sneakiest laugh for one, and two she laughed too damn much. I didn't have a problem with her, but her friend Rain had one with me. And I couldn't stand Rain. Dee and Rain were close, which meant a lot to me. Those two bitches rolled together, and most likely, if I liked Dee now, I probably wouldn't later.

"What you got for me Mrs. Wallace?" Dee asked.

Mrs. Wallace ignored her and looked at me. "So how you doing, Shiree?"

"I'm all right, Mrs. Wallace." I gave her a smile.

"All right, I'll bring you girls something back when I come in tonight."

I learned a lot about Dee that day since it was just us all day. We ran around the house laughing and having a world of fun, like we were toddlers again. I found her to be a little bit goofy with a heavy hand. She was a bully in her own way and Cookie was one of her targets. I got the impression she was trying to figure out if I could be her next target or not. She couldn't figure me out. I was quiet with a few laughs, but I didn't do the kiss-ass thing. My laughs did turn into serious faces at times.

Mrs. Riley was working that day. "Did you girls do your chores?" she asked.

Dee and I both said yes.

Mrs. Riley walked past the living room hollering, "No, B-side bathroom is not done."

Dee who was sitting right next to me, nudged me in my ribs. "Go do your chore."

I nudged her right back. "You do it." She started laughing, and kicked me. I kicked her back. We both swung our legs on the couch and began kicking each other.

Mrs. Riley walked out of the office. "Come on now girls, cut it out, please."

"We're just playing," Dee hollered, and laughed.

"No, you're just playing," I shouted. "You play too much." I walked away.

She ran behind me, laughing as she pushed me.

I pushed her back harder. "Stop playing," I yelled.

"All right," she said still laughing.

Sometimes I thought she was serious, but she was always laughing.

Rain walked in the door at ten thirty that night. Dee and I were sitting in the living room where we had been chilling all day.

"Oh Dee, let me tell you." She threw her bags down, smacked her lips and ran her fingers through her hair. "The boy likes me. He likes me."

Dee jumped up. "Did you see him?"

"Yeah." She smacked her lips again.

"Well, what did he say?" Dee asked excitedly, waiting to hear the goods.

"Nothing."

"Nothing?" Dee asked, disappointed. "How do you know he likes you?"

"Because I know. Don't be mad, Dee, because somebody likes me." She picked her bag up and smacked her lips as she walked to her room.

"What ya'll got?" Dee asked, running behind her.

"None of your business, Dee," Rain's voice echoed from afar. Rain had dark chocolate skin with jet-black long hair, like silk. She smacked her lips every time she spoke as a habit. She was very slim with no curves behind her. But she knew she was cute, and I don't think Jesus Christ could have convinced her she wasn't.

Mrs. Wallace walked in minutes later. She carried a bag that smelled the house of steak, onions, and peppers. As she walked to the kitchen to set the bags down on the counter, Rain and Dee came running out of the room. It dawned on me that Mrs. Wallace was supposed to bring me something back. As soon as I got to the kitchen, Dee was eating her gyro, and Rain had my gyro in her mouth. I looked in the bag to see if there were anymore but there weren't. Rain laughed out loud.

As I walked away, Dee chuckled and said, "That was Shiree's gyro you're eating."

"Oh well, she acted like she didn't want it."

The window in my room had a gate on it. Every day I pushed and kicked on it until it loosened up enough for me to squeeze through it. On my way to the office to clear up a few rules, I noticed Rain, Dee and Miss Stewart crowding the door. As I got closer, the voice from outside the door became familiar to me.

"Shiree cannot go out," Miss Stewart told the girl behind the door.

"But can I just speak to her?" the girl pleaded.

"Phone calls are between six and eight."

"I'm not talking about calling her. Why can't I tell her something right here and right now?"

"Shiree cannot have any visitors. Now, what did you say your name was? Lawanda? I will tell her you stopped by." She slammed the door shut.

I ran back to my room. I ran to the window and

screamed Lawanda's name out loud.

She walked up to the window laughing. "You look like you're in jail behind that. Are you coming out?"

"Yeah, I'm about to come through this window."

She stood there laughing as I struggled to get out. "How did you squeeze through that gate, Shiree?"

"Easy, I been working on it since I been here. Being as though they have to let us out with a key, it's my only way out."

"A key! Are you serious?"

I nodded.

"That is illegal. They can get in trouble for that. So what's up girl?" She got excited. "How you like your new home? How are the girls in there?" She got serious.

"I hate that fucking place, and those fucking bitches."

Lawanda started laughing. "Why, Shiree?"

"Because I just do."

"Did someone do something to you?"

"No, I don't really have a problem with anyone, I just don't trust them. I know they're grimy. And it's too many females to be living with anyways. The staff always tries to tell you what to do. Sometimes I just want to flip the whole house upside down. We got this conceited girl, every time I hear her talk I just want to slap her lips off her." I screamed out loud.

"Calm down, Shiree, calm down. I got something for them nerves right here." She pulled out a nickel bag of weed and waved it in my face.

"Oh yes, what is it?"

"This right here is that funk defied skunk."

We headed towards New Lots train station. Lawanda rolled the weed in a White Owl blunt, while we were standing on the platform waiting for the train. We got off on Atlantic Avenue and smoked the blunt on the way to her projects.

Lawanda opened the door with her key.

Miss Harris came running out of her room while we were on our way to Lawanda's room. "Hi Shiree, I haven't seen you in a while." She stood with her head leaned to the side as if she was concerned about me. "So, you like your new place?"

"Oh, Miss Harris, don't even ask."

"Well, you ain't gonna listen no way, so they'll be throwing you out of there anyway."

Lawanda was getting ready to step in her room. "Lawanda?" Miss Harris yelled like she was getting ready to catch a heart attack. "Where it's at? I smell it."

Lawanda looked at her mother and laughed.

"Lawanda, you didn't save me a piece?" She looked disappointed.

"Here, Ma." Lawanda handed her the little piece of blunt that was left over.

Miss Harris smiled. "Lawanda you got more, don't you?"

Lawanda laughed.

"Yeah you do. Okay, don't forget about me when ya'll smoke it." She smiled happily as she went back in her room.

"Are you going to get in trouble for staying out tonight?" Lawanda asked, bringing up the group home again.

"What could they do to me? Besides, I would already be in trouble for sneaking out. I might as well go all the way out. I hate that damn place."

"But you don't want to keep moving do you?" Lawanda asked.

"No, but I'm not happy there, so what's the difference?"

"The difference is, you might not be happy anywhere."

I was silent for a minute as I thought about it. "You

know what, Lawanda? I think you're right."

Lawanda carried the conversation on. "I mean shit, who wants to be in a group home, foster home, whatever. Who wants to be in a place with people they don't know, or don't need to know? My family ain't shit, but I'd rather be with them than a bunch of strangers who ain't shit."

"And those bitches, I can't stand them," I said cutting Lawanda off.

"Oh yeah," Lawanda spit part of the leaf from the blunt out of her mouth, as she continued to roll up another L, "what's up with them girls?"

I got comfortably positioned on the bed, leaning my back against the headboard as I explained the story. "Okay, there's this one girl name Dee, and she plays too damn much. She's always in my business. When I first got there she was fighting with this girl named Cookie. She slammed Cookie, flipped her, and took her off her feet. I don't know if Cookie just can't fight to save her life, or if Dee is really that bad. But there's something about her I really can't stand. Maybe because she's a bully. I know it, but she pretends like she isn't. She tries to order me around. She hits me."

"Hits you?" Lawanda yelled out loud, losing her focus on finessing the blunt.

"Not like that." I took offense.

"What do you mean, not like that?" Lawanda continued.

"Well, because she plays a lot. When she pushes me she laughs. She's like a goof ball, who thinks we're friends or something."

"Does she have any peoples?"

"She has an older sister that lives in the Bronx."

"If that bitch touches you, Shiree, you bet to stomp her ass out. Wear it out."

"Oh yeah, I know that. Nobody has ever gotten away

with putting their hands on me yet. Shit, you might get away with talking a little bit of shit, but I don't do the hand thing."

Lawanda laughed, "Yeah you're crazy. I knew it. Come on, let's go smoke half of this blunt with my mother."

Miss Harris took a few puffs. "Shiree, come sit next to me. I want to ask you something. Ernest told me a little about you. Is it true your mother died?" She sounded sad and concerned.

Nearly choking on the weed, I nodded.

She sucked her teeth. "Really? How did she die?"

"She was murdered."

"Murdered?" she screamed as her eyes super sized. "Oh, what do you mean, Shiree, who could do something like that?"

"I don't know," I said.

"You mean they never found the person?"

"No," I said.

"Oh that is so sad. I am so sorry, Shiree. And you were young right?"

"I was twelve."

"Oh my God, that is so sad." She began to console me. "And I hear your father is a pervert."

I nodded.

"Did he touch you?"

"He put his hands in my panties."

"Yeah, because Ernest left here one night, losing his mind, ready to go kill your father. We had to calm him down. He ain't gonna have any good luck." She sucked her teeth. "Is he West Indian?"

"I don't know much about him. But his mother was born and raised in St. Thomas."

"Yeah, he's West Indian, and they are some nasty mother fuckers anyways. They believe in that incest shit. But you're a strong little girl. You have been through a lot, Shiree." Miss Harris became real serious and upset. "Ya'll go back in there. I don't want no more of that weed. I'm upset."

On my way out the door, she called me. "Give me a hug, Shiree, I love you, okay? Your father is going to get his; you hear what I tell you." She said all that with a serious look on her face as she squeezed my hand and a tear dropped from one of her eyes.

I got off on New Lots Avenue, and headed toward Cozine Avenue. I wondered what kind of action would take place once I got to the group home.

Mrs. Stewart came to the door, "What's wrong with you girl? You cannot stay out like that. You must sit still and follow the rules."

"I know Mrs. Stewart, I know. I'm going to listen." I kept smiling at her to brush her off and went straight to my room. I went to hang my coat up and noticed I had a closet full of hangers, but no clothes. My hands began to sweat, as I lurked around the room. I thought about the day I unpacked my clothes. Maybe I put them in the drawer... But I knew well, they were gone. One of them bitches stole my clothes. My heart pounded as I walked to the other side of the house where every girl in the house was.

The noise was coming from Rain and Dee's room. I didn't bother to knock. I busted the door wide open.

"Don't you knock?" Rain was the first to speak. The guilt was written on her face.

"Where are my clothes?" I asked in rage.

"We don't wear your clothes, how are we supposed to know where they're at?"

"What are you talking about?" said Dee with her stupid smirk.

I opened the closet and drawers, looking for my clothes. I pulled Rain's drawer out of the dresser.

"Get your fucking hands off my shit."

The whole drawer was empty.

"You can check my stuff," Dee said. "I didn't take anything."

"What's going on in here?" Mrs. Stewart made her way into the room after hearing all the noise. "Who took this young lady's clothes?"

Nobody said anything. "If you know anything please tell me. That is not right, you guys."

I stood next to Mrs. Stewart thinking, You won't get them back like that Mrs. Stewart.

She walked me to my room. "I will write this up. Now you make sure you speak with your counselor, he should be able to help you out. I'm so sorry, sugar."

I sat on my bed putting two and two together. Rain's drawers were empty, which meant she hid her stuff. She hid it so I didn't take hers. And wherever my clothes were, hers were.

I pushed Rain's door open again. When they saw my face they got silent. I walked up to Rain and stared at her. "This is not over Rain. You will pay for this, so don't sleep."

I didn't know where my roommate was. I was glad she wasn't there. I lay on my back looking up at the ceiling. My hands were sweating, my heart was pounding, and my spirit was raging. She housed my clothes. She housed my gyro, what was next? I got out of bed and headed toward the door. I'm going to beat Rain senseless, I told myself.

When I opened my door, Mrs. Stewart was standing there. "Oh Shiree, this came in the mail for you today."

I looked down at the envelope. Ernest, I thought, as I took the letter. Mrs. Stewart smiled at me before she walked away.

Dear Shiree,

What's up sexy? How's life treating you out there without me? I know you're all right because you're strong, but innocent. I taught you everything you need to know about the streets. You understand because you're just like me. We're one. I miss you. You are the only one who cares how I feel or how I'm doing. You're so young, but so different, and so real. I respect your natural, your mind and your beauty. I'm all right. I'm holding shit down. I'm a thug, and you already know that. I just want to make sure you are all right. Hold your head up. You're a survivor. Don't let anybody play you.

E-Lo

A tear ran down my face. I just got played, I thought. If he were there he would have dropped every female in Rain's room. I didn't know who took my clothes for sure, I could only guess. I just knew I had no friends.

I had a sudden burst of energy from Ernest's letter. I hopped off my bed and checked my drawers for my polo sweat suit I slept in. Even though I wore it to bed, it was suitable to wear outside. I grabbed a under wear set, a towel and jumped in the shower.

"Hi Shiree, how are you?" Miss Harris smiled one of her biggest smiles. "You got something for me?"

"No Miss Harris, not today, but you know me."

"Okay Shiree come on in. Lawanda is in her room."

I pushed the door open like it was my room. I saw

Lawanda searching around the room. "What are you looking for?"

Lawanda paused and noticed me standing there. "My money. Lee left me twenty dollars, a bag of smoke and he bought me these jeans off Wall Street."

"I don't even want to hear about clothes."

"Why? What happened to you?"

"Do you see what I got on?" I posed for Lawanda.

"Yeah, a dope Polo sweat suit."

"All right, yeah it's dope, but they're my pajamas and it's all I have left."

"What do you mean it's all you have left?" Lawanda stopped searching and stood still giving me her full attention.

"My clothes were stolen last night."

"Yeah right." Lawanda stood there shocked, and I could tell she was pissed off. "Oh, hell no! We're going up there to fuck something up. Who took them?"

"I don't have any proof, but my instincts tell me Rain took them. Her clothes are gone and she left the house this morning in her pajamas."

"Where does she go in pajamas?" Lawanda asked.

"She has a friend in Fairfield projects. She probably gets dressed over there."

"But don't you two go to the same school?"

"Yeah, and if I ever catch her with my clothes on I'm going to beat her out of them."

"No," Lawanda got excited, "Were gonna beat her out of them now."

"Lawanda nah, I'm dropping it for now."

"You're always talking about dropping it. I say we drop one of them."

"It's not time for that yet. I can't prove a thing. Besides, I won't get my clothes back."

"So what are you going to do?"

"I'm still thinking."

"Well look, let's go on Wall Street take these jeans back and get you a pair. We can get you a shirt with this twenty dollars, and then smoke us a long one."

"All right." I smiled with appreciation. I still thought about the fact that I would have one outfit and a dope sweat suit, which no one knew I slept in.

As we entered the store, I looked around in astonishment. Everything looked nice to me.

Lawanda held up the jeans. "Miss I would like to return these and get another pair."

"What's the problem are they too small?"

"No Miss, I just would like to exchange them."

"Okay that's fine, you can get anything for the price of these, okay?"

"All right," Lawanda said, about to get pissed off.

"Would you like me to take your bag?"

"No, that's okay. I keep all my bags."

I headed toward the Ralph Lauren section and picked up four pairs of jeans, four shirts and one sweater. I knew I didn't have enough money, but I didn't know which one I was going to pick. I walked down to the next rack and spotted a whole Guess outfit. "Now this is dope. I want this."

"How much is it?" Lawanda asked while she browsed around.

"With your twenty dollars the jeans will cover the rest. You go downstairs and exchange them, I'm gonna keep looking," I told her. I noticed she sat her bag down while she browsed, and she forgot it. I headed toward the bag. I looked around quickly then opened the bag wide enough to swipe all four outfits and the sweater into the bag. I walked slowly down the stairs.

Lawanda had just walked away from the cashier. We met up at the door and walked out together. "What is that?" Lawanda scolded me.

"What?" I asked, smiling.

"You know what I'm talking about." She grabbed the bag. "Oh shit! You sneaky ass."

"I had to do what I had to do."

Lawanda laughed. "I knew you were up to something."

As I stood in the hallway waiting to get in, I heard one loud violent voice, and a helpless sad voice. When I finally got inside I stood at the door with my bags watching Cookie and Dee argue. These were the same two girls who were at it when I first stepped foot in the door.

"I was not talking about you, Dee," Cookie pleaded in tears.

Dee stormed over to Cookie, yelling. "Yes, you did. You are always talking shit. You think you're better than me."

"Dee, what have I ever done to you?" Cookie asked wiping her tears.

"Fuck you, Cookie, and your tears. You always want somebody to feel sorry for you."

"Well fuck it then, I don't care any more either," Cookie said walking to her room.

"Oh fuck me?" Dee raged and ran after Cookie.

Cookie turned around to see Dee running toward her.

Dee pushed her into the radiator and Cookie fell hitting her head. Dee jumped on her hitting her upside her head.

"Get off of me, Dee, get off of me. Aaaaaaaaaaaaah." Cookie screamed at the top of her lungs.

Dee was still lying on her, and hitting her on the head.

Cookie began to swing back.

Dee got off of her and stepped back with a smirk. She laughed as she watched Cookie scream, at the same time smashing everything in her room.

Cookie threw all her cosmetics off her dresser onto the floor. She snatched her clothes off the hangers, and ripped her pictures off the wall.

Mrs. Stewart grabbed Cookie, wrapped her arms

around her and walked her to the office. We could still hear Cookie scream from the office. I went straight to my room to put my clothes up.

"Shiree, come here," Dee said standing by my door laughing.

I walked up to her. "What?"

She led me to Cookie's room. "Let's take some of this shit and leave."

I looked down at the camera I saw, and a blow dryer. Lawanda and I always took pictures after she did my hair, and we did need a blow dryer. I looked up at Dee. I didn't trust her; she was Rain's girl. But then I thought, Who knows who took my shit? I grabbed the camera and blow dryer.

Dee kept laughing as she picked out the stuff she wanted. "Come on let's leave."

I followed her straight out the door. We headed down New Lots Avenue. "Where are you going?" I asked.

"It's my sister's birthday. I'm going to her house." As we walked Dee kept laughing.

"What happened in there," I asked.

Dee got excited as she explained. "Oh, Cookie think she is all that. Fuck her right now."

Cookie was all that. She had beautiful hazel eyes, a pretty complexion and a nice shape. And Cookie had nice things. Dee always messed with her knowing that she was emotional and far from a fighter. Sometimes Dee got upset for no reason. It was like she was angry inside and she let it out on whomever she could. I was not the one.

We reached the stairs to enter the train station. "Hold up. Let me use the phone," Dee yelled as she picked up the pay phone and started punching numbers. "Damn, I didn't get any answer at my sister's house. I hope she's home. Come on I'm going anyway."

As we waited for the train, I wrote Lawanda's number down. "Here," I handed the number to Dee, "call me if she's not there and I will meet you." We both got on the train and got off on Atlantic Avenue. She had to switch trains to go uptown.

The door to Miss Harris' apartment was open, so I walked in. I went straight to Lawanda's room to show off the camera and blow dryer.

"Where did you get that stuff?" Lawanda asked. She was sitting on her bed blowing down a L.

"Why didn't you put me on about you weed party going on?" I scolded her.

"What were you going to do, Shiree? Come all the way over here to hit my half of blunt." We started laughing.

"Dee beat Cookie up," I told her.

"Again?" Lawanda shouted. Her eyes grew big.

"Dee started with her for no reason. Cookie went crazy and tore up her own room. The staff put her in the office and that's when me and Dee went through her stuff."

Shortly after I began telling Lawanda about the bugged-out episode that took place at the group home, the phone rang. Dee's sister was not home. It slipped my mind that I had told her to call if she wasn't, and we would hang out together. "Okay, take the #3 downtown and get off on Nevins Street. I will be there waiting for you."

"Okay bye," she responded and hung up.

Lawanda jumped up, "Yeah let's meet this Dee." She grabbed her coat, "Let's go."

Dee walked out of the train station looking lost before she noticed me. "So this is your sister Lawanda you told me about," Dee said."

"Yeah, that's her," I responded.

"And you're the Dee I heard so much about,"

Lawanda jumped in the conversation chuckling.

I stared at Lawanda as if to say, be nice please. "So Dee," I cut her conversation short. "What are you going to do with your stuff now?"

"I'm taking it to the group home with me. Cookie won't do anything about it. Let's go to the group home right now. You, me and Lawanda. Do you want to go Lawanda?"

Lawanda and I looked at each other. "Come on let's go," Lawanda said.

On the way to the group home Lawanda and Dee laughed about the fight. They had plans to humiliate Cookie once we got inside. The plan was to add fuel to the fire.

It was dark when we reached the house. We stood in the hallway, knocking to get in. Mrs. Stewart opened the door enough to stick her head out. "You guy's cannot have any company," she said.

Dee tried to plead with her. "But she is Shiree's sister."

"It doesn't matter who she is, she cannot come in," Mrs. Stewart said before she slammed the door. That did not stop us from knocking.

We knocked until ten minutes later Mrs. Stewart opened it back up. "Why don't you girls listen? You already know the rules, and the girl can't come in."

"Mrs. Stewart," Lawanda yelled, "Can I use the bathroom? I have to go bad."

"I'm sorry, young lady, but you cannot come in here." She slammed the door again.

We all laughed. Dee kept giggling. "Did you see Cookie in the hallway looking scary? I'm gonna beat her again." She kicked the door. "Open up the door." Dee kept kicking while Lawanda and I stood next to her laughing.

The entrance door opened up and we all looked

back. Two tall police officers stood there before they began walking toward us. "What's going on in here?"

Mrs. Stewart opened up the door and Dee went and stood in the doorway. I whispered to her, "I'll be back." Lawanda and I started making our way out past the officers and out the door.

One of the officers looked Lawanda straight in her eyes as we walked by. "You don't belong here do you?" He shouted at her as she walked down the stairs. He rushed over to her and kicked her in her ass with his hard black boot.

Lawanda kept on going and I was keeping up behind her. We were halfway down the street when I looked back and saw Dee exit the building. Both police officers were walking toward her. Where is she going? I asked myself as I watched from a distance.

The officers got closer and Dee began swinging both of her arms in the air.

I watched, confused. I didn't understand what I saw. One of the officers reached on his hip and grabbed his stick. The stick went up and down off Dee's body and into the air. The other officer pulled out his handcuffs and cuffed Dee behind her back, while officer number one was still hitting her in her arms and ribs. Dee was in a corner getting beat and I could hear her screaming. Nobody was around except me and Lawanda was standing from afar.

I started to panic. In my first reaction I screamed, "Oh my God they beating her," and I began to run to her.

Lawanda grabbed me by my arm and swung me around. "Girl are you crazy? Let's go." She started running and I ran with her. We stopped running and started walking to catch our breath. I was in a state of shock. "We shouldn't have left her," I kept saying.

"What were we supposed to do, Shiree? We can't beat police officers."

I thought about what she said, and it made a little sense to me. We got on the train and went back to Lawanda's house. I tossed and turned. I couldn't get Dee out of my head. When I closed my eyes, I saw the police beat her with the stick. I heard her scream. What if she was dead? I still felt like I was wrong because I left her alone while they were brutally beating her. I owed it to her to have run back because we lived under the same roof, which made us family. Lawanda was right I couldn't beat a police officer, but I could have gone inside and told someone. And if I couldn't make it inside without them stopping me, then they should have beaten me, too.

First thing in the morning I walked to the first pay phone I saw and called the group home. I tried disguising my voice. "Can I speak to Dee?" I asked.

"Who is this?" one of the staff shot back at me. "There are no phone calls until six."

"This is her sister," I shot back.

"Hello?" Dee said curiously. When she heard my voice she hung up on me. She was mad at me and I didn't blame her.

I walked to the train station and went home. When I got there the house was quiet.

"You're just in time," Mrs. Riley said. "We're going on a field trip."

I took a seat in the dining room and heard voices coming from the bathroom. I tried to listen. I felt funny vibes. Soon after, Cookie walked out of the bathroom, glanced at me, and went back in the bathroom. I heard the voices clearer. It was Dee in the bathroom soaking her wounds, and Cookie was sitting in the bathroom with her.

Cookie said to Dee, "You know what? You should get your sister to beat her sister's ass and you should beat hers."

Dee did not respond.

I thought, Oh I get it, the whole thing started between them two now they're talking and the beef is with me. I'm not going on a field trip with them. I got up and left.

I walked down the street, furious, talking to myself. "She got the fucking nerve to be mad at me. I didn't have to do a damn thing. In this world you hold your own. I always held mine. If I always expected someone to help me or defend me, I would never do my best. Fuck all those bitches." I couldn't wait to tell Lawanda. I was mad, at the same time I was sad. Everything turned on me, and I wanted to help Dee.

Lawanda was shocked. "Who the fuck do they think they is? Fuck them. I don't know anybody that's willing to fight the police. I damn sure ain't getting my ass beat by police officers."

I tried to get over it, but I still felt a little off. Because, even though everything was cool at that moment, it wouldn't be when I went home. Lee was over so Lawanda was kind of occupied.

I went to the store to get some ice cream. I stuck two Haagen Daz ice creams in one sleeve and one in the other sleeve. I got rushed at the door over the ice cream. I gave Ameanie one, and Miss Harris, leaving me with one.

Lawanda came out of the room to see what was all the commotion going on, when she noticed everyone had ice cream. "Shiree where's my mine?"

"I couldn't take four so I got Coffee ice cream for us to share." She frowned her face up. "I don't want to share I want my own." She went to her room and closed her door.

What is this, lets beef with Shiree today? I shook my head and plopped down on the couch.

Ameanie came in the living room. "Hey Shiree, you

want to go to Far Rockaway?"

"With who?" I asked.

"Just me and Jodie. I'm going to see Mike."

"Okay, I'll go." I was not really in the mood, but there wasn't much else for me to do. Lawanda was mad at me. There was no need to stick around. Lawanda was spoiled. I stole her whatever she wanted. She was my right hand, so she felt like she was supposed to come before everyone.

As we stood in the hallway waiting to get in, I looked Jodie up and down. She was busted and always excited to see boys. The word was she was nasty. She would do anybody.

Ameanie, Jodie and I walked in the living room where we saw three dingy boys occupying the couch and Ameanie's boyfriend, Mike.

I glanced at Ameanie who was always happy to see her boyfriend, and Jodie who was excited over dirty nappy heads. I walked out of the living room into the hall and called out for Ameanie. "Ameanie? Ameanie?" She came out smiling. "I can't do this. I can't stay in this house."

"Why?" Ameanie asked.

"Look at them boys. Uh uh, I got to go."

"Okay Shiree, just wait for a little while. We won't be here that long. We didn't come all the way out here for nothing."

"All right, I will wait for a little while. Didn't you say Mike was coming back with us?"

"Yeah, he is," Ameanie said.

"Well then, tell him to get ready so we can leave."

"All right, come on." We both walked back.

I sat down and began watching everything. Jodie was already in a conversation with one boy. The two boys that were left were both checking me out. I looked them up and down and then I looked at the wall. All three of them needed haircuts desperately. And their sneakers needed to be thrown on the wire. And with all the dirt under them nails, they better not speak to me. Ameanie and Mike were sitting there whispering in each other's ear.

"What's up Mike," I said. "I thought you were going to Brooklyn with us?"

"I am."

"So why ain't you getting ready?"

"I'm waiting on somebody."

"What's your name, Shorty?" One of the dirty boys spoke.

"Oh, hell no. I got to go." I jumped up and ran out the door.

"Shiree?" Ameanie was right behind me, calling my name. "Okay Shiree, we're coming right now. Give me ten minutes, all right?"

"All right I will wait right here."

Twenty minutes went by and I could still hear them laughing and goofing around. I took the elevator downstairs, thinking, This is not my type of party. I waited in the lobby for ten minutes hoping they would come down. It was dark outside and I was not feeling the Rock. If you had a penny you could hear it drop. That's how quiet and deserted it was.

When I got to the train station, there was nobody there, not even a conductor. I was so scared. I made up my mind I was never going back to Far Rockaway. I kept thinking about my mom, and how they found her body in Far Rockaway. It took the train almost forty-five minutes to get there and Ameanie and them didn't show. I went back to Lawanda's.

Miss Harris let me in. "Hey Shiree."

I remembered the days she was tired of seeing me and she would scold me. I think I gained her respect. "Hi, Miss Harris."

"Wait a minute. Didn't you leave with Ameanie and Jodie?"

"Yeah they're coming."

"You left them?"

"No they're with Mike and some other dirty boys."

Miss Harris laughed. "You're so crazy girl."

I found some covers and hopped on the couch. I woke up to voices. It seemed I had missed something. I looked up.

Lawanda stood over me. "Shiree, when are you going to bring my Girbaud jeans back?"

I sat up. "When is your man going to bring my Walkman back?"

"I don't have anything to do with that."

I started to grow angry now because I felt her turning on me. "What do you mean you don't have anything to do with that? That's your man. You knew I lent it to him. You worrying about your pants and don't care about my Walkman, what is this some new shit?"

She picked up my jeans off the floor. "Well I'm taking these jeans then."

"And then I'm going in your room and taking everything I got you," I said to her.

"And then I'm going to punch you in your face."

I stood up on the couch. "And then I'm going to punch you back." We went up to each other and swung. The same time, grabbing for each other's shirts, we ended up at the window, and then we were rolling around on the couch. Her boyfriend Lee came over pinned me down and started pulling on my hair.

Miss Harris came rushing out of her room. She put her hand over her mouth. "Oh my God, Lawanda and Shiree are fighting." She took a double look and spotted Lee in the mix. "Lee, get the fuck off her. Lee stood up. "What the fuck is wrong with you Lee? Huh? Huh?" Miss Harris was flipping. "Those are girls, and they are friends. If Ernest were here you wouldn't have done that. He would of hurt you. "

Lee stood there listening.

"Get out of my face, Lee." I went in the kitchen with Ameanie. She saw my hair was pulled out a little and went to tell her mother.

Lawanda came in the kitchen to see my hair and went off on Lee. "Why would you jump in my fight, Lee? I didn't need your help. It was none of your business." She didn't need any help. It was just something Lee always wanted to do. Even though he was helping her, I was still her dog and always was going to be.

She told me to sit down so she could do my hair. Everybody in the house laughed at us.

The next morning Ameanie was going to school and I was going home. I had to walked past Sarah J High School to get to the train. When we reached the school, Ameanie walked away. "See you later," I said.

She turned around. "You want to come in?" "

All right," I said.

"Wait at that door right there and I'll let you in."

We sat in the gym on the bleachers with Jamie. I was uncomfortable because I knew she liked Ernest, and she had a smart mouth.

Ameanie began setting me up. "Shiree, you know Jamie slept with Ernest, right?"

"Stop playing," Jamie said to her.

Ameanie looked at me and smiled. I shook my head, still not saying anything.

"I mean, so what if I did," Jamie said, taking advantage of my silence.

"Yeah, so what if he did," I said. "That was then, and this is now. Besides you don't really think he wants your fat ass do you?"

"What?" Jamie stood up.

"What?" I mocked her as I stood to my feet as well.

"You heard what I said." And I started dancing. "I'll beat your ass."

Ameanie laughed.

"You aint gonna do shit to me," I said getting my defense ready.

She started coming toward me, talking shit. I didn't move until she got close on me. Before she could put her hands on me, I pushed both of my hands in her face. I pushed her all the way to the wall. I took her whole face and mushed it to the wall, banging her face on the wall again. While she was dazed and trying to balance her huge body, I grabbed her hair and pulled her head down and kept upper-cutting her.

She wiggled, trying to come up. I lifted her up and gave her a good shove to the wall and held her up, losing my breath. I didn't know how much longer I could hold the fat girl up.

Two security guards broke it up and a man in dress clothes stood on the side. As soon as the one guard put his hand between us, I let go and ran out of the gym.

The man in dress clothes ran after me. "Who are you?" he kept yelling. He grabbed me hard enough to stop me and then let go. "What's your name?"

"Lawanda Harris, I said." I looked to my right and spotted Lawanda. She had just gotten to school. She was getting the story from Ameanie and heard me tell the guy I was she, so she stayed afar.

He walked me to the office. "You all right, Lawanda?"

"Yes I am. Could I go?"

When we got to the office, the secretary was asking questions. "That's not Lawanda Harris," she said.

He looked at me. "Why did you lie to me? Who are you?"

I told the truth and I was very nice, so they let me go. I hurried up out of Sarah J High.

On the way to the train I thought it would be a good idea to go to the agency. It was Wednesday and every Wednesday everybody from the group home had to go to group and then meet with their caseworkers afterwards. There were boys there too, because there was a boys group home that was apart of the same agency. They just didn't keep us in the same house. The boys and girls would be together when we went on field trips, which I never attended.

When I got to the agency, everybody was already in group. I stood in front of the closed door, looked to the right and saw my caseworker. The door flew up as this boy walked out.

Cookie stood up and threatened me. She made a fist and punched her other hand.

I guess that was her way of telling me she was going to whoop my ass. I thought, She can't even fight. She letting everybody soup her head up.

My caseworker made his way to me. "Shiree, hi, it's nice to see you. Come to my office." I followed him to his office and we sat down.

He stared at me a long time before he decided to speak. "You know you are going to have problems tonight right? That's what I suspect from what I been hearing."

I nodded. I began to shake from the thoughts.

"Are you going to be all right?"

"Yeah I'll be all right," I said and gave him the look like most definitely. I mean really what was he going to do? I was scared, but what was the sense of telling him that? Was he going to knock them bitches out for me one by one? I felt like whatever happens just happens.

After that I went to the office and asked for my train fare. Group was already over and everybody was gone. I ran into Tiffany in the office who was getting her train fare too. Tiffany used to be in the group home, too, but she wasn't there any more. I was happy to see her. She was always cool and never bothered anybody. We left the building and ran into some other dudes. We decided to put all our train fare together and get a bag of weed.

We hopped the train and went to second Fairfield. We sat in the staircase getting high in the building behind the girls' group home. Tiffany and I laughed about the girls in the group home. We talked about who was phony, who thought they were all that and who couldn't fight.

I sat there just meditating. I knew I was going to go through some shit that night. I didn't know what was going to happen, so I had anxiety.

Tiffany had to get something from the house, so she walked with me. I had knots in my stomach I was so scared. I didn't want any beef. I went straight to my room and Tiffany went the other way.

When she was leaving, I heard her arguing with some of the girls. She was pretty much scared. She pleaded and pretended she didn't know what they were talking about. She made it to the door and on the way out she knew she would never be back so she told them to suck her pussy.

I took off my coat and sat on my bed. I didn't make any plans, because I knew something was going down. My roommate Darlene, was sleep on her bed.

Cookie came alone in my room and said, "Shiree I want my shit back," and then she walked out.

Rain walked in my room with Dee right behind her. Rain said, "Shiree you said you don't like me?" She was smacking her lips.

I just looked at her.

Dee was smiling with that grimy look in her eyes. The same look she had after she beat up Cookie. "Don't lie either," she said.

I looked at her too, like she was stupid. I was too

nervous to argue. All I knew was these bitches better not touch me.

With Rain and Dee still standing at my door, and Darlene still sleep, Cookie felt confident. I could just see how Rain and her girl Dee just threw the battery in her back. Cookie came in my room and stood in front of me. She counted on her fingers. "I want my blow dryer, my tapes and my camera.

I sat there looking at her.

When she got down to her middle finger she swung. Her swing was so slow, I grabbed her long arm as it came toward me and swung her on the bed. I grabbed her by her neck and flipped her over the bed. We landed on Darlene's bed.

Darlene jumped up and Cookie and I landed on the floor. Dee and Rain started kicking me. I sat on the floor easing my way up. They were trying to swing and kick at the same time. I kept swinging hard at every last one of them.

As I was swinging, I saw Darlene standing there with her mouth open. But she didn't touch me.

When they noticed that I wasn't going down, my swings were coordinated and I was making my way up, they ran.

I stood up in rage. I wasn't done. I had just begun. I saw Rain run in the dining room under the table.

Dee ran in the bathroom across from my room, so that's where I went first. Dee stood looking confused. I came full force right at her. I punched her one. She fell in the tub and I turned around to chase Cookie.

Cookie was right next door in her room. I jumped on her bed and started punching her in her face hard. I put her face in her pillow and kept punching.

Sonia from Guyana came running into the room. She jumped on the bed and yelled, "Get off her," and then she punched me on the side of my face.

I paid her no mind; I didn't even look at her. I was trying to demolish Cookie.

Sonia started pulling on me, so I fell off the bed. But I dragged Cookie right with me. As I dragged her I kept punching her. When I let Cookie go, she ran to the other side of the house.

I was running around like a maniac, with a burst of strength. I ran past the dining room on my way to the other side of the house. Rain was no longer under the table.

When I got to the other side of the house everybody was in the room, scared to come out. I ran into Cookie sneaking in the room with a can of spray in her hand. She turned around and held the bottle up.

"What, you scared now? You need some spray? Put the spray down," I said. I wasn't done. I wanted some more. I was pissed off. I thought about my clothes, my gyro and Rain smacking her lips. I thought about Dee testing me.

Miss Wallace was the staff that night and apparently she saw the whole thing. She grabbed me and took me in the office and she went back out. She came back in shaking her head. "Girl you ain't no joke. You hear what I tell you?" She was demonstrating boxing moves. "Wait right hear. Don't you move now."
She was excited. She kept shaking her head going in and out of the office. She was amazed.

When the police came I had to leave the office. We all were in the dining room talking with the police.

I opened my mouth and Rain said, "Stop lying," and grabbed my braids over the officer.

I punched her so hard in her face she let go of my hair. I grabbed her hair tight and jerked her body. She almost flew over the officer. Miss Wallace made me sleep in the office that night.

I sat in my last class playing back the scenes of the night before. They jumped me, I thought. Well, they tried to jump me and got jumped on. The bell rang signaling class was officially over.

"Shiree, may I speak with you?" Mrs. Forest my English teacher asked.

Every student left, and I walked to her desk with her. "You never show up for class. But when you are here your grades are remarkable. It's almost unbelievable. It's not hard to tell you don't do homework or study, but look at your grades. I am disappointed in you. I want you to come to class. Will you promise me?"

I just looked at her. My story was a little bit more complicated than that.

"Will you try?"

I nodded.

"Okay then, I will see you tomorrow."

I smiled and walked away. What she didn't know was, I was done. School was useless. I never graduated ninth grade, they just threw me in tenth. Algebra #2 was my first class, but I never learned Algebra #1. I knew I could take the time to learn if I wanted to, but I got so high I could never get up that early to make it to first period. School was a done deal.

Besides, my life was too dysfunctional to sit home and study. And what did I need to graduate for nobody cared but the teachers.

Leaving the building, I saw Lawanda, Ameanie and Lee standing there. I was so happy to see them.

Lawanda said she knew something happened that's why she came. She saw my hair was pulled out a little bit.

We went to her house and she took my braids out and did my hair in a ponytail with big curl coming out. I had a Chinese bang in the front and a long strip of hair curled under on the side. My hair looked so nice and I looked so pretty.

"Walk with me to the store?" Ameanie asked.

We were on the elevator going back up when it stopped on the eighth floor. Jamie got on carrying a television. Another girl got on with her. Jamie looked me up and down. "Why were you telling everybody you whooped my ass?"

I didn't tell anybody I beat her up, but I wasn't gonna tell her that.

"She did beat you up, Jamie," Ameanie said.

"Why don't ya'll do it again," the girl next to Jamie said.

I couldn't refuse, even though I didn't want to fight the big girl. "All right," I said.

"What floor?" Jamie's friend asked.

"Eighteen," Ameanie and I said at the same time.

When we got to the floor, everybody got off the elevator. Jamie turned her back to me to put the television down. I ran toward her and kicked her into the television. Fuck that, if I had to fight this big girl again, I needed some advantage.

Before she could get up Miss Harris came out. "What is going on?" She had that don't play with me look going on. Everybody respected her. They knew she would smash something. Miss Harris was plain rude and spoke her mind.

Ameanie explained how Jamie wanted to fight again.

Miss Harris said, "Well I can't see little ol' Shiree beating up big ol' Jamie."

"She did, Ma."

Everybody from Miss Harris' house came out. And the Fortunato's came out too. Everybody stood still while Miss Harris spoke. "Go in the house, Shiree. You don't have to keep fighting. If you got beat up, Jamie, you got beat up. And you must have got beaten up if you want to fight her again. Whatever you want to do to her now, you should have done then."

I was relieved when Miss Harris said I didn't have to fight.

Before I left, Lawanda told me she was pregnant. I knew I lost my hang-out partner. I knew Lee was working on that and I knew he was happy. She was getting fat along with throwing up, and she was getting lazier by the minute. But that's my dog, and I was happy for her.

I made it home just in time for dinner. Everybody was at the table. I slid right in a spot and looked across from me at Dee. I gave her a smirk. I was looking good. They stared at my hair because they thought it was pulled out. I smirked at Dee because now she knew my skills. She always thought I was a sucker. She was so curious that she had to try me. They always said, you go around looking for trouble, you're going to find it.

Everything was cool that night. I didn't have any problems out of nobody. Everybody was nice to me. They stayed out of my way and they respected me.

I received a phone call from my Aunt Janna. "Hi baby, how are you?"

"Hi Aunt Janna. How did you find me?"

"You're still my niece. You know I'm not gonna lose you. I don't live in Staten Island any more. I live in Brooklyn now."

"It's been a long time, Aunt Janna, but I didn't forget about you."

"I know baby. The last time I saw you I gave you some awful news. I'm sorry, but I have to give you some more awful news."

I took the phone away from my head for three seconds. I looked up to the ceiling and rolled my eyes. I began to shake. I was a little nervous. The last time I saw her she told me my mother was dead. She comforted me all night. What now?

"Shiree, are you there?"

"Yes, but what happened Aunt Janna?" This time she cut me off and told me the man I called Daddy was dead. She made arrangements for me to come to her house. She said she would pick me up the night before the funeral, and then she hung up.

I guess Miss Harris was right. Daddy was dying. I went to my room and shed a few tears. I understood, but I couldn't believe it.

I left the house and went for a train ride. I got off at the Port Authority, went to a pay phone, and called Caseen.

"What's up sister? What's going on down there?" I could hear the excitement in his voice.

"Caseen, listen, Leroy is dead."

"Yeah right. You play too much, sister."

"I'm serious," I said. "He had cirrhosis of the liver."

"What the hell is that?"

"I'm not really sure. All I know is your liver deteriorates from drinking too much."

"Leroy was not an alcoholic, Shiree."

"I know, but he did drink."

"Not like that though, sis."

"I know. It doesn't make sense. But that's what he told me he had."

"So how do you know he's dead?"

"Because Aunt Janna just called and told me. And the last time I saw him he did look sick. He lost his hair and his skin was dark and his stomach was real big. He had a hospital bed in his room, and he had a maid come to cook for the kids. He really looked sick Caseen. He's dead.

"Stop lying," he said. "Okay fine Caseen. Call Aunt Janna if you don't believe me. She's going to pick me up for the funeral."

Caseen was silent for ten seconds. "So you're serious, huh?"

"Yeah, Caseen, you know I wouldn't lie about something like that."

"All right sister, I'll be down there."

I was thinking to myself on the train ride home. Caseen couldn't believe Leroy was dead. I definitely understood that. It was all too shocking.

I stayed at Aunt Janna's the night before the funeral. When the morning came I reunited with all my family I knew from Leroy. Caseen and Uncle Andre were there. My brothers, Leroy, Troy, Lionel and Kareem were there. Caseen and Uncle Andre sat in the back pew. I sat in the middle. Caseen did not drop a tear, nor did he get up to say his goodbyes. I sat there and watched my dad with my eyes full of water. I could not hold my tears. They came in spurts. As I saw my dad I saw my mom, too. I put both funerals together and let it all out. I went up to him and kissed him goodbye.

My life at the group home remained normal. I was home more often. I got a call from my Aunt Barbara,

another one of Leroy's sister.

Aunt Barbara was cool. "Hey niece."

"Hi, Aunt Barbara."

"Do you remember me?"

"Of course I remember you and Precious, Terell and Sean. It hasn't been that long."

"We want you to stay over for the weekend, and if you like it, you can come live."

"Okay, Aunt Barbara."

"Get ready. I will be there to get you."

Her daughter, Precious, and I were the same age. Her son, Sean, was the same age Caseen was and she had a younger son named Terrell. We were all close growing up.

That Friday we all hung around laughing and joking. Saturday Precious and I went out. Sunday we were up early and I had to return home later on in the day. Precious and I were in the living room reminiscing about the olden days. We talked about my mom and my stepfather, which was her Uncle Leroy.

"I can't believe Uncle Leroy died of AIDS," she said.

"What?" I sat up on the couch and my eyes grew large. "AIDS! He had AIDS?"

"You didn't know?" Precious asked me.

"No I didn't know. He told me he had cirrhosis of the liver.

Aunt Barbara walked into the living room and jumped in our conversation. "No honey he had AIDS."

My heart dropped. I was scared, shocked and in disbelief at the same time. I then was full of many questions. I didn't understand and I really needed to. "Well when did he get AIDS?"

"I don't know, Shiree." Aunt Barbara shook her head and shrugged. "He might have got it from a blood transfusion in 1981. But like I said, I really don't know."

"Did my mom know before she got killed?"

"I don't know, but I don't think so. I heard that's what they were arguing about the morning she left for school. But then I heard he had just found out the day he got admitted to the hospital while your mom was missing."

They told me so many stories that didn't add up. They said that it was said that he signed himself out of the hospital and killed her, and that his cousin Sheeka and her boyfriend may have had something to do with my mom's death. My mother's engagement ring that Leroy gave her was taken off her finger after she was murdered. I jumped when I heard a knock at the downstairs door.

"Go see who's at the door Precious." Aunt Barbara yelled. .

Precious walked to the window and look out. "It's Sheeka, Mom."

"Sheeka?" I shouted. My legs trembled. Knots swelled up in my stomach. I had just heard my aunt say that cousin Sheeka might have had something to do with my mother's death, and now she was at the door.

Aunt Barbara and everyone who was in the house went outside to talk with Sheeka. I went into the bathroom and locked the door. I couldn't wait to go home. None of it made sense. I was full of questions that I had to find the answers to. I began thinking about my mom, wondering what she went through before she passed.

When it was time for me to leave, I pretended like everything was fine, but it wasn't. They thought I was going to move in with them. I was happy to get to the group home. I went in solitude.

"Shiree?" The staff hollered my name from the office.

I ran to the office and waved my hand at Miss Stewart to come to me. I whispered in her ear, "Is that my aunt?"

She nodded.

"Please tell her I'm not here."

Miss Stewart looked at me like, I don't know.

"Please Miss Stewart."

"All right," she whispered.

They kept calling, and I kept saying I was not here. I was not moving in with them. They scared the shit out of me. The staff got tired of lying for me, and the truth was told. I didn't want to speak to them.

"Hello? Is this the 100th precinct?"

"Yes it is ma'am."

"May I speak with Detective Deleon?"

"Hold please."

"Hello, Detective Deleon speaking."

"This is the daughter of Colleen Brown who was murdered in 1991."

"Yes, yes I know. How can I help you?"

"I think my stepfather Leroy killed her."

"Why do you think that?"

"Because I just found out that he died of AIDS. And the only thing that was missing from my mother was her engagement ring that he gave her."

"Shiree, I don't really suspect Leroy anymore. I knew Leroy had AIDS. He told me in the hour of questioning. Give me some more information on your real father. What is it, Sam right?"

I didn't know anything. As I got to know Sam, he was a pervert but that was it. I didn't think he was the killing type. Of course if he was crazy enough to do what he did to me, hey who knows what else he'd do.

I went to my first field trip to the skating ring. "Come on girls," Mrs. Riley yelled. We all raced to the door.

"Oh, you never went on a field trip with us huh?" Cookie asked me on the way out the door.

"No, is it fun?" I asked.

"Yeah, we're about to meet the boys. They go with us on field trips, too."

We were approaching the boys' house. They were outside waiting on us. The two staff greeted and then we walked to Pennsylvania Avenue train station.

"You must be the new girl everybody kept asking were you my sister. My name is James." James walked up on the side of me.

"So you're the guy," I said.

"I'm the guy what?" James asked curiously.

"When I first got here all the staff kept asking me was I your sister and said we look alike."

"How come you never came on any trips?" James asked.

"I don't know. I guess I was sort of doing my own thing. My home girl is pregnant now so I stay in the house more."

"Do you know how to skate?" James asked.

"Not really."

"Oh, I'm gonna be laughing at you all night. Psych! I'm just playing. I will show you."

I laughed at him. I was more like blushing. He was tall, light-skinned, nice built and sexy. He had sex appeal. He was also kind and cool. We skated together and we were focused on each other. It was something about this boy. I didn't want the night to end.

"Shiree, phone! Shiree?" I heard Cookie screaming my name. She stopped in front of my room door looking exhausted, as if she had run all around the house looking for me. "Didn't you hear me calling you?"

"Who the fuck are you that I have to jump when you call?"

Her mouth opened wide then her big hazel eyes went to rolling.

"Psych!" I busted out laughing and threw my pillow in the air. "What Cookie? What?"

She smiled. "Phone, hooker, phone."

I jumped up and ran to the office. "Hello? Who is this?"

"James," the voice answered.

"Oh what's up?" sounding surprised, I sat down. "How did you get this number?"

"Uh, we're in the same group home, remember?

We're just in different houses."

Oh yeah, that was dumb, I thought.

"What are you doing today?" James asked.

"I don't have anything planned yet, I'm chilling."

"Did ya'll get a new girl today?" James asked.

"Yeah she just came in this morning."

"Why don't you and her walk over here? She's my man's little sister."

"Who is your man?" I asked.

"His name is Ronald. He stays in my house, too. Her name is Miesha. Okay?"

"Okay, but she can't leave yet. She's on probation period."

"Nah, it's cool. She's going to see her brother at the other house. Just tell them that all right?"

"All right, bye."

After I hung up I walked around the house looking for Miesha. I found her in the bathroom on my side of the house. "Is your name Miesha?" She nodded her head innocently. She was short and dark-skinned. She didn't have much hair and her gear was off. "Do you want to go to the boy's group home to see your brother?"

"Yeah." She smiled.

"Okay let me know when you're ready." On the way down the street I told her about every girl in our house. "Don't worry. If you have any problems you can come to me. I will help you. She smiled. I meant what I said. I said that because she was young, innocent and respectful.

James and her brother, Ronald, were outside. "What's up sis? You all right?" Ronald didn't know me, but he looked at me and said, "Make sure my sister is all right? I heard how you put chicks in check over there."

I smiled. "I got you covered."

James grabbed my arm. "What's going on, Shiree? How did you like your first field trip?" I blushed looking in his sexy eyes.

"Shit, if there's a trip tonight, I'll go." Everybody laughed.

"Oh, my bad," James said. "This is my boy, Troy and his girl, Shaquanna."

Troy and Shaquanna was hugged up. I heard Shaquanna talking going to the store and then she walked off.

I caught up to her. "You going to the store?"

"Yeah, you coming?" she said. I nodded. I turned around and called for Miesha. "Come on Miesh we're going to the store."

"What are you going to get?" I asked her.

"Some drinks."

"What do you drink?" I asked.

"Do you drink?" She asked.

"Sometimes. I'm drinking today. Do you smoke?".

"Yeah, but I don't have any."

"I got some," I said.

"Good let's get high."

I turned and looked at Miesha. "You don't do anything, right?"

"I am today," she said.

"I'll get you a beer. If your brother says anything, I don't have anything to do with it." I asked Shaquanna, "Does James drink?"

"Yeah, he drinks St Ides."

I grabbed two and we all sat around drinking St Ides.

James was tipsy. He stood up dancing, singing, "The world is mine," by Nas. The whole night we laughed, joked and played around as a group. I got special attention from James when he would grab my hand and spin me around.

James and Ronald, Troy and Shaquanna walked

Miesha and me home that night. I kissed James in the hallway. "Will I see you tomorrow?" he asked. I smiled and went in the house.

Miesha came to my room that night. "I wish I was in your room," she said. "I had fun tonight. You like James huh?"

I blushed because I loved hearing his name.

Miesha was cool and I think I would have gone to the moon for her. I was fourteen still and she had just turned thirteen. She looked and behaved younger than that. But she grew up fast over the weeks. I think she was just shy and frightened when she first came. I made sure she was all right at all times. I made sure she had clothes, hygienes, and that nobody messed with her. Miesha and I were at the boy's group home damn near every night.

One night I called Sam and told him I was coming over there with my friend. He sounded cool and he was okay with it. I wanted to show him how good I was doing. I wanted to see if he changed now that I got older. I wanted to know if he was sorry.

When we got there, he was polite. He asked my friend questions. I think he noticed how delicate she was. He took a few drinks of his rum and got right to what he was about. I'll give you a hundred dollars to finger pop you," he told Miesha. "And I'll give you a hundred dollars to watch," he said to me.

I was stunned and Sam was dead serious. "Come here a minute," he said to Miesha, inviting her into my room, which was off the living room. Miesha followed him.

He came out and asked me again. "You want to watch for a hundred dollars?"

She agreed to it, so what was wrong with watching? After all I was earning a hundred dollars. It wasn't my pussy his hand was in. I watched my father pull her pants down, spread her legs apart and stick his fingers in her pussy. He started putting more than one finger up there and shoving them hard. Then she began to make faces like she was disgusted from him taking too long. As I watched, I felt sorry for her. But she wanted her hundred and I wanted mine. He gave us our money and we left. We went to Fordum Rd and went gold shopping. I still didn't like Sam. My friend was only thirteen-years-old and he didn't care.

Miesha became independent and went places on her own, which was cool. I bounced around everywhere. If I wasn't with James, I was in the basement of my group home with this boy named Marcus.

Marcus treated me with respect, and we were cool. He respected my gangster. He lived in the building next door. We stood in the basement many times, smoking weed and just kicking it. He was one of the realest niggas I knew, the type that if you had any problems, you could go get him, the type that will sit down with you and kick some real knowledge shit. He didn't play games with females.

After getting high with him I went upstairs and ate. If I missed dinner they would put my plate up. Most of our staff was Jamaican so we ate a lot of Jamaican food.

I used to wake up in the morning and flip on everybody. The staff would call James and ask him could he come and calm me down.

One night Miesha and I were on the side of the house smoking a cigarette. We heard a lot of noise and a car drive off real fast. We went to the front, but we didn't see anything. We went inside and went to my room. My roommate Darlene was in our bathroom in the mirror crying. Her face was all messed up, and I asked her what happened.

She just kept screaming, "Those bitches jumped

me."

Rain's cousins jumped her. I left the room and saw Rain in the living room laughing. Rain had an army of cousins I had heard, and they were crazy and would hurt you. I kind of, myself, stayed out of Rain's way.

James and I were both getting off the hook. We would go to a store, walk straight to the cooler and grab a St. Ides. We would act like we were walking to the register and as soon as we got to the door, we ran right out. We started fights around the way. But we had fun. We kissed and humped because I wasn't ready to have sex yet.

I was the only virgin in the group home until I turned fifteen when we did it. I snuck him in my room while my roommate was not there. In that little bathroom after humping I was ready to feel the real thing. I bled a little but it was still good. I was a woman.

As soon as he gave me my first piece, he got kicked out of the group home. He went to stay with his aunt, which was cool. She lived in East N.Y too, on Linden and Williams. I stayed nights over there a lot. I still was living in the group home even though I didn't follow the rules. I stayed out all night, I didn't do chores, and I just didn't care about nothing.

The staff brought in lockers for us. Everybody got a locker with a key. We were able to lock our shit up and nobody could get in because we had a lock on it with a key. Rain brought her clothes home.

When she left, I told Miesha to follow me. I went in Rain's room with a big knife and broke into her locker. I didn't see my clothes, but I knew she was the one that took them. I took all her clothes, just like she took all mine. I gave Miesha some and took the rest with me to James' house. I stayed all night at James' house.

The next night James and I were sitting downstairs when we saw Miesha walking up. "Shiree, Rain is mad about her clothes. She knows we took them. Dee and Rain were talking about what they going to do to the both of us."

I started laughing. I knew Miesha was scared or else she wouldn't have walked to James' house. I walked back up to James and kissed him. "I'll be back, probably tomorrow."

I left with Miesha. I left the clothes at James' house, with the exception of Rain's skirt set I had on.

As soon as we got in the house, I went straight to Rain and Dee's room. They both were sleep, with my radio playing. I snatched my plug out of they wall and yelled, "I'll be in my room if you want me."

I was sure to sleep in the skirt set. She won't take this. If she wants it she's going to have to take it off me, I thought.

The next morning Dee came in my room talking real loud, "Shiree, why did you take Rain's clothes."

I sat up and looked at her. "Don't ask me a stupid question like that."

"Give her back her shit."

"She ain't getting shit."

"When her cousins come and jump you, don't say anything," she said.

"She ain't stupid. If her cousins jump me, she better remember she got to live in this house."

Rain came in my room smacking her mouth like she was bad. "You going to give me my shit."

I stood up, "You want it? Take it."

"I'm going to fuck you up," she said.

"Come on, here I go. You ain't saying nothing but a word," I told her. "You're not going to do nothing, so get the fuck out of my room."

Mrs. Riley came in. "Shiree, please give Rain back her clothes."

"No Mrs. Riley because she took my clothes. She

never gave my clothes back."

Mrs. Riley kept trying to explain something to me, but none of it made any sense. The only thing that made sense to me was she took mine, now I got hers. I could tell she was on their side; all the staff was about sick of me anyway. She sucked her teeth and told me to get up for school.

After she left I just lay there. I noticed she kept peeking in my room. I used to go to school, but I lost all interest. First of all I barely ever made to first period anyways, because I was always late. When I did go the teacher gave me work to take home and I didn't know what the hell he was doing on the board, so I couldn't do it at home. Second of all, they gave us two minutes to get from one class to another before the bell rang. There were five flights of stairs and each flight was two sets of stairs, which meant actually there were ten flights. I had classes on the fifth floor, so I had to walk up ten flights. Not to mention they had certain ways you could go and certain ways you couldn't go. By the time I got to the tenth flight, huffing and puffing, they would tell me I couldn't come in that way. Did they really expect me to go all the way down and around, and walk up ten flights again? I didn't think so. How was I supposed to get to class in two minutes? The hallways were always packed with no room to walk. There was no way you could walk straight to class without stopping or getting pushed.

I heard Cookie and Darlene about to fight in Cookie's room. I got out of bed and went to stop a fight. I tried to talk to them, when two police officers walked into the room.

I tried to explain to the police what was going on. So I stood up and started to talk.

One of the officers pushed me down and told me to shut the fuck up.

My back hit the wall, and I sat up from the wall. "Why did you push me, officer?"

He pushed me again and my head hit the wall. "I said shut the fuck up." He grabbed me by my collar and I hit the floor, landing on my stomach face down. I was dragged from Cookie's room to the dining room. The dining room was carpeted with hard rug, so I could feel the rug burns on my face. He then handcuffed me and stood me up. He walked me outside.

Miesha ran outside, too. "Go get my sneakers," I told her.

The officer looked at her. "Don't bring her shit."

When Miesha came out with them anyways, he told her to take them right back inside.

They drove me to the precinct and handcuffed me to a pole. Now I wondered what I did wrong. I later found out that Mrs. Riley never called the police on the girls who were about to fight. She called them on me because I wouldn't get up for school.

Next thing I knew I was sitting in the G building. They had me sitting in the hall for a while. I did not belong there. I didn't see anybody there who was like me. Those people were not normal. I couldn't believe they put me in a nut house. I wasn't crazy. I sat there watching people drool on themselves. People were talking to themselves. I just looked around in disbelief. I was anxious and wanted to leave, but they had me just sitting. What am I waiting for? I thought. Oh I get it, they're waiting for me to go crazy. I tried to talk to everybody I saw with a white nurse suit on. They didn't look well, either, if you ask me. "Excuse me," I approached a nurse. "I don't belong here. It was a mistake." She looked at me like I really was crazy. "No really." I went on to explain my story, but she cut me off. "I'm sorry ma'am but you have to wait."

By the morning they put me in this room with a little

white girl. She couldn't have been any older than nine. The room was caged in like a dungeon. She looked as if she didn't have a worry in the world. She was not worrying about leaving. The only thing she complained about was her breakfast.

"What are you in here for?" I asked. "I don't know don't know," she shrugged. Later when she told me about how she was going to kill her mother, I knew. I begged to get out of there. The little girl kept staring at me. "Do you want your tray?" she finally asked.

They moved me to another building. I wondered why they moved me from building to building.

When I got the chance to use the phone, I called the group home and spoke to a Mrs. Stewart. "Shiree you can't come back. They don't wan't you back." "They set me up." I yelled. "No Shiree your too bad." I was so mad and anxious I hung up in her face. I could not stay there I didn't belong there.

I called back and begged for them to please come get me.

They made me promise to straighten up.

"I will behave, I will. I promise." I was so happy to get out of there and see the streets again. But my behavior didn't change.

It was no secret that I wanted to be a model. In school I took a couple of pictures and made a portfolio. My case manager called and told me to get ready. He said he was coming to get me to take me to a modeling interview in Staten Island. He came and we got into a cab. We got out in Staten Island at some huge building. We got on the elevator and walked into an office.

A lady greeted us. "Hi Shiree is it?" I nodded. "Well follow me Shiree."

I kept a smile on my face since I was at a modeling interview. I had to show my potential.

She took me into a little room. We sat down and she

opened up a folder. "I don't see your discharge papers for some reason."

"Discharge?" I said out loud. I knew what discharged meant; I began to sense something was not right. "Miss, what am I doing here?" I asked the lady.

"You're being discharged to another facility."

I jumped up and walked past my case manger and headed toward the elevator. "You lying motherfucker," I yelled at him and I kept walking. The elevator opened up and I got in it.

He came up to it. "Where are you going?"

I yelled at him. "You set me up." I threw the bottle I had in my hand at him. It broke at his foot. "Fuck you!" The elevator doors closed.

I got off and saw him. He must have taken the stairs. I went to get in the cab and he told me I couldn't. "This was a one-way trip for you."

"Fuck you. I was born in Staten Island. I know my way around this mother fucker." I began walking to the ferryboat. I was so pissed off I called him all types of faggots, scum buckets and assholes. I took the ferry and the train from the Bowling Green to the group home.

I knocked on the door and Cookie looked out the window. I told her to open the door, but she couldn't. I kept banging until Mrs. Stewart opened the door. "You don't live here anymore."

"Well I can't get my stuff?"

"Where are you supposed to be, Shiree? They will bring your stuff."

"Fuck, that my shit is in there."

"You think that attitude is going to get you something?"

"Please Mrs. Stewart, I'm not going to stay. I need my stuff and to use the phone. "Let me get my shit."

She came out with one garbage bag and closed the

door in my face. I knew automatically that was not all my stuff. "One bag, come on, one bag." I knocked again. "Mrs. Stewart can I call a ride, I can't carry this."

When she let me in, I went breaking in everybody's locker. Only Darlene was there, but she didn't have anything. Everybody had something of mine, and I got my shit back. Now I had two garbage bags.

I called James and told him what happened; he said he would be right over.

He came with his friend and we sat outside on the front steps. The police came and so we did what we always did. "Officer we called the police. These kids were around here starting trouble but they left." "So you guys are all set?" "Yeah were okay," I said. The officer turned around to leave, and then Mrs. Stewart came out.

She spoke in her Jamaican accent. "Excuse me officer." She pointed at me. "She don't belong here."

The officer looked at me with a dirty look. "Oh you lied to me. Stand up. Turn around," he said. He handcuffed me. "You're a stupid liar, you know that."

James stood up. "Officer is this necessary? She didn't commit a crime. They kicked her out she just came to get her stuff. This is her stuff right here. She was just waiting for a ride." Who are you?" the police officer asked. "She's my girl," James said. I came to help her with her stuff, and make sure she get to where she got to go."

The officer turned to look at me. "Your lucky to have such a nice boyfriend," and he took the handcuffs off me. He let James kiss me goodbye, then he put me in the car and my bags in the trunk. He went to speak with the staff and got back in the car. He dropped me off at the agency to be placed. I did not want to leave the group home. Out of all the places I was comfortable there

Chapter 8
Survival

"Hi Shiree, how are you? My name is Mrs. Ryan." I stood there smiling at the new foster lady as she introduced herself.

"Okay Mrs. Ryan, she's all yours," said the agency worker. I called them my escorts, cause that's all they did for me was drop me off. I'm going to go now. By the way you have a lovely home."

"Oh, thank you," Mrs. Ryan responded.

"Good luck, Shiree."

I gave her a nice smile. I had no problems with her. She was nice to me, so I returned the kindness. Not all the agency workers were nice. They usually had me freezing in their air-conditioned cars. They saw my goose bumps, but they didn't care. They just dropped me where I had to go without many words. If they did have something to say it was usually rude, like I was just another statistic. I had no family, so I was nobody, that's how I took it.

"Shiree, these are my two girls. That's Asia," she pointed, "and that's Dasha. They are my foster kids, too, but they're my babies. They have been here forever."

Dasha rolled her eyes as if Mrs. Ryan was exaggerating. "Well come upstairs with me I will show you your room. You will like it here."

We reached the top of the stairs. "Okay, this is it."

It was okay. It had sunlight in it, so that meant a lot to me. It had a full-size bed with a nice spread on it. It had a dresser with a mirror, and a nice size closet.

"This is the bathroom." She led me into the hall, pointing out everything. "This is my room. You don't go in there. It's just the girls and I here, so if you have any problems, you can come talk to me. Come downstairs and let me show you around and tell you the rules."

I followed her down the stairs. She was fat, brown-skinned and wore a wig. I noticed how the other girls were doing their own thing. They went out as they pleased, and stayed in their room whenever they were home. So I did my own thing too.

I walked in the door two hours late. It was so hot and muggy outside, I ran up the stairs to take a shower. As I was entering the bathroom, a voice came from Mrs. Ryan's room. "Shiree, is that you?"

"Yes Mrs. Ryan, I'm home." I hollered back.

"Come here a second, Shiree."

"Yes Mrs. Ryan." I stood by her room door curiously.

"You are two hours late. I have to put you on punishment for that."

"How long do I have to stay on punishment for?" I asked.

"Well, let's see, tomorrow is Friday, that's right on time. You are to stay in this house for the whole weekend."

"Ah man, why do I have to stay on punishment for so long just for two hours?"

"I don't care Shiree. You broke the rules. Now go do what you was doing, I'm done with you."

I got off punishment on Labor Day. I was so lifted off

skunk trees and St. Ides. James' Aunt Venice cooked us crabs and grill food.

"It's almost time for me to go James."

"Damn you just got here." James was upset.

I lay down on his mattress and began whining. "Every time I get here it's time to go."

James began kissing on my neck.

"Ah shit, I'm not gonna make it James."

"Well if you're gonna be late and get punishment anyway, you might as well stay out all night."

"Yeah James, you're right." I stayed out all night.

She sat in the living room on the couch watching the stories. Fat, funky miserable couch potato was what I thought of her. She heard me come in and didn't even look at me. As I started up the stairs, I heard her say, "Pack your stuff, you're out of here."

"Huh?" I paused at the middle of the staircase. I turned around and headed back down the steps. "I have to leave?"

"Yes you do." She still didn't look my way.

"Why do I have to leave?"

"The reason is you stayed out all night. You can't stay out all night in here. That's an automatic out-the-door ticket. Those are the rules."

Funny, but if I knew that, I would have avoided it. She sounded serious, so I headed back upstairs to pack my bags. I carried all my stuff downstairs and stood by the door. She would not take her eyes off the television. Not one time did she look at me, not even during our conversation.

"Miss Ryan, what am I supposed to do?"

She cleared her throat, glanced at me, and said, "Take your stuff and go."

"Go where? I need to be placed somewhere."

"Why don't you go where you were last night? You want to be grown you go carry your ass up out of here."

"What do you mean Miss? Just because I go out that makes me grown? Everybody else goes out."

"Yes they do, but everybody else follow the rules too. I'm sorry, but you have to go."

I kept trying, more like begging her to give me a chance because I had nowhere to go. "You never even told me that if I stayed out I would get kicked out automatically."

"Look little girl, I shouldn't have to tell you that. I told you the rules and you should know when you don't follow the rules there are consequences. These kids here will tell you I don't tolerate any hardheaded grown-ass kids. Now, get your shit and go."

She didn't have to say it no more. I grabbed my bags and left. A tear dropped from my eyes as soon as the door slammed behind me and I heard the lock click. Fuck her, I thought. I was mad at myself for standing there that long kissing her ass. She is just mad because she ain't getting no dick. I started walking toward the train station while I figured out where I was going to go. I had to get on the train anyway. Where was I going? I thought back to my father's house . I knew that sounded absurd, and something was bound to happen, knowing him. But then, I thought, I was older, what could he possibly do to me now? Besides, I would drop my stuff off and stay at James' like I did anyway. I'd just go to Sam's house once in a while.

I got to Sam's building, rang his bell, but there was no answer. I entered the building as someone exited. I knocked, but I didn't get any answer. Shit now what? The building was swamped with Russians and you had to have some kind of money to live in the building. Sam was the only black face in the building so I really didn't have to worry about anyone stealing my stuff. So I left my stuff in front of his door, with a note. The note read: Take my stuff inside for me. I will be back later.

On the elevator going down I laughed at the thought of how you couldn't trust your own kind. It was a damn shame. On the train ride to East NY, I thought about how in all reality, I was homeless. I was fifteen and I didn't have a place to stay. I couldn't depend on James, and Sam was definitely not stable. I didn't like the foster home I was at anyway. I couldn't get comfortable there. I just lost my virginity to James; he
was all I thought about.

James' Aunt Venice came to the door. "James is not here, Shiree."

I turned around and headed toward the old block. I would be sure to find him there.

James jumped off the step and scared me. He grabbed me and put his arms around me. "Where you been Shiree? I missed your yellow sexy ass. Check this shit out. My aunt keeps complaining about what I'm going to do with myself. She said I can't stay with her forever."

"For real James?" I asked out of shock.

"Come on. Let's go get some St. Ides."

"All right, come on," I said, ready to get drunk.

"So what's up with you, Shiree?"

"Me?" I asked, getting hype. "That fat funky lady kicked me out because I stayed out that night."

"Word, Shiree?"

"Yeah."

"Ah man, Shiree. Where are you at now?"

"Nowhere exactly. Nobody came to get me. She just told me to leave. I took my stuff to Sam's house. Come with me over there."

"Okay, we'll leave in twenty minutes."

When we arrived, Sam played it off like everything was cool. He greeted us at the door with a smile and told us to come on in. "How you doing, what did you say your name was again?"

"James."

Sam gave James a handshake. "Have a seat James. My daughter tells me a lot about you." He looked at me and said, "Oh Hun, I put your stuff is in your room."

I think he liked the fact that I needed him; which probably meant that if I needed something, he should be able to get something.

Sam was being very nice to James. He treated him like he treated all his guests. He entertained with drinks and a little music. He seemed interested in James because he kept smiling at him. He began asking questions, the normal questions. How old are you, where did you guys meet and where did he live. Then he came out and asked, "So are ya'll doing it yet?"

James and I looked at each other and then at Sam.

"You know. Fucking. Are you guys fucking yet?"

James smiled, but it was not funny to me.

I answered him, "Yes."

He said, "Oh you finally let go, huh?" Then he turned to James and asked him how did it feel to pop a cherry.

James kept on smiling without response. He was surprised, but I knew James, he was down for whatever.

We were all sitting on the couch looking at one another. The room got quiet. I believe Sam was trying to figure James out. He was trying to determine if James was gullible or not. Why couldn't he just leave us alone? After all he was my company.

Sam's eyes appeared quite dilated to me. And he had a stupid-looking smirk on his face, which usually meant he was up to something. He stood up, "Come James, let me speak to you privately." He walked in his room and James followed him.

When James came out, he already knew he could stay the night. I heard Sam tell James to think about it. Then he came and rubbed me on my shoulder, and said, "You okay, booby? I'm glad you're home. Now let's be a real family. You and I and James can be a family and get some money together. I'm going to bed now. He can stay here, booby."

James seemed shocked. When we went to bed James told me what Sam said, I was shocked. Even though I knew his nasty spirit, I truly still was shocked. Sam did not get better. He wasn't sorry for the things he put his own child through. Sex was his nature; I didn't think it mattered with whom.

James told me in bed that Sam said we could make a lot of money. He wanted to do a family playboy movie. And he wanted us to practice around the house and then fly to California and perform. He said with us three, we could split over twenty thousand dollars.

Sam always had a way of making things sound real good, better than it really was.

The next morning Sam walked into my room without even knocking. He just wanted to peek in on us before he left for work.

James and I had fun together. We wished the apartment were ours. But Sam came home with his manipulation. He was nice to us all day. But when the night came, he was ready for action.

He called us in his room. When we got to his room Sam was in the bed with covers on him. "Sit down," he said, pointing to an empty spot on the bed.

We sat down curiously. Sam focused his eyes with mine. "You know we can be rich right?"

I looked at Sam as if to say, please don't start this.

"James, you remember what we talked about last night right?"

"Yeah."

James dumfounded-looking ass, I wanted to slap him silly. I looked at him and Sam like they were crazy.

"Did you tell my daughter what I said?"

"Yeah, I told her."

"Let me see ya'll do it."

James laughed.

"I'm serious. There's a lot of money involved we have to get this right here first."

Sam went to sit up and part of the covers didn't move with him and I saw that Sam was naked under the covers. What the hell, did he think he was going to be in it? Not that it was going to ever happen. I jumped up. "You and you, too, must be crazy." I left the room.

Sam didn't waste any time. He and James followed me into the living room. I could see in James' face he was down. Sam already knew I wasn't going for it. But he had James going, so he must have thought I was that crazy over James that I might have been down.

James sat down right beside me and Sam sat on the Lazy Boy. "So ya'll don't want to get this money?"

I just kept quiet. I didn't want to piss him off, either while he was letting my boyfriend stay over.

"What are you going to do?"

"I'm not doing that," I said and I think you already know that."

"Okay, fine, I thought you guys like money like I do."

I could hear the disappointment in his voice. He stood up with his tall skinny ass in tighty whities, shook his head, threw his hands up and went to his room.

The rest of the evening was quiet. Sam went to bed, and James and I went to my bed.

The next morning Sam opened my room door, calling James' name. He woke us both up. James turned to look at him half sleep. "Make sure you're gone before I get home," he told James.

Sam came home from work with what I called an attitude. He walked in and spotted me in the living room, lying on the couch. He said hi so low it wasn't worth a response. I watched him pace around the whole house before he spoke to me. I guess he had to get his thoughts together.

"Why did you drop your clothes off here, Shiree? Where were you living before?"

"I was in a foster home."

"What happened at your foster home?"

"What happened to me?" I chuckled. "That's what you want to know now? I got kicked out."

"So what are you going to do now?"

"I'm going to turn myself in to the system."

He went to his room and I sat on the couch. I knew I couldn't stay there.

The phone rang. After five minutes Sam hollered, "Shiree, James is on the phone."

"What's up sexy? Yo, my aunt is bugging me."

"What do you mean, James?"

"She keeps pressuring me. She wants me to leave. She told me that I have to do something. I'm thinking about going to Jobcorp. What about you, Shiree? What are you going to do?"

"I'm going to the agency so they can place me somewhere."

"What you doing right now?" James asked.

"I'm sitting on the couch watching movies. I'm about to go to bed."

"I'm coming to get you tomorrow, Shiree. All right?"

"Okay, see you tomorrow then."

I sat there waiting for James. It was also time for Sam to come home from work. I wasn't sure who would get there first. It was Friday, which meant Sam was coming home with a pack of cigarettes for me and possibly some money. That's what he did every Friday.

When Sam came home from work, I was sitting in the living room dressed and ready to go. "Hey Hun, you all right?"

I nodded. "I'm waiting for James to come and get

me."

"What do you mean he's coming to get you?" He frowned up his face. "James doesn't have a car. How is he coming to get you?"

"I didn't say he had a car, but he's on his way over here and we're going out."

"Well say that then, Hun."

I felt my body temperature go up.

He switched his tone of voice just that fast, from nasty to excitement. "So James is on his way over here now?"

I nodded.

"Here are some cigarettes, Hun." He reached over and handed me the cigarettes.

I busted them open and lit one so quick just like a fiend. I sat on the couch impatiently until the intercom rang.

Sam went to buzz James in and greeted him at the door. "Hey James what's up?"

I was ready to go, but Sam was ready to entertain. "Come on James have a seat. Do you want something to drink? I have beer and liquor."

"I'll have some liquor," James said smiling at me.

Sam came in the living room with two drinks. A drink for himself and a drink for James. As he prepared to sit down he looked at me. "Are you all right, Hun?"

I slightly nodded and mumbled, "Um Hum." I was hardly interested in anything he had to say.

"So where are you kids going tonight?"

"I don't know," I mumbled again uninterested.

"Go easy on that liquor, James. That's no cheap shit. It's rum imported from St. Thomas, Puerto Rico actually. We can get this stuff easy from my Island."

"You're from an Island?" James asked, seeming amazed.

"No, I'm from the Bronx, born and raised. My mom

was born and raised in St. Thomas." Sam cleared his throat. He was getting into the conversation and the time being spent amongst him. "It's beautiful, man. I'm not kidding you. The water is pretty; you can reach your hand down in there and grab a lobster this big. I love my seafood, man. I'm allergic to shrimp, but I still eat them. I have these pills I take before I eat them. I call them my shrimp pills. But yeah, man, St. Thomas is nice. Maybe we can all go one day."

James was sitting on the couch looking amazed. I knew Sam knew I was ready to go, but he kept talking. I crossed my arms and huffed and puffed one time. He turned his head toward me like he was the terminator, staring at me like I was a show on the television. He said, "Stop being rude." He began to talk so I waited.

After waiting fifteen minutes I sucked my teeth.

"Stop it," he said in a calm serious voice as if I was a child.

I rolled my eyes and sat back after giving him a long stare. This man was taking up my whole night, and I had plans. And so I kept whining.

He said, "You keep it up and I'm going to get my belt."

I laughed for a second and a half. "And do what with it?" I got serious. The nerve of him and I had to tell him. "You're not gonna touch me."

He got up and walked toward the chair in the dining room that had a belt lying across the arm of the chair.

Oh my fucking God, I thought as I jumped up and moved quickly out the door. I stomped down the stairs and stood by the entrance door. I waited approximately ten minutes. "Where the fuck is that ass hole," I said out loud, pacing the hallway. I rang the intercom to see what was taking James so long.

"What do you want, Shiree?"

"What do you mean? Tell James to come on."

"James is talking to me right now. He said for you to come back upstairs."

I screamed at him. "Put James on. You act like he's your boyfriend." I kept ringing the buzzer thinking James would have sense enough to come down the stairs. But he didn't.

I walked to Coney Island Avenue to use the pay phone and call the house.

Sam answered. I could hear in his voice he was tipsy. Anytime the alcohol kicked in that's when he became manipulative and ruthless. "What the fuck is wrong with you? You need to stop your mess. Here talk to James but you need to stop this shit."

Before Sam could even finish, James got on the phone. "Why are you disrespecting your father?"

"What? What is wrong with you, James, for real? My father asked us to have sex with him, but I'm disrespecting him?"

"Just come back to the house, Shiree."

"No! For what? We're supposed to be going out remember?"

"Your father is upset. He is hurt."

"James, listen to me, I don't give a damn about how he feels. He is using you. He is fake and he knows you can't see it. He is manipulating you. Can't you tell that my father doesn't have it all? He is lonely and miserable as they come."

"Come back to the building and we'll leave together."

Sam opened the door and I glanced at James sitting on the couch. "Come on James."

James sat there with no intention of moving.

When Sam got tired of standing there holding the door and listening to me beg James to get up, he walked away from the door and grabbed his belt. I ran out the exit and down the stairs.

I walked back to Coney Island Avenue again to use

the payphone. James answered the phone. He continued to stick up for Sam. I knew Sam loved every bit of it.

I held the phone listening to James. "What's wrong with you, Shiree?"

I screamed at him. "Fuck you! Fuck you! You stupid mother fucker." I paused to hear what he was going to say. He was just listening to me, so I kept going. "You are a sucker. Word up! Are you my father's keeper? Are you my father's keeper?" I heard the dial tone. "Hello? Hello?" I slammed the phone down so hard I broke a nail. "Damn it!" I turned around and kicked a garbage can into the streets.

It felt like fire was shooting through my veins as I walked to the subway. I didn't know what train I got on because I didn't look, I didn't care. The first train that pulled up, I got on it. I didn't know where I wanted to go. I didn't really have a place to go. Since the train stopped at Atlantic Avenue, I got off and caught the 3 to East New York.

The first thought that came to my mind was to go to the block. I ran into Shaquana and Ronald sitting on the stoop in front of the boys' group home on Flatlands. I got greeted as usual. James and I came around once in a while. We usually were low key and did our own thing. Everybody was joking around except for me. I sat down on the stoop and began thinking. Everybody kept asking me where was James. I couldn't tell them he dissed me for my father. So I would just wait for him to show up. It was getting late and I knew the moment would come.

Shaquana got up and said, "I'm going home. See ya'll tomorrow. You'll be around tomorrow, Shiree?"

I nodded.

"All right, I'll see you tomorrow then." Then she walked away.

I stood there because I had nowhere to go. I thought James would show up. He knew I had nowhere to go. Ronald looked at me. I got the impression he knew I was homeless. I was so embarrassed. I looked at Ronald and said, "All right,

Yo, I'll see you." And I walked off, heading to Shaquan'a building in Starright City. I reached the building and hesitated to ring the buzzer. I couldn't hack the position of being homeless. It wasn't my style to need anyone. Feeling secure and stability meant everything to me. With the thought of lying down right there in the doorway or sitting up on the steps I rang the buzzer.

"Who is it," Shaquana yelled.

"It's me, Shiree. I need to use the phone." I heard the door unlatch and I entered the building.

Shaquana met me at the door and guided me into the kitchen. As I went in I said hello to her grandmother who was wide awake in the living room watching everything moving. There were four little kids running around, so I knew grandma wasn't going to sleep no time soon. I told Shaquana what happened. She really wanted to help, but I knew I couldn't stay. She didn't have to say it, because her expression and her grandmother, who kept calling her into the living room inquiring about me, told it all.

She said, "Shaquana? When is your company leaving, these children got to go to bed now."

So I left and went back to the boy's group home. I threw rocks at Ronald's window.

He peeked out, "What are you doing out there Shiree?"

I shrugged my shoulders, looking sad, "I don't have nowhere to go. Did James come by Ronald?"

"No, he didn't, and what do you mean you don't have nowhere to go?" He waved his hand and shook his head. "Never mind that, climb up here." He snuck me in and hid me under his bed. I was so uncomfortable. I started making plans for the morning. It was time for me to go to the agency and get placed.

When morning came, I went straight to the agency. I told the people I got kicked out of the foster home.

After I waited for thirty minutes a lady came to me. "Shiree, I'm sorry but we cannot place you. Your father said he did not want you in the system anymore. He said that he was perfectly capable of taking care of—"

I cut her off. "But Miss, he just threw me out."

"I'm sorry, Shiree. There's nothing I can do."

I kept trying to explain my story to her, but before I could get it all out all I saw was her back as she walked away from me. I wasn't surprised on Sam's part, but I was more hurt that the lady dismissed me and didn't care enough to help me. I would have cursed her out but I didn't have any energy, so I just left.

I stood in front of Sam's door and slid my key in the lock, but the key would not budge. I was in disbelief. How could he have changed the locks so fast? I was so furious I went downstairs to go smoke a cigarette. I had to think about what I was going to do. I was tired of running around in dirty clothes. I couldn't even wash my ass. After thinking so much, I walked off to go to James' house. I hated the fact that I really needed to go there, but I had a set of clothes, under gear and a toothbrush over there. But being that he dissed me last night I didn't want to see him.

James' Aunt Venice came down the stairs to let me in. I went upstairs and grabbed my bag from James room then went straight to the bathroom. James was still sleep when I came in and when I left. I felt fresh and clean. At least I didn't look like I slept on the train or underneath somebody's bed.

Just as I hated to go to James' house, that's how I felt about going to Sam's. I never was the type to kiss some ass, not even a little bit. I always felt like, it is what it is.

I could hear the television going in Sam's room. The aroma from whatever Sam was cooking was in the hallway, so I knew he was home when I knocked. Sam opened the door and looked me up and down like I was at his door begging for some money. I walked in and stood by the door.

His eyes were still looking me up and down. He said, "You can't stay here." He put one hand on his head and shook it as if he had a headache or something. "You know Shiree, I tried everything. I let you lay up with your boyfriend. I even buy you cigarettes. But what do you do for me? You don't even have any respect for me." His voice got louder. "You don't care about me. You care about your friends more than your own father. You want to be with your man? You love him more than me. So then you go and live with him. I'm done. I'm tired."

Who the fuck do he think he is? I stood there saying to myself. The world does not revolve around his ass. I had a few words for him myself. "If you want me to leave, Sam, then why did you call my agency and tell them not to take me in because you could take care of me?"

He denied it all. "What are you talking about? They must have meant that I was capable of taking care of you. That may be why they wouldn't take you."

"So are you telling me that those people lied to me? Why would they tell me that?"

Sam got really angry and screamed at me. "So you're calling me a liar, Shiree? Is that what you're saying? See, that's what I mean about you, everybody comes before me. Your father ain't shit, huh?"

"Damn sure ain't," I hollered as I grabbed my bags and went out the door. I wasn't gonna kiss his ass. He was a natural liar and I knew about it. I cried all the way to the agency. I was going to try my chances. I mean, after all Sam said, I couldn't stay. So I belonged to the state. I walked up to the first lady I saw, dropped my bags and said, "Oh ya'll going to place me. My father's house is not an option for me. He kicked me out, too. Last night I slept under a friend's bed and rode the train until I couldn't stand it. I have nowhere to go. I am homeless, and my father is a pervert. That's the reason I'm fucked up now. I'm going to sit down right here and I'm not leaving here until you find me a place."

I was placed far away from my usual atmospheres. I didn't know where the hell I was. I didn't see any street signs, nor did I see any buildings. I saw grass. I saw a great big field with little small houses all over. I went straight to a nurse's office. I had to strip. I was searched for weapons, checked for lice, tuberculosis, a positive pregnancy and damn near everything else. Basically they wanted to know if I was healthy, had any deformities, or was I a threat to the facility.

Looking around the facility, I felt like it was a threat to me. I felt like I was in jail. The kids I saw walking around the field didn't look too nice. After a thousand and one questions I was sent to Dorm A. Two staff, not one, escorted me and they had on uniforms. Walking in the dorm I was given the rules.

One staff spoke. "This is the boy's lounge. This is there whole area. You don't come up here for anything, you understand?"

I just looked at her like she was crazy.

"Follow me now." We walked towards the back. "This is the girls lounge. Most of the time, this is where you are. Come with me. I will show you your room."

We went into a room with three beds in it. She pointed to the far bed on the left, right by the door. This is your bed. Those towels, clean sheets are for you. She walked out of the room and I followed her. There are two bathrooms. One right here and there's one on the other side. Showers hours are between five and six in the a.m. and five and six in the p..m., no sooner or later. You are to be in the lounge no later than six o'clock in the a.m. This dorm is the strictest dorm we have here. It's called probation. Your stay here is two weeks, although it can be longer. If you have any trouble following the rules and you get written up, you will start your two weeks all over again. And trust me, you want to get out of here. Any questions?"

I looked at her and said, "Yeah you sure this isn't jail?"

She laughed, but I didn't find a damn thing funny. She cleared her throat and said, "I'll tell you, a lot of these kids here came from jail. In and out of jail. The judges gets tired of seeing their faces so they send them here. We straighten them out here. When you get used to it, it's a really nice place. But you want to mind your business, and don't get involved in that he-said-she-said business. I see a lot of that up here. Once you make it to the other dorms you can do more things independently. All right?"

I nodded in confusion.

"Okay, go in the lounge and sit down. The rest of your crew is at lunch; they should be back any minute now."

I was confused. How did I get here?

I walked to dinner in a line with the girls from my dorm and a staff. The cafeteria was in a separate dorm by itself. The kids, who roamed the field freely, looked like jailbirds. The dudes had limps in their walks. They walked around with their radios rapping. The girls walked in groups. Their groups represented afro puffs, excessive gel hair styles, attitudes in their expressions and trouble. It was like one big ghetto.

At dinner we sat at a long lunch table. The staff

stood up at the head of our table and watched us eat. In about fifteen minutes, finished or not, chow was over.

Every day we did the same routine. A staff yelled really loud and banged on our room door. "Let's go! Get up! Time to get up!"

It was always at five o'clock when the bathrooms opened. You were to shower only if you wanted to, and make sure that you're a.m. chore was done and your ass was in the lounge by six o'clock.. After breakfast we went back to our lounge and sat there for about an hour. Then a staff would tell us to line up to take a long walk to a green house to play with flowers and plants. Planting flowers was not my type of thing. We did activities for two hours every day, except weekends. Then we would walk back to our dorm and sit in the lounge until lunch at eleven. After lunch, back in the lounge and just sit until dinner. All we did was move around like soldiers and sit in the lounge. We were not allowed in our rooms until five o'clock. At that time chores had to be done as well as showers by six o'clock. And lights were out at eight o'clock. But that was only enough time to take our shower and do a chore. By the time we finished our chore and sat on our bed to read a book, they came by talking about lights out. That's when I had the most peace, when it was dark and quiet.

I lay there disbelieving how my life was turning out. I never thought I would end up in a place like that. I felt like a dead mouse in a trap. All I could see in my head was the streets of N.Y. The fast cars riding down Linden Blvd. and the bright lights, and the corner stores with the Puerto Ricans hollering, "Momi, Popi." But that place was totally country. I wasn't getting use to that; I would run away. Especially after I saw two staff take a girl, put her arms behind her back, and drag her across the floor while she squirmed to get up, leaving her face with rug burns. Then they let her know that the girls from dorm B were going to finish her off. I knew I was leaving.

Three girls came up to our table at breakfast. I took one look at them and turned my head the other way. Suddenly I couldn't taste the French toast I was eating.

"Who you?" one girl asked one of our new girls we got the same night that poor little girl got dragged around. I guess she saw it all her first thirty minutes there. She was so shook she got on some sucker shit.

"Who am I?" she asked nervously, pointing to herself.

"Yeah you, I'm looking at you, right?"

"My name is Nicole," she answered. She tried to take a bite of her toast, but it missed her mouth and fell off her fork.

"Where you from Nicole?"

"Queens, LaGuardia."

"Are you new or something?"

"Yeah, I came in last night."

One of the girls from her little clique who was standing there with her hand on her hip smacking the shit out of that gum asked her what happened last night.

Nicole said, "I don't really know. I just saw two staff dragging a girl. That was wrong."

"No," the bully responded, "it wasn't wrong. These girls come up here getting smart with the staff, thinking they don't have nobody. But that staff is like my mom and when that bitch get out of Dorm A, I'm going to step to her." She looked at me. "What's your name?"

I saw her looking in my face because I was looking in hers when she asked me. I gave her a look like "yeah right" then turned my head. Knots were bubbling up in my stomach. My hands began to sweat. I started plotting in my head what I was going to do to her if she touched me. But I was not going to answer her questions. Before I turned to Yolanda and asked her why she wasn't eating, I looked toward the girls who were looking at each other like, what you gonna do?

The staff who walked up to the table from running his mouth with another staff apparently didn't know what was going on. "You girls ready?"

Everybody jumped out of their seat ready to go. I heard if you acted crazy, got mad, and started screaming because you couldn't take it anymore, you would be shipped out on the first bus smoking to the nut house. I heard that it was not the place to be, and that where I was was heaven compared to it. All the kids who got sent would keep calling, begging to get back.

I always got depressed on the van rides they took Dorm A on. The music always depressed me. Certain songs brought back a lot of memories. I wanted to cry as I watched all the sights we were exposed too. We went skating one week, and for the first time, I sort of enjoyed myself. I noticed that down the street to the right was New Jersey. But to the left down the street was a bus to New York City.

Yolanda and I became tight. She was a good person and I liked her. We shared a lot of interests and agreed on a lot of things.. One agreement was we were going to run. She and I were both Virgos, born in August. My birthday was on the 28th and hers was on the 29th.

I woke up in a bad mood.

"You did not do your chore Shiree Brown." The staff came to me in the lounge with an attitude.

"Do you have to call me by my last name? Shiree is good enough. I know who you talking to. Shoo, ain't like there's no other Shiree in here. And I did do my chore." I rolled my eyes.

"Cut the attitude, Ms. Brown. Brown is your name, isn't it? What's the problem, you don't like it? Worry when I call out your name, okay? And the bathroom is not clean."

Getting smart right back and stroking my head, I said, "Well, I cleaned it and I'm not cleaning it again. I ain't no slave and I don't clean up behind people, just myself."

The staff walked away after saying, "Your choice, you all will just sit there until you do. Nobody will eat."

Nicole sucked her teeth. I jumped up and got in her face. "What, you starving or something? What you sucking your teeth for. You that hungry I'll make you eat them teeth. You need to be trying to avoid going to eat the way them girls punked you in there."

Yolanda grabbed my hand. "Come on, Shiree, let's go do your chore."

I started yelling with tears running down my face as I left the lounge. "I'm sick of this place. I'm tired."

Yolanda comforted me. "We up out of here, yo. We ghosts. The bus is right down the street. Because for one, we get too many write ups, we're never gonna make it out of this dorm, and two, I don't want to leave this dorm. I want to leave this whole field."

"Yo, Yolanda," I said, "Doesn't this place look like a college or Jobcorp or something?"

"How the hell you know what college or Jobcorp look like? You ever been?"

"No stupid, but I saw flyers and commercials on television."

"Well I ain't ready for college right now. I'm ready to JJ go."

We both busted out laughing. I said, "You crazy girl, where you from?"

"I'm representing Queens."

"Queens ain't fucking with Brooklyn," I told her."

"It's not where ya from it's where ya at. And right now, home girl, we're locked up." Just then Yolanda got serious. "Okay, how we gonna do this?"

"All right, boom, tomorrow when we go to activities we're just going to jet from there."

The very next time we went to activities we sat in the greenhouse playing in the dirt for a while. Then we stood outside for five minutes trying not to look suspicious. Then we took off running. We made it off the field and ran down the street.

"Come on, Yolanda, come on." I turned around to see if she had caught up when I noticed a van. Two reasons made me think it was the staff. One, it favored the van, two it was slowing up. "Oh shit, Yolanda, that's them."

"Ah man, fuck!"

"I'm not going back, Yolanda."

"Me either."

Staff pulled up on us in a van. "Now where did you girls think ya'll were going. We didn't give ya'll permission to go anywhere. But we knew you two was gonna try to run. Come on let's get in the van now."

"I'm not going back there," I yelled.

"What?" The staff got offended and he stopped the van. He grabbed my arm. "Okay, let's go now."

"Get off of me. Shit, I can walk on my on. Don't be fucking pushing me."

"Well walk up then, girl, and I won't have to push you."

Yolanda and I sat in the van with screw faces. The staff was laughing at us. "You guys won't never make it out of Dorm A."

I yelled at him, "We don't give a fuck. We're not trying to make it out of Dorm A, We're trying to make it the fuck out of here."

"Well, guess what girls, you never will."

As he walked us back to the lounge I whispered to Yolanda, "This is jail." She shook her head in disappointment.

We got our trust taken away, which meant we could not be left alone. Days went by and we were just so anxious to hit the fast streets of New York. She and I both were mad, but glad to have each other. Getting caught did not discourage us. "We'll just try again," we said. "This time we'll just do it in the middle of the night. We'll do it when they'll expect us sleeping."

While shifts were changing, we tied sheets together and the girls in the room helped us down. We ran faster than Forest Gump did down the dirt road. My heart pounded. I was scared and just wanted to get out of there. I kept looking back.

We were almost there when I saw a van coming. There was nowhere to hide. I wanted to cry. As the van approached, we shook our heads and slowed down. There was no sense running.

When entering the dorm, we had to walk through the boys' lounge to get to the girls' lounge or rooms. The whole dorm must have been awakened, and they were talking about us. The staff brought us in with our hands behind our backs, and the boys were up sitting in the lounge laughing at us. They called us the runaways. I did not find anything funny. It seemed to me like we were stuck. After awhile we made the best of our lives. We were not going to make it out of the dorm any time soon.

We all rode on a yellow school bus to a big public pool. The bus parked and let us out in a big parking lot and we walked through the changing room to get to the pool.

When we got to the changing room I said, "We can leave right now, want to?"

She looked at me and smiled. "Hell yeah, nobody ain't thinking about us. Look at all these people."

We ran out of the changing room into the parking lot and paused. "Which way do we go," I asked.

She pointed at some woods. "Let's go through there."

"Okay let's go."

We ran through the woods with smiles on our faces. We were so happy. "We made it, we made it." We kept yelling and jumping up and down.

"Watch your step," I told Yolanda, "We still got to get through these woods."

We walked through the dark woods for a half hour. "There go some lights," I yelled to Yolanda. "Were free!"

As I got closer things didn't look right. "Oh shit!"

"Oh shit what?" Yolanda yelled out catching up to me, because I stopped in my tracks.

"This is where we came in at. We're right back where we started. We were standing in the same pool parking lot when we looked over and spotted one of the staff, as the staff spotted us.

"Ah man, run Yolanda, run." I ran in the back of a house and Yolanda followed me. We ran until we couldn't run anymore. We stood at the end of the yard, which was the beginning of a pond. By the time we went to turn around and get out of there, the staff was entering the yard with some of the boys from our dorm.

Yolanda stood there. I started to run back, as if I was going to charge them. I got halfway and I saw a boy from my dorm come my way. He stopped me in my tracks.

"Get out of my way, you don't have nothing to do with this."

Another boy and two staff came toward me full charge. One grabbed my arms and the other one lifted my legs up. I looked for Yolanda by the pond, and that's when I noticed I was up in the air. I kicked one boy in the face who was holding my right leg. I grabbed the one on my left and kept punching him in the face. They still carried me to the bus.

I squirmed and hollered all the way on the bus. "Ahhhhhhh! Get off of me! Get off of me you fucking idiot!" I got on and went crazy. I kept hitting the seat, crying out loud. I cried and screamed and swung my hands around. I screamed and cried all the way until I got in front of the dorm. I wouldn't let anybody touch me. And I hated all the boys for helping the staff. They were in the same boat I was in. Didn't they want to leave? Did they like it there?

Everybody exited the bus except Yolanda. She tried to calm me down. "Shiree, cut it out."

I kept crying. "I can't take it anymore, I can't."

"Well, you better straighten up now because that staff right there," she pointed, "just came out of the nurses office. And remember the nut house. You don't want to go there do you?"

My head was already lifted from when Yolanda pointed out the staff that walked out the nurse's office. As she was reminding me of the nut house my tears instantly dried up. I walked off the bus rolling my eyes. I was heated. Yolanda was right behind me to make sure I remained cool. I think she knew I was on the edge. And she was right.

Yolanda and I cried and laughed together. We knew one day we would bust out of there. I decided to call my father. I told him how unhappy I was and about how I had a friend and we tried so hard to run away.

He asked me questions about her. She was my age, was very nice and yes she was pretty.

I asked him to help us escape.

He said he would come up to see me.

For the first time in my life, I was happy to see Sam. He met the staff, and they loved him. They found him intelligent, smart, and respectful. They didn't know him like I did. He had a lot of people fooled. The staff let us outside to visit. They let Yolanda go too. Sam and I were standing under a shaded tree. Yolanda was waiting for me by the benches.

"Is she a freak?" Sam asked me.

I wasn't even surprised; actually I knew something like that was coming. "I don't know," I said, trying to pretend his words didn't bother me when they did.

"Well does she talk about fucking her boyfriends?"

"No, she never talked about boys."

"What, she like girls or something?"

"I don't know. I don't think so. She never said that."

"You think she would give me some pussy?"

"I don't know, Sam. You have to talk to her yourself." But deep down inside I kind of felt like she would—to get out of there she would. I was a pretty good judge of character. From what I learned about Yolanda, she was a gangster bitch. I felt like she been on the streets for a long time, long enough to know that you had to do what you had to do to survive. That's how I viewed her, and I respected her. She never crossed me.

I stood two feet away from Yolanda and Sam, while they talked. I could imagine what he was saying to her. I hated him. They both walked over to me when they got done.

I tried to convince Sam to help us get out of there. "Sam, with your help we can get away. See, the bus that goes to New York is way down the street. We'll never make it in time before they come looking for us. But if you park your car at the bottom of the hill at a certain time, we could come out and meet you. That's the only way we'll get away."

Sam put his hands in his pocket took a deep breath. "We'll think of something, Shiree, okay? I promise." Then he reached in his pocket and pulled out a fifty-dollar bill. "Here sweetheart, I'll keep in touch."

As he walked away I yelled, "What am I supposed to do?"

He turned around as he continued to walk and said, "I know you, you'll find a way."

Later on in the evening one staff lady took us and a few other girls to a plaza. There were a lot of stores. As the staff and the rest of the crew were entering the store, I heard, "Come on you guys."

"Nah, we'll wait out here for ya'll." Yolanda and I had our trust back, so we were able to do that. We stood there exchanging our war stories when a cab drove by. "Oh shit, Yolanda, look a cab. I got fifty dollars."

We looked at each other, laughed out loud and ran for it. We jumped in the cab. "Yes, yes, yes, to New York City baby," I said to the Arab.

After fifteen minutes the cab driver pulled over and said, "Okay New City, that will be thirty dollars."

"What!" I blurted out loud, "This is not New York City." His accent pissed me off because he was talking stupid so he was sounding stupid. "Yes New City, You say New City."

"I said New York City. Listen, just take us to a bus that goes to New York City, you know Manhattan and shit."

"Oh yes, I know, Manhattan. You want a bus go to Manhattan. Okay." He let us out at a bus stop. I handed him my fifty-dollar bill and sat there waiting for my change. He put my money in his pocket and said, "Okay you can go now."

"Give me my damn change then."

"No, no change. That's fifty dollars. You go to New City and here too."

"No, you went to New City. I said New York City. I can't help it you don't understand English too good, but we still need money to get on this bus."

"Okay here, get out my cab."

We were a little nervous waiting for the bus. "We didn't make it yet," I said.

"Yes we did stupid. They ain't gonna find us here, We're nowhere near that place. We have been to New City and shit."

When the bus pulled up, we grabbed each other and started jumping up and down. They said we would never get away. Look who's laughing now. I looked at Yolanda and said, "That was some fucked up shit."

She laughed. "I agree, we had one fucked up experience."

Chapter 9
Streets

I liked having Yolanda around the house. It was like having a sister. I had someone with me at the place I despised. With her there I felt safe. It took the attention off of me when it came to Sam. I felt sorry for Yolanda. He called her in his room at night and she stayed for a while. He told me that Yolanda had some good pussy but she needed to step her head game up.

I was shocked to know she did that with him. I guess that's what she did to stay there. Even though she fucked him, she wasn't there for him. She was there for me. She was my friend, and we were very close. We hung out in Queens around her hood. She met James and some of my friends. We were happy.

Sam suddenly became unhappy. Sam's jealousy was not surprising to me, but it took my friend by storm because she gave her body up to him. She was nice to him. So when he told her she had to leave, she felt belittled. Pussy, lips, and thighs were not enough for him. He needed attention, and to feel loved. He wanted Yolanda to act like a wife. But you cannot make someone love you. And that was selfish. We had an agreement. But that's how Sam was.

I knew it was coming. Every day his jealousy grew stronger. You saw it in his face and heard it in his voice. I hated him for that and blamed myself for it happening. But then, I believed we made our own decisions. After all I never pressured her; neither did I suggest it.

Shaquana told me about James cheating on me while I was away. So I didn't bother with him much.

After Yolanda left, I found another friend. I met Fantasia around the way and we had a lot in common. We were broke and were on our own. She didn't have a place to go. And I couldn't stay at Sam's anymore.

When he left for work in the morning, I had to leave. Other than that I had to sleep with him if I wanted to stay. That's how he presented it to me. One day he came to me, after I started to get comfortable. I was sitting on the couch listening to Celine Dion.

He walked in the living room asking if he could he speak to me. "You could have all this." He pointed to his nice apartment. His hand covered the whole layout, the loveseat I was sitting in, the Lazy Boy, and the coconuts hanging from the ceiling. "I will put my weekly pay checks in your hand. But you have to pay the bills around here."

"What are you talking about Sam?" It sounded good; what was the catch?

"You have to take care of me, though."

How the fuck could I take care of him? He was the one talking about giving up the money. He wasn't handicapped.

"All I'm talking is a few times of the week, just take care of me."

"Sam, what are you talking about?"

"Some sex, babe, some sex." He sat there staring with the long face, looking pitiful.

All I could do was shake my head, because I knew he had a problem. In some little way I felt sorry for him, even though I was the sad one. It was me who suffered pain and abuse from his problem. After he said that, I left his house for the streets. And on my path I thought. Why couldn't I have all that by just being his daughter?

Fantasia was staying in a crack spot on Franklin Street in Crown Heights. You could have pretty much gotten anything out of there. Crack, high, fucked and sucked. Anything went in there. There were no rules. Which made me wonder— what the hell was Fantasia doing up in there?

"Who is it?"

I didn't say anything. It wasn't like any of those crack heads knew me. The door opened. "Oh my gosh." I blurted out by accident. But the thin, frail, black-ass lady with a nappy, twisted-ass weave in her head didn't seem to hear me she was so fucking high. I'm saying to myself, Damn she fucked up. All she had to do was take it out the same way she put it in.

She finally spoke. "We're all out. Come back in about twenty minutes and we'll be straight."

"What?" I snapped, getting offended. "Do I look like I smoke to you?"

"Shit, I don't know. Crack doesn't discriminate. Pretty girls smoke crack, too. Shit, you just don't know. Babies smoke crack now. What the fuck you come here for if you don't wanna get high. This is a crack spot," she yelled.

I rolled my eyes, getting impatient. "Is Fantasia here?"

"Who? Fantasia? Who the hell is Fantasia?" she yelled into the apartment. "Anybody know Fantasia?"

I looked into the apartment and saw Fantasia get up off the old raggedy couch.

"Girl, what are you doing sleeping on that dirty couch?"

"I got to sleep somewhere."

"Fantasia, that is not somewhere, that is anywhere. Sleeping on that shit is like sleeping outside on some trifling mattress."

"Now, I wouldn't sleep outside, so some pervert could come fuck with me."

"They can fuck with you in there. I know about that spot. They sell more pussy than a pancake house sells pancakes. You guaranteed to get whatever you want up out of there."

Fantasia got hyped. "Not me, I'm not giving it up. Besides, aint no nigga dumb enough to mess with me after I sent that one dude running out of there with one hundred and fifty stitches across his face. You know how we do it." She pulled two blades out. Her name is clapper, and his name is trigger."

"No, that's how you do it. I don't use blades. I'm not cutting nobody, but if you touch me I will hurt you." We both laughed. "Come on let's go."

"Where we going," Fantasia asked.

"To Flatbush."

"Flatbush?" Fantasia repeated looking puzzled. "What's in Flatbush?"

"Some money."

"Money?" she asked.

"Yeah some green."

"Yeah," she smiled, "let's do it.

Flatbush was definitely diverse, and I loved it. If you ever felt like leaving the country but didn't have the dough just go to Flatbush. Jamaicans, Haitians, Africans, Trinidadians, you name it. All the foreign foods you could eat, beef patty cocoa bread, rice, beans and green bananas. The Rasta music played loud on the streets. Anywhere in Brooklyn, Reggae was popular. Flatbush had some real Buju Banton, Shabba Ranks looking mother fuckers. The reason I loved Flatbush, because it was different. Foreign people were different, and I was a different kind of girl. It always seemed to me that anywhere born out of America were the kindness of all people. They had the most hospitality and they stuck together more than Americans. But they weren't to be fucked with either.

"So Shiree, how are we supposed to get this money?" Fantasia asked while walking up the stairs to exit the train station.

"Easy," I said. "We are going to find out who's holding big, and we're going to get down with them." We had to play it cool. We didn't want to seem desperate. We just need to play cool. "Come on, we gonna walk over to Beverly Street and just hang." I pulled out my Walkman and popped in one of my famous Reggae tapes. I got real excited when I heard "Big Things a Gwan" by Daddy Screw and Donovan Steele. I stood up and did the pepercede. Then I did the bogo, dropped down and whined my waist all the way up like a centipede. Then I started prancing around like I saw the real Jamaicans do.

"Yo shorty, who taught you how to move like that?"

I turned around and saw this light-skinned guy with curly hair. "Those are some dope moves. Who taught you?"

"It's natural, baby. I just move like that. The music makes me do all that." I chuckled. "What's your name?"

"Mario."

"What's up Mario? We need a connect."

"What kind of connect you need umm, um?"

"Shiree, my name is Shiree and we need some crack."

"You smoke crack?"

"No I don't smoke crack, I sell crack."

"How old are you, Shiree?"

"How old do I look?"

"I don't know, umm seventeen?"

"Almost. I'm nineteen."

"Stop lying."

I busted out laughing. "Okay look, don't worry about how old I am. I need to speak to the head nigga."

"What are you going to do with weight, Shiree?"

"Okay Mario listen, I have two spots, one in East New York, and one Downtown Brooklyn. My weight man is suffering from a major drought so I have to shop somewhere else, feel me?"

"Yeah, I got you, Shorty. Just hang around and I'll get back at you, all right?"

"All right, Mario, we'll be right here."

Fantasia ran up to me, "Girl, he is fine. Don't you think so?"

"Yeah, he's cute, especially with that accent."

"What do you think he is, Shiree?"

"Well, he ain't Jamaican, so he has to be Haitian."

"Who's Shiree?"

I hopped off the stool. "I am."

His accent was nice, too. He had a confused look, and in a smooth sexy tone he asked, "You want some crack?"

"No, I mean yes, but some weight. I don't smoke the shit, I want to sell it."

He grinned at me. "You ever sold crack before?"

"Yeah, I have."

"Where's your spot?"

"Downtown in Wycoff projects."

"Okay, let's go right now."

I was so nervous. I never sold before. I didn't even know a crack head. But I went along with the flow because I was sure going to try. "Hey, what's your name?" I walked up to catch up with him as he walked fast to the train station. I was following him, and Fantasia was following me.

"Jackface." Jackface had a flat face with a low top

fade, a cool walk and a cool accent. He was Haitian.

We entered Wycoff projects. These were my projects; I did know it and I did rest there occasionally. So I walked in there like I knew what I was doing. I didn't know any crack heads but I knew what one looked like. I spotted a lady standing by the back door and I walked up to her. I ran ahead of Jackface and Fantasia. "Excuse me Miss, I got some butter for sale. I'm gonna be on the eighteenth floor posted."

Her eyes grew wide. "Okay let me get something right now, what you got?"

I put my index finger up, "Hold up." I hollered for Jackface. "Talk to her," I said and went to press the elevator.

When Jackface walked away from her I could hear her calling me. "Yo Shorty, come here."

I went to see what she wanted.

"Yo, you one of the Harris's girls right?"

"Yeah." I nodded.

"Okay, well, I know where you at, I'll be up there."

"All right," I said and got on the elevator Fantasia was holding. As soon as we got to the eighteenth floor and stepped off the elevator the other elevator opened up and five fiends rushed us. They were ready to get high and they had the loot.

Customers came fast. Before I knew it Jackface's whole pack was gone. I could tell he was impressed. I was standing in the staircase talking to a fiend. She was telling me how cute I was. She said there was some money in Gowanda's projects down the street and around the corner.

Jackface came over to me, after I noticed him getting to know the customers and conducting business. "Shiree? We're all out."

"So what do you want to do?" I said. "There's some money down the street in Gawonda's projects."

"Okay, let me call my man. He'll bring us some more butter over."

Fantasia followed me. When I moved, she moved.

After doing business with his man, Jackface came over to where I was standing. "Here Shiree."

I called Fantasia over who was all up in some dirty boys face. I looked down at the bag of capsules Jackface was handing me.

"You sell two of these for five dollars." He handed Fantasia a bag of straight up chunks. "These are ten dollars a piece." She had a bag of dimes. "Here take this number and call me when ya'll done or if you have any problems."

This was easy I thought. I looked around; there were crack heads everywhere. They were thirsty. They began hawking. Most people wanted capsules because it was only five dollars for two. So I had the most customers. I looked over at Fantasia who had a line going on over her way. My line slowed down, so I went over to Fantasia. A lady walked up to Fantasia with five dollars. Fantasia handed her two dimes.

"What the hell are you doing?" I yelled at Fantasia in shock.

"What?" she replied. "Two for five right?"

"No, I'm selling two for five, these capsules." I pulled out my bag to show her. "You have dimes, Fantasia, those are ten dollars apiece. Ah man! How many did you sell? We fucked up on our first chance," I yelled.

When Jackface got back, I told him what happened. He said it was all right, but I noticed the disappointment in his face. He brushed it off and directed us to follow him. We jumped in a cab and got out on Ditmas Ave. I was content sitting on the steps in the building with Jackface. Fantasia was on the top step asleep with her head in her lap and her coat covering her.

"How can she do business asleep? She's weak I

don't need her?"

"Well she's with me, so she goes wherever I go."

"I don't care, she can stay, but I'm only doing business with you." He chuckled to himself.

"What's so funny?" I asked.

He shook his head and laughed again.

"What?" I said.

"I laugh because she sell two dimes for five dollars." I defended her. "She didn't know."

"Oh no? She didn't know? How did you know?"

I got silent.

"That's my point," he said. "This is the streets. Ears open, mouth closed, watch and observe. I notice that about you."

"What you notice about me?"

"You're very observant and you pay attention. You're not easily manipulated. Most of these girls out here are gullible, say stupid things and do stupid things. I admire you for doing what you're doing. Getting this money. Most girls would rather lie on their back. You can get plenty money out there that way. But look what you're doing instead. And you're very pretty. Do you stay downtown?"

"Yeah, why?"

"Well, if you want to get this money, I got a spot out here in Flatbush. We're trying to open this spot up right here, that's why it's moving so slow. But you and your home girl can stay with me tonight until I find ya'll a place."

"Okay," I said. That's exactly what Fantasia and I needed. We didn't have a place to go.

"All right let's go," he said, nudging Fantasia. "Hey sleepy head, you ready to go?" Fantasia nodded her sleepy head.

I got Fantasia and me off the streets for a minute. Jackface took us to his apartment on East 22nd and

Clarendon. Things worked out perfectly because neither one of us had a place to go. He shared a room in the basement with his sister, Michelle, who was pregnant. She didn't really speak English. It was a small room with two beds, a TV and VCR. Jackface's bed was on the right, just a mattress with no box spring or frame.

After introducing us and showing us where everything was, he noticed that we were tired. "You two sleep here on my bed. I will sleep on the floor."

The next day when I woke up, it seemed like Jackface had been up for hours and maybe he wanted us to get up. I woke Fantasia up and ran straight to the bathroom that was outside the room. I freshened up the best I could and went back to the room. Jackface was standing there with a knot of money in his hand. "Here is some money for some clothes for you two."

"Okay," I said as I took the money and signaled for Fantasia to leave.

We walked to Flatbush and bought a few outfits out of V.I. M.S. When we got back, Michelle was cooking Haitian rice and peas. I walked in and exchanged a smile with Michelle. "Here, Shiree, taste my food." She extended the spoon with rice on it.

"That's good. See, that's what I'm talking about. You foreign people know you can cook. When is it gonna be done? Because I'm ready when it's ready." Everybody laughed.

We ate, and we showered. I had bought more than a week's worth of panties and bras. I bought some dope outfits; the new Air Max, a toothbrush and my own toothpaste. Jackface asked me was I ready.

"Yup," I said. "I was born ready."

"Okay, let's go."

We walked to 23rd and Avenue D. As we entered the building Jackface said, "This is my spot."

"Hey Jackface." Some dude walked up to him and they spoke in their language.

"This is Shiree and her friend Fantasia," Jackface introduced us. "And this is Animal."

Indeed, he looked like an animal, and he was wild like an animal. He wore baggy jeans, a fitted shirt, and leather motorcycle boots with the buckle. He was dark-skinned with no hair on the sides, but a little on the top. On the top he had three skinny braids, and that was it. While Jackface was a smooth cool kind of dude, Animal was wild and moved around a lot. Their accent, and language made their style official. It was everything to me. I respected how they looked out for one another like a family. We met the whole crew and there were a lot of them. They had the building moving productively. Jackface worked from seven until three; then someone would come and relieve him, and so on. It was an around-the-clock business.

I watched them go in and out of the mailbox. That's where they kept the crack and the money. I guess that was to fool Five-o. I watched crack heads go in and out of the building.

The building stayed crowded. Not for a minute did I catch the building empty. It was like a candy store. They wanted to establish the new building like that. That's where Fantasia and I came in.

Jackface took us to the first building he took us to on Ditmas. He gave me a stack of dimes, money to eat and he left. Money came slow, very slow. Fantasia and I sat there. We was getting paid to sit there, it didn't matter how much we made.

I was happy to be somewhere where I wasn't always worrying or stressing. With Jackface I felt safe and normal. He was a very sweet guy. He gave us shelter, food and clothes. I wasn't stupid; most guys I encountered had a thing for me. So I knew Jackface liked me, but what I liked was he never mentioned it. He respected me. We always talked as a way of getting to know each other. We grew a bond.

Fantasia stood from a distance staring at me. "It's Friday we get paid today right, right?"

"Yeah," I said. "Even though we sit at this building all day and were not bringing back much money. I'm tired of getting paid, but not really helping the business grow. I don't want to seem incapable. After a while our services will no longer be needed." I stood up. "I have a plan. Let's go downtown and pump the left over crack."

We went to Wyckoff projects and finished the whole package. But we had to stop going there because the police started doing rounds after someone shot that boy down and left him dead. You never knew what time the police was coming, so it just wasn't safe. But that did not stop us. We walked down the street to Gowanda projects and pumped our crack.

We made a few dollars in Gowanda. But this guy walked up on us and said, "Ya'll selling in this building?"

Without any hesitation I responded, "Yeah why?"

"Ya'll can't sell in here. This is my building."

I turned my head away from him without a response. I felt his stare on my face for about ten seconds and then he left.

"What are we gonna do, Shiree?" Fantasia asked nervously.

She kept staring at me like I was crazy, but my pride kicked in. I sucked my teeth and said, "I ain't going nowhere. I stood for ten minutes and said, "Come on let's go."

"Where are we going now?"

"Shopping, let's go shopping." Since we were getting rid of the entire package Jackface was a lot happier, and we got our cut. Fantasia and I did our own thing. We went shopping, hung out, went to Haitian restaurants, manicures, pedicures, we did it.

That night we went to the room to shower and change Jackface handed me a beeper. "What do I need this for?" I asked him.

"It's communication, that's how we keep in contact. You have been busy, so if I need you I'll page you. Are you leaving again?"

"Yeah, Fantasia and I, we'll be back."

"All right," he said be safe okay?"

"Yo what's up Mario?" I spotted Mario walking toward Fantasia and me. I looked at Fantasia. "Remember him?"

"Hell yeah, he hooked us up."

"Hey Shiree, how you doing? I see you're still around."

"Yeah, thanks to you I been straight."

"So the connect worked out all right? I heard you're working with Jackface. That's my boy."

"What are you doing right now, Mario?"

"I'm just chilling, mon."

"Come with us downtown then." We still had seven dimes left over from earlier. I was surprised Jackface didn't ask for the rest of the butter. I left everything we made on the bed before we left.

Before we got to Gowanda projects he stopped at the corner by the store and looked up at the building and shook his head. "I'm not going in there, mon."

"Why? Just come on."

He shook his head and he was dead serious. "I will wait right here, you go."

Fantasia and I went to the building. Ever since we first went to Gowanda projects Fantasia had been saying her boyfriend stayed in there, but we never saw him. "Here take these seven dimes I will be right back." I handed her the small bag with the seven dimes in it and I left to hang with Mario.

When I went back in the building, I looked around for Fantasia. I didn't see Fantasia in the lobby. I went in the staircase and saw Fantasia on the top flight bent over holding her stomach. I stood at the bottom of the flight with my mouth open. "What the fuck happened to you?"

"They just robbed me."

"Who just robbed you?" I was in a state of shock as I walked up the stairs to where she was standing. "What about the seven dimes, did they take that?"

"They took it," she whined.

I stood next to her. "Calm down, all right?" I heard a loud noise and turned to look. Three dudes came busting out the exit door. I was getting patted down. I started thinking about all my shit that was about to get ran. I cooperated. I didn't say anything, I didn't move.

Another set of dudes came through the same exit door. Apparently the two sets were not together because they began to bang on each other.

I ran down the stairs and out the building. I gave Mario my pager and my gold, and ran back to Fantasia. I noticed her talking to a dude and I went over to her. "This is my boyfriend," she said. "He wants me to stay with him."

"Boyfriend? Stay with him? Where was he when you was homeless sleeping in crack spots without pay?"

Her boyfriend walked away.

"Fantasia you're just going to leave me? I have to go back to Jackface by myself and tell this man I don't have his shit?"

"I'm staying here, Shiree. I think I'm pregnant."

"You stupid bitch!" I smacked her to the ground. It sounded like wind.

When she fell her boyfriend came running toward me. "She's pregnant."

Before I could even turn all the way around he punched me with one hand and grabbed my hair with the other. I lost one breath for a minute, and regained it the next. I ate his punches as he dragged me down the hall by my hair. I kept kicking him and swinging my hands in the air as I got dragged. "Get the fuck off me! Get the fuck off of me!"

Just when I thought I was about to die, a voice came from the door. "Let her go!" Everybody looked toward the entrance door. Mario was standing there holding a forty-four. He cocked it. "Didn't your mama teach you not to hit girls?" Mario spoke to the boy that finally let me go. "Come Shiree, let's go."

I got up and we left. "How did you know Mario?"

"You came running out the first time. Remember you told me to hold your stuff. Then you never came back out."

"Thanks, Mario." I gave him a hug.

I was thinking on the whole train ride back to Flatbush. I couldn't believe Fantasia played me. All that nigga of hers wanted was some pussy and my money she had in her pocket, and then when he got done he was going to throw her ass out. Where was he before, when she was living on the streets? He was probably the one who robbed her dumb ass. I was going to have to go by myself to tell that Haitian boy that I didn't have his shit. At first I thought about not going back. But in reality I didn't have anywhere to go.

I went to a pay phone and called Caseen. I told him the whole story, and that I was scared, because Haitian niggas didn't play that.

"Wait a minute, wait a minute, hold up," Caseen replied, as if he couldn't believe it. "You got robbed, some dude beat you up, and the nigga you were with pulled out a four-four on the dude. Where's the dude with the four-four?"

"He's gone now. He made sure I was okay and he left."

"Well, first off you got to thank that nigga for me. Second of all, what the fuck are you doing selling drugs?"

I got mad. I was beat up, betrayed, by my damn self, and had to face this dude about his shit. I never felt good about falling short of anything. And now my brother was chastising me. "Caseen I'm about to go. I don't want to hear that mess. I'm out here, and you already know that. I called you for some advice."

"All right, all right, sis, calm down. Now what did you say now? You was robbed seven dimes right?"

"Right," I replied.

"Okay, sister, that's nothing. That's petty cash. And by the way you tell it you been hitting him off larger than that. The man paid you large and double for you and your friend. And I can bet all my dough he likes you, so I trust that you have nothing to worry about. So just go back and tell him what happened and let me know. But on some real shit, you need to let me come down there with my boys, a few of those thangs and lay them niggaz down."

I stood at the pay phone laughing. Everything felt better. "You crazy, brother."

"I'm serious."

Jackface wasn't at the room so I went to 23rd and Avenue D. He was working late and business was producing. As soon as I walked in the building he saw and ran to me before I could get to him. "What happened to you Shiree?"

"I got robbed."

Jackface got loud and hysterical. "What? At the building?"

"No, the projects downtown."

"Why did you go down there without me? That's why I put you in my spot. I got people you don't know watching out for you. Who did this to you? Take me to him." Jackface looked serious and mad. He headed toward the door, ready to go.

"No Jackface, it's over."

"Your face look like that, they take my shit and it's over? No, no over."

"I was fighting with Fantasia's boyfriend. He did this to me. That was already taken care of. But somebody else robbed Fantasia for seven dimes."

"Why Fantasia boyfriend hit you?"

"Because I slapped Fantasia."

"What happened with you and Fantasia?"

"She got robbed, and then she told me she was staying down there with her boyfriend. And so I slapped her."

Jackface shook his head. He got on his cell phone and spoke for twenty seconds in his language that I was beginning to learn a little. He told someone to come and relieve him so he could leave.

Jackface didn't care about the seven dimes at all. He was pissed off about my face. He took me to a restaurant where a lot of Haitians hung out. We ate, talked and laughed. I met a lot of nice people. That night his friend Herby came to stay with us. Jackface and I slept in the bed together while Herby slept on the floor. Jackface and I had sex that night and he told me he didn't want me selling drugs no more. But I would still get paid. While he was at work, I went shopping. I hung out at the restaurant he took me to on 22nd. He would get off work and find me there if I wasn't at the room. The lounge played reggae music.

Jackface fell in love with me. He became over protective. And there was nothing he would not do for me. He stayed concerned about me and he protected me, but his sister and I stopped liking one another. She was ugly, with no hair and no man. She was seven months pregnant and miserable. She stayed in our business. But I was not the one to take lip. Jackface always took my side. She wanted me to leave. He told her that I didn't have to go nowhere. He reminded her who paid the bills.

Jackface, Herby and I went to the club one night and danced until I got tired. Jackface went off for a minute. After that we left. Jack face was talking to a tall light-skinned girl outside the club. She had her hair in box braids in a barb. She favored Tony Braxton. Jackface walked off.. Then Herby and she began to talk. It looked strange to me. Later I found out she was Jackface's ex-girlfriend.

That morning everybody left the room, while Jackface and I were still sleeping. The curtains were closed, so it was dark in there. We had sex and just lay in the bed under the covers. Until his sister and Herby came in with Jackface's ex-girlfriend I recognized from the club, and a tall dark-skinned girl. They came in real loud.

Jackface and I sat up. I had on a tank top and silk boxers. I sat against the wall and Jackface got up. He was talking with them in their language. They were all Haitian.

Michelle hung a picture on the wall. When I looked the second time, I was shocked and wondering what the hell was going on. Then they began to praise the picture. They ran up on the picture yelling "Yeah! Yeah! Yeah!" The tall dark-skinned girl walked by the mattress that I was sitting on, and turned her back to me. The mattress was huge and I was against the wall, so her butt was not in my face.

I sat there quietly watching them. I gave them looks like, I'm not scared and I dare you to touch me.

The tall dark-skinned girl got the impression I wasn't scared and all she had to do was touch me and I might flip. Those were the looks I gave her.

Jackface was talking with them and he was even smiling. I didn't know what they were saying. I only knew a few words.

I sat there pissed off and couldn't believe Jackface was letting them do that. It seemed to me he was down with them. But it was no time for emotions. I had on my defense spirit. I had to defend myself. All I had was myself, as usual. And I would never let anyone hurt me. I knew his jealous-ass sister set that up, with her gorilla-looking self, having a baby.

Jackface sat next to me, and the girl sat next to him by the wall. He was sitting between us. He began touching my legs under the covers. I pushed his hands off me, and rolled my eyes at him. He actually smiled in my face.

His ex-girlfriend looked at me, and in her accent she said, "What the fuck you looking at? Don't fucking look at me."

I got up, stepped in front of her, and snatched her braids. I yanked and yanked while I upper-cut her ass.

The tall dark-skinned girl ran toward me from the side with an umbrella.

While still holding on to the girl, I threw my leg up and kicked her in her stomach, like a home run on a good kickball game.

She fell on the floor and never approached again.

I lifted my foot again and triflingly kicked the bitch I had in my hand..

Jackface tried to pull me off her, but I just pulled harder.

When he finally pulled me with enough force, I fell with her braids in my hand.

I was still mad, so I turned around and out of rage I

threw the TV and VCR down on the floor.

Michelle grabbed a cup of water, speaking Creol, with the attempt to throw water on me.

I turned to her and raised up on her. "Bitch, you throw that water on me I'll kill your fucking baby."

She didn't throw that water.

I went and stood on the mattress and did not say anything. I watched the crowd. I was not to be fucked with.

The girl was very upset. She went to the bathroom to see her face in the mirror. She came back going crazy. She was screaming in her language. Her braids were pulled out; she had a bloodshot eye and scratches all over her face.. She spoke Creol to her friend and then her friend left. She came back talking.

I understood what she was saying. I knew mount venee meant I'm coming. So when I heard venee, I knew some more girls were coming. I stood there. I was not the type to run and leave, but I couldn't wait to get out of there. I was nervous, but I had to finish it so I could go.

Three girls came. The boldest one walked up to the mattress popping shit to me. I gave her the grill I first gave the other girls. She went to swing at me.

I swung too and grabbed her hair. I never let her go, while the other girls tried to swing.

Jackface and Herby were breaking it up. It was a lot of pushing and shoving.

The tall dark-skinned girl ran up on me twice and ran back. The first time she ran on me, I felt a cut across my stomach. When she ran on me again, I felt a cut on my face. After I felt that I went crazy. I broke the whole party up. I pushed everybody who was pushing and shoving. I started throwing some mean blows to whoever was in my way.

Everybody backed up. The other girls tried to come

up and fight me but Jackface and Herby stopped them. The first girl that swung on me I grabbed and never let go. I had her on the floor the whole time by her hair. She got up and I had her bow bow in my hand. She wanted it so I threw it at her.

She was mad and too scared to approach me again. So she tried to hawk spit on me.

I didn't move an inch.

She missed and made a mess on the wall.

I stood there looking at them like they were stupid.

They left and I got dressed and packed my little bag. Jackface and Herby laughed and spoke in English. They were saying, "Man, she beat them girls up." Now they want to talk English.

He stopped me while I was walking up the stairs to leave. I looked at him in disgust. "You have a lot of nerves trying to act like nothing happened." I spoke with emotion, because I was hurt.

He sat down and hung his head low. His eyes were full of water. "I love you Shiree." I stood with my hand on my hip. I didn't feel him at all. "Well I'm about to go," I said. I headed down the stairs. He stood up. "Shiree!" He kept calling me. I kept walking.

I took the train downtown. I lifted my shirt and showed Lawanda a long cut underneath my breast that went straight across. I had a very little cut on the side of my left eye. I did not look bad at all.

Lawanda rounded the whole projects up. We had about fifteen girls who were ready to go to Flatbush and fight.

"Nah, nah," I said. "I'm straight. I'm always straight after a fight. They jumped me, yeah, but I handled mine."

Instead Lawanda, Ameanie and Lee came with me to the hospital. We sat in the waiting room for a long time. And I went back there refusing to get stitches and so we left.

I was real shook up about what happened. I really felt alone and wanted to be around some family. I still had some money that Jackface gave me. I got on the greyhound to Syracuse.

My family was pretty large in Syracuse. I had lots of uncles, aunts, and cousins. I was around a lot of family all the time. I could have stayed anywhere. I stayed with my Aunt Gina who lived in a complex in Liverpool called the Willows. My Aunt Savannah and her man Alan stayed there, too. The lifestyle I indulged in was very different from the city. I did not walk far, nor did I ride the train. There were no trains there. I really didn't go anywhere if it wasn't with a relative.

Alan had a car that he constantly hopped in and out of, simply because he was a businessman. For him time was money. He was a fast man living a fast life in the fast lane, and Savannah was down with him. She didn't give a fuck as long as she got what she wanted. Whatever she wanted she got. If she wanted sneakers she got it, a coat got it, that chain someone was selling got it, some crack—got it. She was spoiled got everything she wanted, but she was chasing her high. Savannah and Alan ate the best of foods. She had the finest things in life. Things most bitches could not afford, and would die to have. That was because Alan could get a hold to anything he wanted. He would go into the leather limited and put four leather coats under his coat. I called it leather unlimited. He went in just about any store and took shit the same way he took clothes. Savannah had a closet for just her shoes. Every day she got brand new leather.

But she and my Aunt Gina were addicted to crack. And it didn't make her habit better by him selling it. If he wouldn't give her any crack, she would sell her shit. It didn't matter when she sold her clothes and coats, Alan would just replace them. He didn't want her to smoke like she did, because she was beautiful and sexy. She looked good in anything she wore. She was a bad chick with a loud mouth, and the type to pick up knives and throw things. She got crazy like that sometimes because she wanted some crack.

He would give it to her to stop her from yelling or to get her out of his face. Alan sold a lot of crack and had players on the corner selling it for him. He was hitting that stem, too, just like them—in fact with them. He was not like them, though, I give him that. He indulged in it lightly. He knew when to stop. He liked it, while they were in love with it.

My Aunt Gina would twitch her mouth around and always was scared to leave the bathroom. I was exposed to a lot of arguing, cursing, fighting and drugs. My aunts hung out in bathrooms. Savannah often tore up Gina's house when they argued. Gina was not a fighter and never wanted to fight Savannah.

I was also exposed to money and material things. Caseen's sister-in-law, Tracey, one of the best beauticians in Syracuse, did my hair. Every day I went to the mall with Alan and Savannah. I always got something out of what he stole. I would point out what I wanted.

They went to different stores and I got more stuff. Sometimes I was in a position where I had the opportunity to steal something, too, and I did. Later in the day, I rode around with Alan. He stayed riding because he would sell his clothes. And he had players on the street selling his crack.

I sold some stuff and some I kept for myself. I watched my wardrobe stack up. I had a nice leather coat and bag, with cash in my pocket. That's how I did my hustle. And every family member I saw I asked for ten or twenty dollars. They could have given me money today, I would still ask tomorrow. I saved every dollar I got.

See, money was all around me. People smoked crack, they had to get their money from somewhere, even if they had to steal it.

I stacked my cash and thought it was time to go back home. I called Miss Harris' house and Ernest had just got home from jail. I called James' house and his aunt said he was leaving for Jobcorp in two days. I made my mind up. I was going to see James first and stay the night with him. Then when he left, I would go to Ernest's house.

I wound up going to Ernest's house first and I never got a chance to leave. I stayed all night and I knew James was leaving in the morning. I had sex with Ernest that night. I did not sleep with him because I wanted to, but because I felt like I had to. He was my first true love. There was a time I thought life was worthless without him. But after he left, I broke my virginity and fell in love again. I became sexually active with James and Jackface and I had feelings for the both of them. I loved Ernest because he was there when I was going through a trial in my life I couldn't bear alone. I was vulnerable and inexperienced with life. He taught me the streets and how to be brave and courageous. Most of all he loved me at the time I needed love. I just was not in love with him anymore. Now I was grown and very much experienced. I was a different person from when we first met.

From his knowledge he still believed I was a virgin. He did not know anything about my life since he left. And I did not want to tell him. I played like I was happy for a few days, but I couldn't take it anymore. The truth was he was like a stranger to me. And I was in love with a different man. I was also mad at him, because I didn't get the chance to see James before he left. I still thought about James.

I had to get out of the house, so I left. I walked to Atlantic Ave and caught the # 2 train to Flatbush. I went to the restaurant on 22nd. Everybody asked me where I was all that time. They were happy to see me, and it felt good to be back. It brought back a lot of memories. And I looked better than I did before. I had the construction Tim's fly leather with a strap, and a fly hairdo. I looked better than fly. I looked luscious. I had light skin, with big gold bangle earrings.

I saw Jackface and he begged me to go home with him. He told me how depressed he was when I left. I still had feelings for Jackface and I went home with him. I still couldn't get over how he let those girls come up in there and jump me. I knew him as a sweet guy, and he was sweet that night. We laid up for two days and then I went back downtown. I took a shower and left that night for Flatbush.

I felt like going to the club, so I went to the Ark, had a few drinks and left. I went back to Jackface's.

The next night we hung out at the restaurant. Monique walked with me to the store to get a beer and some loosies. The man wouldn't sell us the beer or cigarettes because we didn't have identification.

Monique rolled her eyes. "You saw my i.d before." "I don't care about before," the Arab said. "I need to see it now."

She screamed at him, "You dirty Arab."

Animal came in. "Yo, what's going on."

Monique cursed and threw things.

"Get out. Get out my store. All of you, go."

Jackface and Herby came in.

"Out my fucking store, out, out."

We went outside the store and saw fruit in the front. We threw the oranges and apples at the store. The man came out and Animal threw a garbage can at him.

We heard the sirens and saw the lights and we all ran. Monique and I ran one way and the boys ran another way. We jumped over fences and ran until the police caught us.

They took Monique and me to the precinct where we saw Jackface, Herby and Animal. We laughed at each other. They took all of us to central booking charged us with assault, robbery and use of a firearm.

The store man said we tried to rob them.

We all stood next to each other in court about four hours later. We were released for lack of evidence.

I was already in downtown Brooklyn and I needed to clean myself up so I told them I would meet them in Flatbush. I went to Ernest's to take a shower and get dressed, but when I thought I was leaving, Ernest told me I wasn't. I was anxious to go because everybody was waiting for me.

Ernest held me down and sat on me. He took a green marker and marked my face up.

"What's wrong with you, stupid. Get off of me. "He wouldn't listen so I spit in his face. I tried to run out the door, but he caught me.

We were fighting in the living room. He pushed me into Miss Harris' china cabinet and it shattered.

I kept yelling, "You see, you see."

When I made it out the door, he ran behind me. I ran in the staircase, and started out on the eighteenth floor. I flew down each flight like I had no feet until made it to the eighth floor when Ernest jumped on me. I screamed, so he got off me.

I ran out into the hallway, banging on somebody's door yelling, "Call the police. He's trying to kill me."

Ernest peeked out one time, but then I didn't see him any more. The elevator took me straight to the lobby, where I snuck out the back door exit. On my way down the street I kept looking behind me terrified. I began running when I saw Ernest from a distance. A car garage was wide open, and so I flew inside. "My boyfriend is trying to kill me. Please help me." I told the mechanic. He shook his head as he quickly walked me towards the door. "No Miss, you can't stay here."

Since he was kicking me out I knew it wasn't much time. So I ran to the train station and went back to Flatbush for the night.

The next day I went to my father's house to see how he was doing. After talking with him, I called James aunt. She told me that James would be home on a visit for the Thanksgiving and Christmas holidays. This meant he would be home in four days.

I laid low between Sam's house and Ernest's until James reached Brooklyn. It was time to give him a call. "Where you at?" James asked sounding hyper. He was already drinking; I could hear it in his voice. "Come over here girl, now." "Okay. I'm coming now, bye."

We fucked all night and got drunk like we always did. James and I had sex more than we did anything. And that's all our life consisted of. And the sex was so good we often hollered I love you. But the sex was what we both loved.

I went to Ernest's and then back to James'... That's all I was doing was going back and forth; that's how I stayed happy. One pissed me off and I would go to the other. While James and I stayed between the sheets, Ernest and I never had sex again after that one time.

While I was at Ernest's house getting dressed, there was a girl there named Kim. I didn't know her, but anyone at Miss Harris' house was cool with me.

Miss Harris was throwing evil looks. "Kim it's time for you to leave. I don't mean to be funny. I know you are a friend of my kids, but I don't want nobody in my crib right now." She was in one of those moods where she would go off, start screaming, and the whole house would shake. But Kim had nowhere to go.

I felt sorry for her so I took her with me to James' house. James and I went on the block. He hooked Kim up with one of his boys. We left them fucking and went back to his house.

In the middle of the night I heard a knock at the door. I sucked my teeth. "Vernice," I tried to whisper. "Tell that girl downstairs that I'm not here." I really didn't feel like lying up with him, so I left him and went to see Jackface. It seemed like it wasn't working out with any of the dudes. I had low tolerance for everybody. Life was fucked up and nobody was benefiting me. I was so tired of running, looking for love and feeling unsatisfied. I felt James falling out of love with me.

I loved Ernest, but not the way he wanted me to, or how I used to. Jackface and I were always arguing and fighting. I never felt the same way toward him after that fight with his ex girlfriend. When I got to his house, we began arguing and he smacked the holy hell out of me. After I tore his room up I tried to leave, but he stood in front of the door and took my boots off my feet. After he went to sleep I found my boots and left.

I went to Shaquana's house in Starright City to sit awhile, get the latest news around the way, and to call Ernest. I called Ernest at his sister Dee Dee's. He was anxious for me to come over

I was really happy to see Ernest for the first time in a long time. As soon as I got there he was standing in the doorway waiting for me. He ran passed me. "I'll be right back, don't leave." Fifteen minutes later I turned around and Ernest walking in the door. I did a double take as I saw James behind him. What the hell is James doing here, I thought to myself. My heart dropped. I was so nervous. I never wanted either one of them to find out. I did not want to hurt anybody.

We sat at the table looking each other in the face. I

was so nervous. I never wanted either one of them to find out. James grinned, but Ernest was really hurt. "So, that's a nice watch you have on James." I shook my head in embarrassment, knowing that the watch James had on I gave it to him after giving it to Ernest. "So what you wanna do Shiree?" Ernest was serious. "You want us both?" James grinned and agreed with everything Ernest said. "Let's go for a walk," Ernest said.

We walked down Pennsylvania Avenue. I noticed we weren't getting anywhere. "So who do you want Shiree? Ernest said. I grew frustrated. "Stop right here and let me use the phone." I wanted to walk away with James, but I didn't want to hurt Ernest more than I already had. I began to call Sam. "Sam." "Hey Hun."

"I need you to do me a favor."

"What is it?" he asked.

"You know how I feel about James right?"

"Sure, I know how you feel about him."

"Okay, I'm gonna put him on the phone and you tell him okay."

"Tell him what?"

"How I feel about him."

"What? Why don't you tell him."

"Please, I can't"

"Look, I'm not doing that."

"Please." I begged. He was silent. "Are you going to do it or what?"

"No I'm not." I hung up on him. "Ooh," I said out loud. "I can't stand him." I thought to myself, if it was a orgie I was asking him to join he'll be all for it. I left Ernest and James both standing there.

I jumped on the 2 train and took it to the last stop uptown. I didn't get off because I didn't know where to go. I stayed on and rode it back downtown.

I slept on the train till dawn. After hours of exhaustion I walked to the nearest pay phone to call

James. I thought about how I was with James and Ernest for seven hours. "James."

"Yeah." He didn't sound upset with me.

"You sleep?"

"Nah. Why you left like that yesterday?"

"Because I didn't want to hurt anybody. I'm coming over okay?"

"So what that mean you want to be with me?"

"Yeah."

"All right, you coming now?"

While we were between the sheets the phone rung and I answered it. "Hello."

"I guess you made your mind up." It was Ernest. My heart dropped.

I handed the phone to James.

Ernest convinced James to go down the street to his house and to bring me along.

I shook my head. There he goes again being somebody's Flunky. I went down there with him, but I felt weird.

Ernest took me to the side. "I'm not giving up that easy.

"Why are you doing this?" Ernest looked at me with that grin that always meant he's up to something. "I got this," he said. James is dumb. He don't deserve you."

"So why did you call us to come down here?"

"I'm using him." I'm just using him." I sat there playing the dumb game until it got dark and James and I left, back to his house.

I kept shaking my head. "What?" James said.

I was mad that I wasn't getting any attention. I was mad because he was being nice to Ernest. He was being stupid. "You so stupid," I told him.

"Stupid? Who you calling stupid?"

"Ernest don't even like you."

"You just mad."

Oh now he starting to talk stupid, I thought.

"Ernest told me he was using you. You think he really give a shit about you. Someone his girl wants to be with. He loves me to death."

I started screaming at him, because damn how stupid can you be? And I couldn't stand a dumb-ass person. I never knew he was that damn stupid. "What's wrong with you James? Why would you want to sit and chill with my ex lover? Someone who is in crazy love with me?"

He tried to curse me back. "Oh what's wrong with me? No what's wrong with you? You did this shit. That's your man."

I was raging inside and I pushed him. I stood there as he came towards me. He put all his might in his right fist and gave it to me in my eye. I fell in the corner and grabbed my face. I grabbed a steel iron lying in the corner. I got up and swung it at him three times.

He tried to block with his hands and all I saw was blood. The iron fell and I ran out of the house. On my way back to Dee Dee's house where Ernest was tears just came. Ernest and I talked all night.

Laying around Sam's house I found out that I was pregnant. Jackface, was so happy after he found out. But it wasn't his. We had stopped having sex for a while. And before I got with James, I had just got over a period. James was going to be a daddy. He was back in Jobcorp when I told him. He was happy, but it wasn't enough for him to leave.

Chapter 10
Enough

I was tired of running the streets and tired of guys. I despised Jackface the most. I fell out of love with him and he fell deeper in love with me. He knew I was at Sam's apartment. Every day he called. He just had to see me. Sam was at work.

I was lying in the Lazy Boy flicking channels on the cable remote when the phone rang. "Hello?"

"Hi Shiree. It's Jackface."

"Hey, what's going on?" I responded, truly uninterested. Once upon a time I really dug this dude. But now I just want to lie there. I didn't want to see his face or hear his voice.

"Can I come see you?"

"Not right now, Jackface. I don't feel like company. I'll talk to you later, all right?"

He didn't answer me.

"All right?" I repeated, only louder.

"All right," he said.

I hung up. I was relaxed on the couch for twenty minutes when the intercom rang. I pressed the button to speak. "Who is it?"

"Me, Jackface."

I rolled my eyes and I did not buzz him in. When I sat down, I got a knock at the door. I was furious. I swung the door open, and stood there ill, grilling him. "Didn't I tell you not to come over here? Why didn't you listen? I don't want to be bothered." I slammed the door and went to sit down.

I was disgusted. Day after day I was mentally disgusted with Jackface and Sam. And I was physically disgusted with myself. I was constantly in the bathroom peeing, and constantly in the kitchen eating. Eating was the only thing that made the nausea stop.

When Sam left for work, I was on the couch. When he returned home, I was on the couch.

Sam needed stimulation and excitement. You could not just sit around him. "You know, Shiree, it's best for you to go back to Syracuse with your family."

"Well, why didn't you leave me there in the first place?"

"Look Shiree, I tried. You are my daughter. I wanted us to be a family, but it won't work. You need to go because you can't stay here."

"I'm not staying here. Don't worry I'm leaving." I lay there thinking, I get it. He wants me to need him or fall.

He walked around the apartment grilling me wherever he saw me. I didn't have to say anything and he would find something to pick with me. "And tell your friend, or your boyfriend, Ernest, whoever he is to you, not to call my house anymore. I don't like him. The punk mother fucker calls my house questioning me."

"What did he ask you?" I asked curiously.

"Don't worry about what he asked, that's not the point. He don't question me." Sam went to his room. He didn't like Ernest because Ernest knew about him. Ernest wasn't the type of guy you could manipulate.

I made up my mind that I was tired of the bullshit. I called Caseen and explained the whole story. I didn't tell him everything because he was already trying to resolve the problem with violence.

"Yo, word to my mother, I'm gonna pop that dude. I knew something was wrong with him. I'm coming to get you. I'm getting on the bus tomorrow."

I took Sam's gold watch to the pawnshop. "Two hundred and eighty dollars," the Chinese estimated.

"All right, I'll be back tomorrow." I put the watch back in its case. At least I knew what it was going for.

Sam left for work in the morning and almost every day he came straggling in at lunchtime. Then he went back to work.

Caseen went straight to Staten Island. I set it up to where Caseen was on his way to Brooklyn around Sam's lunch break. I was on the couch when Sam returned on his lunch break. As soon as he left I jumped up and packed my suitcase. I ran to the pawnshop and pocketed my two hundred and eighty dollars. By the time I got back I ran into Caseen in the lobby.

"What's up sis, you ready?"

"Yeah, let's go upstairs for a second."

Caseen was amazed with a cassette player Sam had. Everything bought was worth something.

"Take whatever you want." I emptied Sam's water bottle and took all the change and left the pennies on the floor. I was off to Syracuse for a new start. I couldn't take the shit I was going through. The streets were moving too fast for me. Sam felt like I needed him, and he wanted me to need him. He thought I was a weak vulnerable child. He abused me. He took advantage of me and he used me. He wanted my dignity and my pride. I can still hear his voice telling me; it was okay to sell my body for money. That a woman has what it takes to get money. As long as a woman has lips, hips and fingertips, she'll never go broke. He told me there was nothing wrong with incest. When I told him I wanted to go to modeling school, his idea of it was taking naked pictures of me.

I had enough of my ugly daddy.

Caseen sat on the window side on the bus to Syracuse. I could hear the Wutang coming from his headphones. He was bopping his head as he stared out the window.

My thoughts always ran deep on long bus rides. For some reason my mind flashed back to the month of October in 1991.

That night when Mama was first missing, Aunt Gina told everybody that Sam threatened to kill Mama. She said that's what Mama had told her during her visit at our house, which had only been a week before she disappeared. Her memory was vague, so she only knew bits of pieces. What she did know was that Mama was on the phone with Sam. Mother told Sam that she was home alone, which was not true at all. In fact Aunt Gina was in the room right next to her. And what he didn't know was that Mama had him on speakerphone. So when he heard a noise he said, "Colleen you got me on speaker phone? Are you lying to me?"

And quickly Mama said, "No."

Shortly, Sam confessed, apologizing to Mama for what he did.

After they hung up Aunt Gina asked Mama, what did he do to be sorry for?

That's when Mama told everything. Mama said Sam took her somewhere, his job was involved and so was Coney Island. Trees surrounded them; he chose one tree and began to carve his name in it. He carved Sam loves. Then he gave mama the knife and told her to carve her name underneath.

She asked him why was he doing this to her, and how he knew she was about to get married.

That's when he threw her down and said to her,

"Carve it in the tree or I'll carve it in your chest."

At that moment she said in a desperate voice, "My brother knows I'm here with you."

Sam let her up and she began looking for her wallet. She told Aunt Gina that she never found her wallet and she knew Sam took it. Mama also said Sam came by on a later day with some papers he wanted her to sign. He said they were divorce papers, but she knew he would never give her one. One day he told her he would kill her before he divorced her.

She signed the papers without reading them, because she wanted to hurry up and get out his car before dad caught her. She had no clue what she signed. Her words were, "I probably signed my life away for all I know."

I was twelve when my aunt told that story. I'm thinking, three years later I'm starting to remember. I remember going into Mama's room, and I saw Aunt Gina lying across the bed, while Mama was on the speakerphone. I was the noise Sam heard, and Mama shushed me out of the room.

Now I'm remembering the night Mama took Caseen, Leroy, Troy and me to Uncle Andre's house in the Bronx. That was a very unusual move for her because we never traveled without Dad.

When we arrived to Uncle Andre's house, Mama left, and I didn't recall her coming back that night. Uncle Andre was the brother who knew where she was. And when I saw Mama the next day, I asked her for a dollar. She told me she did not have any money. But knowing it was September, almost time for school, I knew she had school shopping money. So when I asked about our school shopping money, she told me she lost her wallet ands tears came to her eyes. I asked what was wrong, but all I got was nothing.

Now I understood and the picture was quite clear.

Mother was not robbed nor raped. She was stabbed seventy-two times. Stabbing is a crime of passion. Someone evil who had a vendetta with her did it, someone who really loved her at one point. But why did Sam do it? Not because he wanted her, they were separated for nine years. And that's why police couldn't find a motive. But there could be numerous reasons why people don't want to divorce. Maybe he didn't want to pay alimony, or child support. Everybody knew he had some kind of money. My eyes began to roll in the back of my head; my body became rigid, and tense.

It was noticeable because Caseen nudged me. "Are you all right? You don't look so good. Don't worry, you'll be all right, sis. I'll take care of you."

But all I could think of was how I was going to take care of Sam. This was hard for me to take. I lived with him after Mom died. He manipulated me, and I kept running back. Yes, he is sick enough to kill my mom. Now I see why he wanted to lay down with me. I must have reminded him of her. But then again, he has been a pervert since the beginning.

We reached the bus station in Syracuse and took a cab straight to Caseen's apartment. Caseen must have told everybody we were coming, because everybody was at his house waiting on us.

Aunt Gina grabbed me and put her arms around me. "Look at my fly niece." She showed me off to her friend she had with her. Aunt Gale was like "Heyeeee." She always stretched her hey.

Caseen's baby's mother, Melinda, was there. She hugged me and said, "What's up girl?" I was happy they were still together, and to see my niece. I picked her up for about five minutes and put her back down. She was still in her sleeping months anyway.

I went outside to smoke a cigarette.

Aunt Gina followed me. "Give me one."

"Give you what?" I asked. "You want a cigarette?"

"Damn, what's wrong with you. What you thought I was talking about? You shouldn't be smoking pregnant anyway. What are you going to do with a child?"

"I don't know, Aunt Gina, what am I suppose to do?"

Aunt Gale came down and said, "What ya'll doing down here?" She had the phone in her hand.

"Oh let me see that phone, please auntie."

"Damn girl, why you seem so shaky?"

They all went upstairs to dance to Caseen's loud music. I lit another cigarette and called Lawanda.

"Hi Miss Harris is Lawanda there?"

"Shiree is that you?"

"Yes Miss Harris."

"Hi Shiree, where are you?" After I told her she said, "Syracuse? Okay that's good. Your family going to help you?"

"I don't know."

"You don't know? Poor baby, you'll be all right. Don't you forget about us, we're your family down here too, ya hear? Okay here's Lawanda."

"What's up, girl? Why you didn't tell me you were going to Syracuse?"

"I don't know, it just all happened so fast. What's up with you?"

"I'm ready to get this baby out of me, that's it."

"Lawanda, I'm getting ready to come back down there tonight."

"For what? You just got there."

"I'm going to kill that mother fucker."

"Who?!"

"Sam ass. He killed my mother. I know he did. I know he did now. I put it all together." I told her everything I knew.

All she could say was, "Oh shit! You're right. But you can't just kill him."

"Why the fuck I can't? He just killed my mother."

"Wait until after I have my baby, so me, you and Ernest, could tie him up and make him talk."

"Okay, I'll wait." After I hung up my nerves could not wait.

Caseen came downstairs and said, "What you doing girl?" He grabbed my arm and pulled me upstairs. I could tell he was real tipsy now.

When we got upstairs I pulled him in the room. "What's up sis?"

"I need a hundred dollars."

"What you need a hundred dollars for?"

"For these boots I saw." He reached in his stash and pulled out two hundred dollar bills. "You might as well get an outfit, too." He kissed me on my cheek and starting acting crazy again. "Come and see your room." He opened the door; I saw bags, boxes and clothes everywhere. "Well not yet, but I'm going to clean all that out, don't worry."

Everybody was dancing, carrying Moet and Hennessey bottles. I thought back to how my family carried on at occasions like this one. But considering we had the more civilized members over, rather than the real crazy ones, everything would be okay.

I went downstairs to smoke another cigarette. I took the phone with me to call the bus station. A bus was leaving in exactly one hour.

I just sat down and pretended to be happy. When it was almost time, I pulled Aunt Gina's friend to the side, and said "Hey you driving?"

"Yeah why?"

"Can I get a ride?"

"Oh, sure, sure."

"Okay but listen." He looked me in the eyes. He was tipsy. "Don't tell nobody about your giving me a ride."

He pointed his finger at me. "Got ya."

"Okay, so leave now and if anybody asks tell them your going to the store." I went and kissed my niece, grabbed a pocketknife I spotted in the room, and then I snuck out the door.

Chapter 11
Kings County

It was dark on the Greyhound bus. I sat on the window side and stared out the window. I asked myself was I really sure Sam killed my mom. I began to think of all the things I knew about him besides the evidence I had just discovered. Sam was quick with criticism, and he always had to win, regardless what the stakes were. He's possessive, jealous, controlling, suspicious, and cold and could be easily moved to violence. He needed to feel superior. He would much rather have his pride than love and happiness. And when he couldn't seduce you, he would try to intimidate you to do what he wanted.

Sam opened the door and stared at me. If looks could kill I would have been dead. I saw a little space in the doorway, so I barged my way in. "You give me one good reason why you're here. You steal from me, and you got the fucking nerve to walk your ass in my house. Where's my watch, Shiree?"

"Fuck your watch, Sam, because I don't know what the fuck you're talking about, and I didn't come over here for that. I want to know what happened to my mother."

He paused and stared at me. His look was as if he never imagined me asking such a question.

"I know you killed her, Sam."

"Where you get that shit from?"

"Don't worry about that, you owe me an explanation."

"How can I have done it if I was at work?"

"Oh, so that was your alibi? Well I don't buy that one. You could have punched in, but you and I both know anyone could have driven that bus for you."

"Anyone could have killed your mother. Leroy could have done it."

"No, Leroy could have not done it. Leroy was not evil like you are, and he didn't have connections like you do. Leroy would have been caught. And most importantly, I am his alibi."

"Oh please, like he couldn't get someone to do it for him."

"Like you got somebody to do it for you, huh Sam? Besides, Leroy had no reason to kill her."

"What reason do you think I had?"

"Why wouldn't you give my mother a divorce? You threatened to kill her."

"Divorce, Colleen never wanted a divorce, she loved her last name."

"You're a fucking liar. That's what you do best. My mother was engaged to Leroy, and they were going to get married. She asked you for a divorce and you told her you would see her dead first. I know about you taking her wallet. I know about you carving your name in the tree, and how you threatened to carve it in her chest.. Why didn't she make it home from school, Sam? You were supposed to meet her that day at her school. You were taking her to buy me a coat. How about the papers you tricked her into signing? You killed her."

Sam charged me. His hands were going straight to

my throat. He wrapped his hands around my neck and threw me to the floor. He squeezed my neck tight, while I gasped for air. He screamed, "Who were you talking to, and who told you that?"

I choked and squirmed. I thought I was going to die. I reached in my pants for my knife. My arm couldn't go up too far, so I stabbed him in his leg.

He hollered as he let me go and grabbed his leg.

I got up and kicked him in his face. "I'm not going to kill you yet, you're going to tell me what happened to my mother."

He lay holding his leg in a puddle of blood. "You bitch, I was good to you. I let you lay up here with your man. I let you bring your friends here."

"Listen you faggot, don't run that dumb shit on me. You let my friends come and hang out, only to accommodate yourself. You try to make it your party. It was your chance to manipulate some young minds that didn't know any better.. You're a psychopath, Sam. That's how I know you killed my mom, and you will pay for it."

Sam jumped up and grabbed me by my hair.

I swung my knife and sliced him across his arm. Then the knife flew out my hand as I fell.

He banged my head against the floor. He dragged me by my hair to the kitchen.

I kicked and punched, but I was still sliding.

He grabbed a knife. "I could kill you right here, right now and get away with it. You already cut me up, and I live here, you don't. None of your clothes are here, and you belong to the group home anyways."

I was ready to die that night. I didn't care anymore. The thought and flashes in my mind of my mother getting stabbed to death in some dark alley, made me ruthless. So I wasn't scared to die or do twenty-five to life. But I preferred to kill Sam and do life.

I shoved my knee in his balls, and he dropped the knife. I wasn't able to get to the knife in time, so I dug my fingers in his eyes.

He screamed like he was on fire.

I kept digging until I heard the police say, "Get off of him now!"

I let Sam go, and he got right to his act. "She came here to kill me, officer. Look at my leg. She cut me up."

"Did you cut him?" One of the officers asked me. When I did not respond, he immediately arrested me and read me my rights.

Sam was sent to the hospital to get stitched up.

Before we left pictures were taken of the house, Sam's arm, leg and my bruises. I had a huge knot on my head along with a huge bald spot. One of my eyes was swollen and my neck had deep red marks on it. But nobody bothered asking me if I needed medical assistance.

Even though I was fifteen, they still had me at seventeen in the computer, so I was taken to central booking. I knew I was going down for attempted murder and that would be a long bid. I wouldn't care about sitting in jail if Sam was dead.

The judge asked me how did I plead, but I couldn't answer.

"Young lady, I'm talking to you."

I didn't know what to say, all I knew was to be silent. My body was tense and I was in a state of shock. Bail was set at ten thousand dollars cash.

When the court officer turned me around to take me back, I saw Lawanda. She must have called my brother and he must have told her I left. She knew exactly what I was going to do and she knew I was in jail. That's why she was my home girl, because she was smart. I felt like Mom did when it came to some sense. I hated a stupid motherfucker.

A court-appointed lawyer came to speak with me later on that day. He asked way too many questions that I did not answer. "Mr. your assistance to me is worthless. I will get time anyway. You don't work with me. You work with the District Attorney, the judge but not me."

"But are you able to afford an attorney." That's when I began to really feel aggravated. "It don't concern you, so you minds well go about your business."

Just as I began to accept my new living arrangements, a CO came by my cell. "Brown, bail."

"Bail?"

"Are you Shiree Brown?"

"Yes."

"Well you're being released." She unlocked my cell and led me down a long hallway.

A man called my name. I looked at him and the three other men and one woman who seemed like were all down with him. They all wore long white doctor jackets in regular clothing. "Shiree, I am Doctor James, and we come to escort you to Kings County Hospital."

"Hospital? Ain't shit wrong with me."

One doctor reached for me, and I punched him straight in the eye. I got charged by the rest of them. I kicked one in the face when they tried lifting me in the air onto the stretcher. I got the female doctor's hair wrapped around my hand and kept pulling and pulling, just like Sam did to me.

First they restrained my legs, and after they got my hands out of Miss Doc's hair, they restrained my hands too. But that didn't stop my thick spit from shooting straight out of my mouth and onto their faces. I enjoyed every bit of it, since they had me tied down, Who the fuck they think they are? But I couldn't win.

I saw the syringe in the air and hollered, "I'm pregnant, I'm pregnant." That did not stop them from injecting me with some two-second knock out shit.

Sam had the charges dropped. He admitted to hitting me first, and that it was a mutual fight. From the pictures it all made sense, because I had just as many bruises as he did.

Sam was afraid that I knew too much about Mama's death. He felt threatened by me being in jail. I could have easily got someone to look into Mom's case. And so he convinced them that I was crazy, and I belonged in the mental hospital.

I woke up in a dark and gloomy room, tied down to a bed. I looked around, and thought, they actually kept patients with depression or schizophrenia. This room would make any person depressed, or go crazy. I guess the real solution they trusted must have been medication. Because a nurse came in with a plastic cup with water in it and about three pills. I knew that I could not swallow a pill, but even if I could, I was not going to take any of their pills. I looked at the fat-ass nurse like she had two heads. I was still stuck and I couldn't speak.

"Hello I'm the nurse. The doctor prescribed some medication for you." What she had for me was nothing more than three mental pills. I opened up my mouth for the pills, and when I got enough water I spit it all over her face.

She started screaming, "Oh my God, yuck" as she wiped it off. "Your crazy."

"Yeah that's why I'm here right? Why are you so surprised? I thought you knew that, you see me tied down don't you? Fat bitch!" I began kicking and screaming. "I'm pregnant, you stupid mother fuckers, and all you people know is retarded people pills. I'm pregnant, I'm pregnant. What about food?" I lay there and cried myself to sleep.

I woke up to another lady nurse, cute petite and pleasant. She seemed like she wasn't on anyone's side, just there to do her job pleasantly. She came in with a tray of spaghetti, meatballs, salad and milk. She released my restraints so that I could eat properly. I thought maybe she was afraid that I would spit in her face if she tried to feed me. Or maybe it was about got-damn time after two days of restraints. There was a table and chair in my room, which favored a jail cell.

Little cute nurse suggested I sit there. I just looked at her, like if you don't get your bony ass out of my face. I wasn't sitting at a table, and I wasn't eating any food.

I just lay there in a fetal position, staring at the wall, and thinking about everything I had experienced since my mothers death. I pictured how beautiful Mom's face was, and how she would go crazy if she knew what her daughter was going through. My tears were salty and uncontrollable. My head felt very heavy and I could not eat. I was not hungry. As far as I was concerned, my life had no value. Even though my unborn seed grew inside of me, I couldn't imagine life getting better for me.

The petite little nurse came back to pick up my tray. "You haven't touched a thing. Come with me, the doctor will see you now."

I sat down and looked directly at the doctor, wondering if the lady was going to further piss me off. Maybe she'd let me go.

"Hello Shiree, my name is Dr. Holmes, how are you?"

I gave her a phony grin and said, "Such a question." I was already growing angry, she just didn't know it.

"Shiree, what is going on?"

"Well let's see, Dr. Holmes, I think you know very well what's going on. You brought me here."

"It seems as if your father has some great concern about your mental state of mind. He says you tried to kill him, and threatened to kill yourself because your mother is dead."

"Listen miss, that's a lie. The mother fucker is a fucking liar, and he's the sick one. He's very sick."

"Well Shiree, I notice your anger you carry, and I was informed on how you have been reacting since you've been here."

"Well Miss Dr. Holmes, I am human and we all get mad. Okay? And if a mother fucker put their hands on you and tried to take you against your will, and your psycho father lies on you and has been nothing but a nightmare in your life you would be angry too."

"Oh Miss Shiree, you are very angry, and I'm sorry I cannot let you go like this. I strongly doubt you will be leaving any time soon. Perhaps your father was right. There is a way we deal with our anger, and you need to learn that."

"What? My name is Shiree, Shiree Brown, bitch, and I'm not going to bite my tongue, or pretend like shit ain't going down when it is. Some things are acceptable, and some things just are fucking not, and sometimes I might have to put my foot up someone's ass to release my anger."

As soon as I stood up and started pointing my finger at her, while I shook my head left and right with my hand on my hip, the guard outside the door who had been there all the time, rushed inside and grabbed me.

"Get your fucking hands off me, you fucking toy cop. All you mother fuckers on them crazy people pills. That's why ya'll so calm, I know. Deal with reality on your own."

Toy cop forced me in my room, where I continued to curse, yell, storming around my room giving them the satisfaction they wanted.

All together I had given up. My bed was all I knew. I wouldn't move, speak or eat. I was so depressed my bones often ached. I was weak and purely flushed. I wouldn't even get up to use the bathroom. I lay in my urine and feces as if I had no control.

It had to have been a long week. I recalled a Nurse Pam who walked in my room. She struck me as unusual. This lady was black, sincere, very worried about me. She did not fake her concerns. When she first set eyes on me she yelled out, "Jesus." I believe tears fell from her eyes. She laid her hands on me and said prayers. I remember her holding a small black book, known as the bible.. She often read me scriptures. I could hear her asking God to heal me from my awful disease. Pam spoke to me even though I never responded. She told me she had faith that I would be healed. She told me to fight, and that the devil was a liar. I heard her tell me repeatedly I was beautiful, too pretty for any man's prison. She brushed my hair, and washed my face. She was the only nurse who would run me bath water, force me out of bed, walk me to the bathroom, and help me in the tub. I usually laid in the water with no intention of doing anything, not even the intention of getting out. Then she'd take me out, and lay me down on clean sheets. Before she left she put oil on my head and said a prayer for me. I remember her arms around me, and her kiss she planted on my forehead.

That night I saw a shadow lurking on the other side of the room. When I turned around to see, I saw a beautiful in a beautiful white dress. "Mama?" I jumped out my bed and ran to her, and fell to my knees. "Mama, oh my God it's really you."

"Oh my beautiful baby, why are you giving up on yourself?"

"Mama I can't go on without you any longer."

"Oh sweetie, yes you can. You are my smartest and strongest child. I always believed in you and I always will. You have special talents. Don't throw that away. You can do anything you want in this world."

"But Mama, you're not here."

She lifted her hand and placed it over her heart. "I'm here, sweetie, in your heart. No one can ever take that away. My time is up. I served my purpose in life. Whatever God had me down here to do, it's done now. But your job is not done yet. Live your life to the fullest. Fulfill your dreams and make me proud."

"What about Sam, Mama?"

"Don't give Sam anymore power over your life. God will deal with him. You have to forgive him one day. Don't become him, or let him change you. You must defeat the enemy. You have new life within you and you're neglecting it already. Feed it, nourish it, love it, this baby relies on you now. Trust God, honey, you'll get out of here. And you are a winner, so don't you ever give up in anything you do." And then she left.

I kept screaming, "Ma, Ma," but she was gone. I cried a few tears, and then I got up.

First things first, they cannot have my life. And that's when I knew sometimes you got to fake it to make it. I got to act like I'm on these niggas' level to get up out of here. It means stop going wild on these bitches and be nice.

"Praise God," Nurse Pam hollered as she wrapped her arms around me. "Look at you! I prayed for this day." She grabbed my hands, pulled me out of the bathroom and positioned me on the bed and sat down beside me. "What on Gods great earth, is going on with you? How did you get here, and why?"

I said to her in such a confused voice, "Oh Nurse Pam, it's a long story." I looked in her bright big brown eyes as she held me in her eyes. Her arms wrapped around me felt kind of uncomfortable. I knew she cared about me, but I wasn't use to that.

"But poor child, you're so young and so pretty to be like this." She squeezed me tighter and said, "God is going to work it out. You have to get out of here; this is no place for you Hun."

"Can you get me out of here, Nurse Pam?" I asked her.

"No sweetie, you have got to get yourself out of here. I can only help you and be here for you. Where are your folks?"

"My mother is dead and my father is a pervert. He cares nothing about me. He is how I got here. Yes I tried to kill him, because I know he killed my mom. But I'm not as crazy as he convinced these people here."

"No you're not crazy, honey. And let me tell you something. Your mother may not be here, and your father may be real unfatherly. But the Lord promises to be your father, a father who will never leave you or forsake you. One you can always count on, and he can do all things only if you believe in him. You need to believe now that he will restore your life, so that you can get out of here and live on. You need to forgive your father, not for him, but for the Lord and yourself. The deliverance is within you. You don't need the bitterness you carry around because of him. It will only keep you down. It is your past now, and you must leave the past behind you to live your future." She kissed me on the forehead. "Now you get some sleep."

After she tucked me in I asked her, "Why do you go out of your way for me? No one else does, and that's very rare that you see that. Why do you even care? You're just a nurse."

She said, "Yes I'm a nurse, but I am a Christian first. I am a Christian who works as a nurse, you understand? Now you get some sleep. I'll see you tomorrow afternoon. When you get up in the morning, you thank God for another day, for healing you. You ask him for wisdom and he will give it to you. God is a loving God."

Nurse Pam worked the three-to-eleven shift, and it

was time for her to go. Pam was different than any Christian I met. Christians were the phoniest people to me, the biggest hypocrites. They were always hollering about God this and God that, but were the first ones doing ungodly things. They gossiped and were always judging people. They always talked about what they did for people, when it was supposed to have been from the goodness of their hearts. And what takes the cake is how they're never there for you when you need them, but they love you. Pam seemed different, genuine. She didn't play, she prayed.

I tossed and turned all night. I could not wait until morning came. I knew I had to be nice to everyone in order to get out of there.

I got washed up for breakfast. Nurse Jenny brought my tray to me. I told her good morning, and she looked at me like I was crazy. After eating everything on my tray, and instead of waiting for them to pick my tray up, I took it to the nurse's station. While I was there I asked one of the nurses for Dr. Holmes. I expressed great determination to speak with her. Instead, I was told that Holmes was the boss around there. She'd call when she wanted me, and that I couldn't just see her when I wanted to. Just asking for Holmes, I was given dirty looks, eyes were being rolled at me, and smart remarks were made.

Who the fuck they thought they were talking to? I was ready to fuck somebody up. But I knew it would have never gotten me out of there. They kept on bickering about Dr. Holmes, making jokes. I simply told both bitches to have a nice day and walked on.

When lunchtime came, I was disgusted to see the same two nasty nurses with my tray in their hands. They stood in my doorway laughing, said to enjoy before they left.. They were trying to play me and I could have played back. My tray would have ended up in one of their faces. Thank you, but no thank you. But they would have told Dr. Holmes and I would have never gotten out. See, skanks like that I don't trust handling my food. I didn't eat that shit. They were amazed when I brought my full tray to the nurse's station. I smiled at them and said, "Thank you."

I was so happy to see Nurse Pam. She noticed the anxiety and my misery. "What's wrong honey?"

"I am so hungry."

"Why didn't you eat your food?"

"Nurse Pam, the nurses don't like me and they keep messing with me."

"So what are you saying, they didn't feed you?"

"No, I mean yes they brought my tray, but I don't trust people like that. They'll do something to your food, believe me."

"Oh, child."

"No, for real, Nurse Pam."

"No child, I believe you. The devil is a lie. But precious child, don't let them still your joy. And you have to kill people with kindness. Let them be as mean and nasty as they want to be, just don't let them change your attitude. You be nice to them anyway."

Pam left and came back with two salami sandwiches, chips, a Pepsi and a book called Mama by Terry McMillan. She said, "Get full, child, and read some, so you can occupy some time. Books are very delightful. It will take you out of this place. I got some more stuff for you." She left and came back with clean sheets, washcloths, towels, pajamas, lotion from bath and body works, and another book that read the bible.

"Oh thank you, Nurse Pam."

"You're welcome, child. I want you to take a hot bath or shower, clean up, relax yourself and your mind. You can thank me by reading your bible, but Mama you will really enjoy. I will be back to bring supper later, so you don't have to worry, okay?"

"Okay Nurse Pam, thank you."

"No thank the Lord, honey."

For two weeks I did not eat breakfast for fear of the nurses who did not like me. I waited for Pam to bring me a late lunch and supper during her shift. Every day she had something new for me. She brought me slippers, a Walkman, meditation tapes, crossword puzzle books. And she made me read my bible. Then Dr. Holmes sent for me.

"Hello Shiree, how have you been doing?"

"Well I'm not crazy about this place, and I don't want to be here. Being as how I don't have much of a choice, I make the best of it."

"Do you know why you're here Shiree?"

"Yes and no Dr. Holmes."

"Talk to me, Shiree. Why do you think you're here?"

"Well, I mean, I know this was my father's request, and not at all his concern. But I'm going to tell you like this, and you can accept it or reject it. I met my father when I was eleven; at twelve my mom was killed. My father took custody of me. I was devastated because he put his hands in my panties. Later on he busted my nose to rip my clothes off me. He constantly tried to manipulate me into being a freak, which is exactly what he is. If I bring friends over to the house, male or female, he tries to get sexual orgies going on. And this is my father I'm talking about.. In my book that's not mentally healthy. You think maybe we got the wrong person in here? He may have killed my mom. I'm not a hundred percent, but that's what I believe. Dr. Holmes, I'm not crazy. I'm a young girl without guidance. I have been in and out of group homes and foster homes. I have been homeless. I may need help, but not mentally. Yes, I have been through a lot and you can see how tired I am."

"Shiree do your hate your father?"

"No I don't."

"Did you try to kill him?"

"Truthfully, at the time I don't know what I felt. I don't think I minded him dead. But I went to his house to get an explanation. He put his hands on me first, I just defended myself."

"Why should I let you go?"

"Because I'm no threat to society. I'm not a threat to myself or anybody else. I don't want to be confined to a room. I can't go to church here, or to the library. I have important things to do. My baby will soon be here. I need to be thinking about him or her."

"Shiree, if I let you go, what will be the situation between you and your father?"

"Dr. Holmes, I forgive him for everything he did to me, and it's out of my hands. He doesn't have to talk to me, but he does have to answer to God. When I leave here, I will be on my way to Syracuse, New York, to start a life for my child and me. I do have goals and dreams."

"Okay Shiree, it was nice talking to you on a more humbled level. You will be all right. I will see you soon, okay?"

"Okay Dr Holmes, thanks for speaking with me. I really wanted to say, "Bitch, let me up out of here. You know ain't shit wrong with me."

Chapter 12
The Visit

Nurse Pam came to my room and informed me that I had a visitor.

"Visitor? As in someone I know outside this place?"

"Yes girl, come on to the visiting room."

"Lawanda? Oh my God look at you. You look good, girl. And who is this? My God baby? What's her name?"

"Leasia Shiree Harris."

"You better had put my name somewhere in there."

"Girl, I caught hell pushing her ass out."

"She's so pretty."

"Anyways, when you getting out of here?"

"I don't know, I have to play my cards right."

"Yeah, because your ass is going wild on these people up in here."

"How you know?"

"For one, I know you. Two, I call up here every day. I tried to get them to bring me up here. I told them I was going to blow Kings County up if they didn't let you go. I had to calm down until I had this baby, though. Let me tell you something, you got to kiss these crackers' ass, just to get the fuck up out of here. Cause I know you, and you can't be acting like yourself. You'll have these mother fuckers putting you in straight jackets and shit, the way you be spasing.

"I know, girl. I did all that already and it got me nowhere."

"So when you going to do it?"

"Well I have been doing good. There's this one nurse in here, she's a Christian, and she's been teaching me about God, reading the bible and shit. She even buys me things."

"My God, let me find out Kings County turned you out. No Shiree, God is good. It's just that once you commit, you can't smoke weed, cigarettes, none of that.. You have to give that lifestyle up, and you're only fifteen."

"Well, Lord knows I'm not making any promises now. I'm just trying to get to know Him, believe in Him, you know."

"Yeah I know. Your brother calls me every day. We was going to bust you out of here."

I laughed for like ten minutes, because I knew my brother and friends were crazy.

Lawanda filled me in on what was going on in the streets. Dee Dee's boyfriend, Fat Jody, just bought her a Benz. Fat Jody lived in Wyckoff projects for years. He always was crazy about Dee Dee. But she never cared too much about him, just the money and expensive gifts he gave her freely. Ameanie was pregnant, and Ernest went to jail for robbing some Jew. And everybody was glad he went to jail for that, because he was on his way to jail for murder. When he found out I tried to kill Sam and Sam wasn't dead, and I got sent to the nut house, Ernest was going to finish the job.

I couldn't stand sitting in my room anymore. I finished reading Mama by Terry McMillan. I got tired of listening to my Walkman. I was ready to go. I stood in the hallway all day. I was the only normal person in there. The whole place was filled with nuts, including the nurses and doctors. All the patients were doped up. They walked up and down the hallways with no laces in their sneakers, looking like zombies. But the nurses kept telling me to get to my room. I asked them why they did not have a library with books, or a church to attend to. They must have really believed we were retarded. I grew so tired of the four walls, and I started to go in the hall and curse the nurses out. Until Nurse Pam came in and told me Dr. Holmes wanted to speak with me. I was happy and overwhelmed at the same time, because Holmes needed to just let me go.

"Nurse Pam, when you give your life to the Lord, is it true that you can't smoke cigarettes anymore?"

"There's a lot of things that the Lord doesn't want us to do. But Lord knows you just don't stop overnight. He first wants you to believe that he's the one and only God, and that no one comes before him. Then you take it one step at a time. He will give you Holy Spirit, and with that you will know what's right and wrong. You can ask God to take the taste of cigarettes out your mouth, or say Lord, help me to change. That's all. You have to talk to your father. The idea is to get a relationship with him. Now go see Dr. Holmes, good news I bet."

I ran to Dr. Holmes' office.

"Hi Shiree, how are you?"

"I'm hanging in there, Miss."

"If I let you go, Shiree where are you going to go?"

"I'm going to live with my brother in Syracuse."

"Well we're going to let you go. There's no reason to keep you. Just a minute." She picked up the phone pressed a button and handed it to me.

"Hello?"

"What's up, sis?"

"Oh shit, what's up brother? Listen brother they letting me go."

"I know. I'm coming to get you, I'll be there Friday morning. All right?" He told me that I was crazy.

"I guess so. I'm in a nut house."

"All right, hang tight. I'll be there early Friday."

I was the happiest I ever been since I got there. "Jesus, you are good." I danced all over my room. Just when I was about to cut up, Jesus saved me. Just when I sat down exhausted from jumping around, nurse came in hollering, "Visitor."

I ran to the visiting room with a Kool-Aid smile on my face. I couldn't wait to tell Lawanda the good news. I got past the door and stepped in the room. Well I be got damn, I said to myself.

Sam must have read my mind. "What happened to your smile? I'm not who you expected, huh? Who were you expecting?"

Well if it wasn't the devil himself. I saw what Nurse Pam meant, the devil was always trying to get in the way of God's work. But not today, I thought. "I'm just a little surprised to see you, Sam." I sat down at the table. My hands were on the table and my legs were shaking underneath. Suddenly I became cold. I think it was all in my mind. I was nervous as hell and I still had feelings of killing him. I began getting flashbacks of the time I lived with him. In my head I kept saying, this sick mother fucker, what the hell do he want?

"So how have you been, Hun?"

"I'm sure you know everything that goes on with me in here, Sam."

"Don't start that, Shiree. I just asked you a question, hun, that's all."

"I can't complain, Sam. I have been hanging in there."

"So, what's this stuff about God, you're into religion now?"

"Yes I am. God is good."

"Girl please, you can't sit here and tell me anything about God. Because I know there is no God. Have you ever seen him?"

The moment I heard Sam speak against God, I knew he was a demon. "Sam how could you dog my belief?"

"Listen girl, believe in what you want to believe in, many people do. All I'm doing is telling you what I know. Like I told you before, the bible is man-made. It has been around for ancient years. When you die, you go in the ground, nowhere else. You're dead. You can talk to Him all day; He's not going to respond. I make my own life in this world. I got my house because I worked for it. Nobody didn't give me a damn thing. You think I'm going to live like some saint, like nothing exists on earth just to be saved and go to a heaven nobody's seen. Please! That's bull. Shiree, why were you telling these people that crap about your mother? Why are you telling that story?"

"Why did you come here, Sam?"

"To see how you're doing. You're my daughter."

He couldn't be serious, because it was too funny to me. What it was, he knew I was getting out. He wanted to push enough buttons to make me perform. He wanted Kings County to keep me. But I had a trick for him and whoever else that was scoping the visit. "Sam I really would not like to talk about that. It's the furthest from my mind. I like to think of my mother as resting in peace. And whatever happened to her is not for me to take on or worry about for that matter. She's gone. I can't change that. But I can change how I live my life now, and raise my child up."

"Listen to yourself. You're only fif teen-years-old. What are you going to do with a baby? You can't even take care of yourself. You honestly think your family is going to help you?"

I wanted to tell Sam to go fuck himself, and to get the fuck out. Cause he really couldn't talk about anybody being a parent. But instead I told him I was very tired, exhausted and would like to lie down. I told him to have a nice night, I would pray for him, and that he should try Jesus.

When I got back to my room, even the nurse that night began fucking with me. "So you're going home huh?"

"Yes I am."

"Don't come back," she said.

"Now you and I both know ain't shit wrong with me."

"Now wait a minute, be honest with yourself. When you started shitting on yourself, you didn't think something was wrong with you?"

My heart skipped a beat. I paused and held my composure. I almost leaped the three feet she was standing away from me and wrapped my hands around her neck. I put my hands on my hip and phony grinned her. "I know one thing. You never washed me up, nor changed my sheets. To be a nurse, you sure haven't said as much as two words to me. What do you think about that?"

She rolled her eyes and walked out.

When the morning came I was up dressed and ready to go. They can have this room. Give it to someone who needs it. There was no doubt in my mind I would miss Nurse Pam. She was strong and different because she kept shit real. There was plenty sisters around there, but she was the only one that cared whether I got well or not. She knew I wasn't crazy or violent, but that I was just in the valley. And I made it. I had the Lord to thank, who I learned more about than I ever knew. And I had Nurse Pam to thank for that. She taught me patience, love, how to ask and I shall receive if I believed, and how to seek the Lord. She taught me how to live on, regardless of what I've been through, regardless who liked me, cared about me or who didn't. It was my future and it depended on me. Can't anybody hurt me unless I let them. I learned how to get out of ugly situations, out of the valley. I love this lady. And she came that morning even though it was not her working hours. She came just to tell me she loved me, too. She wrapped her arms around me. Then she walked me out of the dark dungeon-looking building and led me to my brother. "You take this little black book. I put my home number, cell and address in it." She looked at Caseen and scolded him. "You promise to take care of her. And Shiree, you find you a church now hear? Stay up in the word." Tears rolled down her face as she reached for one last hug.

I got in Caseen's car and never looked back, not even at Nurse Pam. I knew then that the world wasn't fair, but God was.

Author's Note

Sometimes we're born to dysfunctional mothers or fathers who become dysfunctional role models and we suffer from their lack of common sense, knowledge, and most importantly morals. Some of us have been raped of stability, normal lives and even sexually. We have been abused, neglected and talked down to. All of that will hurt and can even leave burdens on our hearts. It can cause us to act out in ways that make us hurt ourselves even more.

We can't change what happened to us in the past. But the future is definitely our choice. We can blame our perpetrators for our past, but we are responsible for our future and can't blame anyone but ourselves for anything that happens in it. There are major consequences for sulking in self-pity. The world will stay the same, nothing will change, because if we live in the past there will be no future, and life will pass us by. If you don't go to school when you are supposed to, when you decide to go back later the road will be much harder. And secondly if you continue to dwell on the past you will never fulfill your purpose in the world. Everyone has a purpose in life and once you find it the victory is yours. There's hope for people like us. There's life after the pain. We can still live normal lives. We should be more equipped for the disaster in the world. Let your struggles be your lessons, and your downfalls your stepping stones. Only the strong survive.